The Clue of the Dancing Bells
A First Ladies Mystery

by

Barbara Schlichting

www.barbaraschlichting.com

DARKHOUSE
BOOKS

THE CLUE OF THE DANCING BELLS
A First Ladies Mystery
by
Barbara Schlichting

The Clue of the Dancing Bells
All rights reserved
This story is a work of fiction. Any resemblance between events, places, or characters, within them, and actual events, organizations, or people, is but happenstance.

Copyright © 2017 by Barbara Schlichting
ISBN 978-1-945467-02-8
Published August, 2017
Published in the United States of America

Darkhouse Books
160 J Street, #2223
Niles, California 94536

Table of Contents

Edith Roosevelt: CLUE OF THE DANCING BELLS

A First Ladies Mystery

By

Barbara Schlichting

Chapter One

The first time I met Gina, I knew we'd be fast friends. We were both about the same height, and with red hair cut in a similar short style. When you find someone who could be your doppelgänger, you don't want to let them go.

Gina lived alone in a house across the street from Aaron and me. She worked as a bookkeeper part-time for a local liquor establishment, a kind-of dumpy bar and lounge called, The Establishment. Gina and I would gossip on sunny afternoons as we tended to our yards. It's a great way to really get to know someone.

I knew she was finding it hard to make ends meet, so I asked her if she'd want to make some extra cash by helping me with my display at a National Parks Exposition in Saint Paul. She jumped at the chance, making it a win-win for me. I would receive much needed help while being able to assist a friend, and I also would get to spend some time doing something fun and exciting with her. The plan was a perfect solution! I picked her up and we drove across town to my store, The First Ladies White House Dollhouse Store. After parking in the back, I looked over at Gina and smiled.

"It'll be a minute."

"Don't mind me helping?" Gina said. Unbuckling her seatbelt, she opened the car door.

"Of course not!"

We climbed out and bounded up to the back door. She waited while I punched in the code. "We've had a number of break-ins recently," I explained. "This new security system seems to have taken care of that unfortunate issue." I twisted the handle and pushed the door open, allowing her to enter first.

"Is your happy hubby working security?"

"Yep. Aaron will be around to check up on us. It's hard for him, working his regular hours as a Minneapolis cop as well as security at the National Parks expo this week, but the extra cash will be nice. My name is down on the contract for the expo as Olivia Reynolds, so don't be surprised if I'm called that and not Liv."

"All right. Any extra cash is nice. Thanks for thinking of me for help this week," Gina said. "I love all of your doll houses."

"Thanks." I took a quick glance around the room. "Hi ladies! I'll be in and out over the next few days, so don't worry. Grandma and Max will take over while I'm gone."

"Do you always talk to your dolls like that?" Gina asked. Her hands were on her hips, head cocked, as she eyed me suspiciously, but with a sparkle in her eyes. "You're not losing it, are you?"

"Not in the least," I huffed. I marched right over to Edith Roosevelt, who stood on top of the bear rug inside of the oval office. "You should be proud of your husband, Edith. The National Parks is the best thing that ever happened to this country."

"Bully!" Gina said. She winked. "Liv, you're a nut."

"I do enjoy my dolls, but we better get moving," I said to Gina. Turning back to the dolls, I said, "Behave yourself, Mrs. Roosevelt."

The showroom had multiple long tables where each of our featured dollhouses were on display, with two houses per table. James and Dolley Madison's White House was one of my favorites. Furniture was sparse in its rooms, since most were destroyed during the War of 1812. The state dining room and the president's offices were on the first floor. The interior walls were replaced with wood instead of brick after the war, which actually made the White House unsafe, causing an almost continuous remodeling over the years since then. The most recent improvements, such as the famed Rose Garden, or the West Wing were part of efforts to make the White House safer.

"Dolley, you look beautiful today." I waved a kiss to the Mr. and Mrs. Madison miniature dolls. "Be good, you two. Don't go making out in front of customers, please. I don't need an X-rated store."

"You're hilarious," Gina said. I got the feeling that Gina was easily amused.

I had prepared everything we needed for the event in boxes stored in the workroom. "I have miniatures to show at the booth, and a few pieces of memorabilia on the side. I hope it'll bring more people to the store." We scooped up the boxes and carried them out to my car.

"It will. These little ten-by-twelve houses are fun. Little girls will love them," Gina said. "The X is always fun to go to. I've gone there for a few concerts."

"Yep. I like the Xcel Center. Aaron loves to go to hockey games there." After buckling up and starting the engine, I turned toward the downtown area and passed over the Hennepin Avenue Bridge, which took us toward the signs for Interstate 35W. I turned onto the ramp and headed toward St. Paul. I noticed that Gina massaged her temples a few times and shut her eyes.

"Got a headache brewing?" I asked.

"Yeah. Might have to take more pills."

"We'll be there soon. If it's too noisy, just take my keys and lie down in the back of my car. Or there could be some quiet place at the arena for the participants to relax." I gave her a smile before exiting.

"I will. Thanks." Gina sat up straighter and yawned. "Don't know what's come over me today, but I'll be fine."

"Well, at least we know where our booth is. We can get started setting up right away. I could have done it last night, but I just didn't feel good about leaving the dollhouses. I wasn't sure about the overnight security. I'll grab the minis. Mind getting the smaller box?"

"Got it."

We climbed from the car and headed toward the main door of the arena entering with a number of park Rangers dressed in full uniform, making me smile at the sight. They looked wonderful in their distinctive dress uniform of gray shirts, green trousers, and brown hats. The Rangers first came into existence to protect animals from poachers and to also render assistance to travelers, since then they have expanded their services. The Rangers come from all walks of life. It always makes me feel proud to see them.

It has been said that the National Park system was the one thing that we did right as Americans. I said a silent 'Thank you' to Theodore Roosevelt for getting the ball rolling on nationalizing them.

"Let's get settled," I said. Gina followed me as I led the way to my small booth toward the back of the vast space.

"I bet my two cousins are here," Gina said, looking around the room.

"Really? Who are they?"

"Harry is a Ranger, and Sunflower is a jingle dancer. They definitely look more Native American than I do, since I'm only one-quarter Native American."

"That's fascinating. See them?" I asked as we glanced around the area.

"Nope. I'll look for them later."

We continued walking through the vast hall. Passing near the many stalls representing each national park, I couldn't help but stop a few times and read the various headlines, or gaze at the breath-taking photos. An extra-added booth for a Theodore Roosevelt impersonator was rightly called 'The Bully Pulpit'. The posters on the back of the booth were of President Roosevelt campaigning across the country, giving speeches from the rear of a train, and around them were photographs of his audiences showing cowboys on horseback and range cattle in the distance. It was an awesome sight.

"Hear that?" I asked. A jingling sound caught our attention as we reached the booth.

"What a spectacle to see. The dancers are so beautiful and elegant looking in their costumes."

Dozens of Native American women stood in a wide circle, dressed in sparkling dresses and wearing handmade bead jewelry. Some wore feathered headbands, and most wore jingling ankle bracelets, and moccasins. It didn't take long for the drum team to set up the drums and make sure they were ready. Each drummer wore the costume of their native tribe. The many vivid colors brightened the room, while the dancers' voices brought music to my ears. The drum beat and the chants were different from anything I had ever experienced.

"Look at them all. See, the drummer is setting up for the opening ceremony."

"I wonder if Sunflower and my friend, Bambi will have a chance to come by the booth afterward?"

"I'd love to meet them."

"Hmm…" Gina's eyes sparkled. I turned to look in the same direction and knew why. The Ranger she was looking at was certainly handsome in his uniform.

Soon the miniatures we brought were set up in the display booth and a portfolio filled with pictures of my dollhouses was properly arranged. Beside them, I displayed a set of Theodore Roosevelt personal riding spurs. At the last moment I had decided not to take the rest of my TR items with me, including a purse that had belonged to Alice Roosevelt. She was the president's first child. He had been a widower when he married Edith.

"I want to take a look around before the opening ceremonies," I told Gina. "How about you?" We were sitting on cushioned folding chairs behind the table in our booth as visitors began to filter into the vast room. "My hope is to see the main speaker, John Muir's impersonator. I'm dying to meet him."

"How about if I go looking around first, then you can go?" Gina stood. "I'd like to find out about the jingle dance, and maybe find my cousins."

"Let me get a cup of coffee from Wrangler Jean's real quick. I need a good strong cup. Be right back." I scooted out from behind the booth and headed for the coffee booth. Since it was a mere hop-skip-and-a-jump from my place, it didn't take long to reach it. A line had started, and I was in fifth place. Several minutes went by before I was able to make my purchase of 'One-eye-shot'. With the first sip of the caffeine-infused drink, my eyes became wide-open. Though I had wanted to make a quick circle around the show floor, I decided to wait until after Gina had a chance to look for her cousins.

I hurried back to the booth where I found her chatting with someone.

"Liv, this is my friend, Bambi. She's invited me to watch the rehearsal later today. I used to be a jingle dancer, but that was a while ago."

"Of course! How fun. Your performance must be after the opening ceremony?"

"Our dance session is tonight. We have a few steps to rehearse, and we'll do that after the ceremony," Bambi answered with a smile.

"You should definitely go, Gina. I'm fine here on my own."

Bambi said her goodbyes and left. Gina pushed her chair aside and stepped out.

"I'm off to find my cousins. I won't be long."

I watched as she wove through the booths representing the framework of America.

"Hi." I waved to the women seated behind the booth for the National Historic Site for the First Ladies, located in Ohio. Our connection was my business. We'd corresponded many times over the past few years, becoming friendly. I was looking forward to actually meeting them in person.

I saw a rather robust man moving behind the Teddy Roosevelt booth. From a distance, his walrus mustache and huge smile reminded me of the former president, and I knew he must be the Roosevelt impersonator.

Glancing toward the dancers, I saw Gina speaking to a few of them. I wouldn't be surprised if she joined them during a demonstration.

I picked up my phone and sent a quick message to Grandma, asking how things were at the store. She responded almost immediately that she'd just sold a TR house, and the purchaser would be stopping by my booth. I responded with a quick 'Thanks'.

A man with a long beard and unruly hair approached Wrangler Jean's. The cut of his suit told me that he had to be John Muir's impersonator. He also appeared to have slept in it.

After another few minutes, Gina returned

I moved my chair aside to enable her to get around me. "I bet you want to dance now," I said with a smile.

"Yes, I do. In fact, one of the gals is going to come over with information about how to join an area dance group. I just might join." Gina frowned. "I have sort of a headache. An aspirin just might do the trick." She reached for a pill bottle from her purse.

"I hope that goes away. It's noisy and it'll make the headache worse," I said.

"I had to stop dancing because I was needed on the ranch. It's a cultural type thing. Good for the community. The woman I spoke to is from North Dakota and had lived near me before I moved to Minnesota." Gina set the bottle down after removing a pill.

"Good for you." I stood. "Someone bought a house at my shop, and plans to come over here today and meet me. Just thought I'd let you know. If she does happen by, tell her I'll be right back."

"And, if it's during the opening ceremony, I'll tell her you'll be back when the speakers are through. Right?"

"Right." I took off, and my first stop was at the First Lady booth.

"You're Liv, aren't you?" A woman held out her hand, and I shook it.

"Sure am. Finally, we meet. But tell me, who is who?" I asked, nodding to each.

"Alice."

"Belle."

"Ruby."

"A pleasure." I smiled and said, "You three must try and make it by my store before leaving town."

"We'll try, but I'm not sure if there'll be time. Our flight out is within two hours of the closing ceremony," Alice said.

"Dirty shame." I waited a moment. "I always wanted to visit it."

"I look forward to it. Canton, Ohio, isn't too far from Minnesota. It became the home of the First Ladies Library in 1998. It had been the home of former first lady Ida Mckinley and is where the president passed away," Ruby said.

"How interesting. I'll have to visit it when I next travel. I'll put it on my 'to-do' list. I hope to have time later to become further acquainted. Thank you."

I gave a slight nod, and walked toward the many park booths. Quite a few were represented by Rangers. Each of the fifty states had small displays featuring their National Park. I figured that Yellowstone was the first displayed, since it was the first National Park. A gigantic photo of Old Faithful was the main image and looked so natural like it was before me. With the snow-capped mountains in the distance plus the many wild-life photos, I knew that I definitely wanted a return visit. My mouth dropped open as I stared at it. From there, I circled on to the Yosemite booth and was again impressed. I continued on my quest to see them all until the overhead speaker announced the opening ceremony.

As I walked over to the area, I did feel a little bit guilty about leaving Gina behind, but she hadn't seemed to mind. An argument, loud enough to be heard over the background noise, caught my attention. I was near the dancer and drum area, and I decided to take a peek behind a portable partition. A Ranger and a dancer were arguing, but I couldn't catch what they were hollering about. I wanted to move closer but decided against it. It wasn't any of my business. Just as I stepped back, they noticed me. Hurriedly, I backed out and continued to the opening ceremony with hopes of Aaron being able to join me.

Just then my phone chirped for an incoming message. I looked and it was from Aaron. 'Bz now. Meet you later'. I responded with 'ok'. I figured he was up to his eyeballs with security detail and not able to meet. Continuing to the ceremony, I found a lone seat right down the center aisle. The audience was a sea of Ranger uniforms,

Native American dancers and drummers, with public spectators filling in the open spaces. Contented with my seat, I searched the audience for a glimpse of my husband. When the TR impersonator stepped to the podium, a hush came over the crowd.

Since I had a close seat, I realized that the likeness was superb. When he cleared his throat and began to speak, I was transformed back to the early turn of the century. The power and strength behind his words left me mesmerized. He spoke of the need for preserving our wildlife and land, and that we are the caretakers. It was exciting and exhilarating.

Next came John Muir's impersonator, a soft-spoken individual who spoke of the power of the land and how it protects us all. He spoke of meeting President Roosevelt and the time they had camped together under the stars at Yosemite and discussed the wonders before them. He told TR how he could change the future of the earth by signing legislation to preserve the land for future generations. He recalled how the president eluded his Secret Service to have the time alone, and how he found the peace overwhelming. Their adventure ended with TR's promise to do what he could to save the land from destruction.

The final speaker was a Native American, who spoke also of being caretakers of the land and Mother Earth, and that we are all one body. His final wish was for all of us to love the land.

When the speakers had finished, I felt abruptly transported from the past and into present day. I waited a few extra minutes for the crowd to thin out before standing. While I waited, I watched as the impersonators leave through a side door. I hadn't known that the door was there until that moment, then realized that there must be doors of this nature throughout the room.

I took a moment to locate Aaron before returning to my booth, and found him knee-deep with work. I blew him a kiss and headed back to my booth. I slowly navigated through the crowd until I found myself at a food booth, *The Rough Rider,* near my booth. My stomach growled, and I decided to pick up two burgers, one for myself, and the other for Gina. I chose the Yellowstone, which had plenty of cheese and onions on the burger, and the other was the

Bully from the TR Park—which had raw onions and buffalo meat. I also stopped for two cold drinks before heading to my booth.

Nearing my booth, I noticed that Gina looked as if she'd dozed off. I wondered how that could've happened, given the noise level.

"Gina!" I called. Her hand was on an orange juice container in front of her. "Gina!" I called once again. My heart raced as I quickly dashed to her. "Hey!" I set the beverages and sack down. "Gina!" I slightly touched her shoulder, and she slumped onto the table. "OH MY GOD!" I shouted, and then screamed.

Chapter Two

Ruby from the First Lady booth helped me sit down and handed me a water bottle. The medic teamed arrived quickly, hooked Gina up to an IV and wheeled her out. As far as I knew, she was going to be fine. As soon as Aaron was by my side, Ruby left.

"Is she going to make it?" I asked. He sat down beside me. "What could've happened?"

"No idea. What can you tell me?" Aaron's quiet voice and soft demeanor calmed me, and I stared into his eyes. "Any ideas?"

"None." I shrugged, and ran my fingers through my curly hair. "Don't know." I picked up Gina's spilled pills from earlier and placed the bottle into my bag. "She was fine. She had a headache earlier and had taken a couple of these pills."

"I'm sure that she'll be fine," he said. I leaned closer just as his radio transmitter sent a message. He turned the dial, and said, "I'm on my way." Standing, he said, "I've given Maggie a buzz, and she's coming to sit with you. I'll keep you updated. Gotta run."

"Thank you." Maggie was my best friend. I blew my nose and wiped my eyes dry knowing that I'd soon feel better once she arrived. *You're fine. Gina's fine.* I reached for the water bottle and realized that I needed to eat. I had many hours to go before leaving and it sounded like Gina would make it. *Think positive!*

When Gina had returned earlier, she didn't have anything in her hands, but now an empty orange juice container sat on the booth table. I placed the juice container in one of my house storage boxes on the floor with her purse. By now my Yellowstone burger had grown cold, but I ate it anyway. I started to regain my energy and enthusiasm with each bite. The crowd thickened. I am happy that I'd cruised the displays earlier.

My phone chirped once again, and I noted it was Aaron. It read 'no news'. No news is good news. I responded 'thx' and sent it. Sitting straighter, I kept my eyes on the crowd, and chatted with anyone who'd stop.

"Tell me about the TR White House," a woman asked who stood beside a Ranger.

I began with my usual tale about how First Lady Edith found it small and stifling for raising children so she had the upstairs family area remodeled and added the kitchen. She also wanted her husband to have a sanctuary. She was very astute.

"Oh really?" the woman said. "Tell me about Alice. I hear she was a spitball to raise."

"She was nicknamed Princess Alice. I have a purse of hers at home." I realized that I had both of their interest. "Come to my store and have a look around." I handed each a card and watched the Ranger stick it inside of his pocket and the lady drop it into her purse as they walked away.

I craved chocolate. I needed something. Sitting alone did that too me. I gave Maggie a buzz. She didn't answer, but I left a message asking her to bring a candy bar.

Wrangler Jean's, next to my booth, was busier than a cowboy during roundup time, and I hoped for some of her customers to spill over to my booth. I rearranged my miniature houses, and made sure they were all looking 'smart', dusting them with a tiny cloth. I noticed that the First Lady National booth was also busy. I waved to Ruby and caught her eye. After a few minutes, she walked over.

"Doin' okay?" she asked. Her brown bobbed hair was all the style. She wore blue jeans, a red shirt, and a vest with the U.S. flag print across it. All three of the ladies wore a similar vest. On the booth wall was a huge Victorian hat.

"I'm fine. A little rattled though."

"You alone for the duration, or what?" Ruby picked up a card. "Mind?"

"No. Not at all." I took a breath. "I think she'll be okay, but haven't heard yet. My friend's going to come to sit with me."

"Good. Was that good lookin' man wearing a uniform your hubby?"

"Yep!"

"You got lucky. Tall, handsome—what more could a gal ask for?" Ruby spoke, and I giggled. "Want me to stay till your friend comes?"

"I'll be okay." I smiled. "I'll come over to your booth when I hear something."

"Good."

I began to think that Maggie wouldn't show. It was already four and the doors stayed open until nine. A gathering of all representatives was scheduled for the next night. I listened to the jingle dancers and the drumming from a distance. Occasionally drummers and dancers came over to our area. I admired the beautiful orange, yellow, and white dresses with tinkling bells the women wore. The dresses glistened and sparkled from the overhead lighting. Young children wore similar outfits including boys, who wore vests and leggings decorated with beads and tinkling bells. Most of the men and boys wore feathers in their hair and wristbands.

My eyes lit up when I noticed Maggie coming across the vast room toward me. In her hand was a small box, and I couldn't wait to see what she brought.

I stepped aside for Maggie to have a seat beside me. She set the box down before scooting in. As she did, she asked, "Heard from Aaron?" I shook my head. She enveloped me in her arms. "It'll be fine, just wait and see."

"I hope so." Just as I was about to open the box, my phone rang. I could barely hear Aaron's voice, and I held up a finger, "It's Aaron and I can't hear him. Hold on." I got up and moved behind the flat back of the booth, which blocked the background noise. I held my palm up over my other ear to better hear. "Speak up!"

"Baby girl, she's dead." I could hear concern in his voice. "Just now got the word. Thought I should call. I haven't called my sergeant yet."

"Oh dear God," I whispered. My heart leapt into my throat, and I could barely speak. "You know how or why?"

"Nope. It's considered 'questionable' given the situation," Aaron said.

I walked around to my chair and slowly sat, internalizing the information.

"Now what?" I asked Aaron.

Maggie saw my eyes and gave me a tissue, then turned her attention back to a visitor to the booth.

"I'm sure that you'll be questioned."

"Probably." I took a deep breath. "She was such a nice person."

"Yes, well—save it all for the detectives," Aaron said.

"Here we go again." I disconnected and slumped forward in the chair. Dazed, I couldn't believe Gina was dead.

When the customer walked away, Maggie turned to me and asked, "What's the verdict?"

"Dead." Tears filled my eyes. "She seemed so happy and she didn't look sick by any means. She mentioned a headache, but that's not unusual."

"They'll get to the bottom of this."

"At least it doesn't have anything to do with me this time. I couldn't be hiding anything—no clues—nothing that someone would want." I sniffled.

"Let's hope you won't have to eat those words." Maggie nodded. She shoved the box in front of me and I scooped out a chocolate cupcake and bit into it with delight.

"It can't happen again. Three times? No way." I shook my head and held up a cupcake. "This is heavenly." I smiled with every bite. "I don't have anything for anyone to want to kill me over. Trust me." I was referring to my two previous adventures. The first was searching for the original copy of the Star Spangled Banner –an adventure that almost got me killed. More recently I had been on a quest to find the only copy of Lincoln's Lost Speech–the speech that propelled him toward the White House.

The hours slipped past, and soon it was time for us to pack up and leave. Unfortunately, I only had too few boxes. I hesitated to leave my minis, but when I saw the women from the First Ladies booth had left the Victorian hat decorating their booth, I decided that the minis were safe.

"I'm bringing the empty orange juice bottle I found next to Gina to Aaron, just in case. Depending on how the autopsy goes, the police might want it." I scooped it up, along with her purse, and we left to find Aaron.

We wound our way among the remaining crowds lingering near the various booths until, at last, reaching security where Aaron stood.

"Here. This is what Gina was drinking from in case you guys need it," I said. I handed it to him.

"Thanks. I'll take care of it." Aaron took it, We said 'goodbye' then gave each other a quick kiss.

"See you later," I said.

Maggie and I left. Only after leaving the elevators and finally stepping out into the fresh air, did I feel better. We hugged, and we arranged for Maggie to join me the following day about eleven o'clock. She even promised to bring more of the chocolate cupcakes.

The drive home brought me back via 35W and then exiting onto the main drag, Main Street in Northeast Minneapolis. The area was known for its Catholic churches and large population of Polish/German immigrants during the turn of the previous century. I grew up on the other side of town, the South Side, where Swedish immigrants settled.

It didn't take long before I passed the old Grain Belt Brewery and turned into our small development. I opened the garage door with the remote, and drove inside, shutting off the car and then lowering the door. The clock read ten pm. I decided that a hot shower plus a cup of hot chocolate to help me sleep was in order.

Aaron found me half-asleep in bed when he got home. "Talk to me," I said. "How could this have happened to Gina? She can't be dead." I sighed and pulled the sheet up to my shoulders. "I can't believe it."

"It's up in the air until all the facts are known." Aaron sat and removed his shoes and socks. "It seems weird to me, and I told the detectives that also."

"They know you're a regular cop?"

"Yes." He leaned closer and kissed me. "And they also know about our past history." He scratched his head. "What I'm sayin' is this—you'll be questioned right away."

"Figures." I yawned. "It gives me the creeps."

"Chances are, it was just a simple death."

"Nothing's that simple." A streak of fear raced through me. I started to shiver and he pulled up the blanket. "I might be asleep before you come from the shower." I looked into his eyes and he kissed me.

I fell asleep immediately but woke during the night and never did sleep soundly afterwards. My thoughts streamed from TR to FDR, and then to the teddy bear that had been a big part of solving a mystery regarding Mary Lincoln. I thought of all the events that surrounded Teddy Roosevelt, from bears and fighting cowboys to the Panama Canal and his Bull Moose speeches. I rolled closer to Aaron and calmed down. Eventually I managed a few more winks of sleep before the morning alarm sounded.

Since I was on my own this morning, I got up and dressed early. Aaron had special hours and duties and had left before I was up. I wanted to stop by the store and see how well Grandma faired yesterday, deciding to pick something up to eat along the way. I headed out the door wearing a sundress and lightweight sweater. As I backed from the garage, I couldn't help but to glance over at Gina's house and my heart seemed to almost stop. I gulped and took a deep breath before continuing on my way.

Five minutes later I parked behind the store, and jumped out of the car. I opened the backdoor, entered, marched straight to the showroom. I wanted to do a quick check of my messages and also take a look at the sales. I sat down in front of the computer and got it running. As it started humming, I perused the sales receipts and noticed that two houses were sold—the historic White House, which would be the early house where the Madison's resided, and Edith Roosevelt's. I was pleased. I glanced over at the wall shelf and noted that the jingle dancer figurine, pictures and other smaller items were as they should be. The computer was ready, and I logged into my account. I had only a few messages and zipped through them easily, then logged out.

"Morning," I said, walking over to the houses. I stopped in front of the historic White House. "Dolley? You haven't been pinching snuff, now have you? Ladies of today don't do that type of thing." I leaned closer to the dolls because it seemed as if they whispered to me. "How wonderful, President Madison. She made you ice cream with strawberries? I'm happy for you." I winked at him before moving away. At the Ford White House, Mrs. Ford, Betty as I thought of her, looked sprightly. "Have you been dancing on top of the President's desk again?" I thought I saw her nod. "Good."

I walked to the counter, and taking a sheet of paper, I left a short message for Grandma.

Was it a good day or not? T. or F.?

Did anyone ask if Mrs. Washington was still alive? Y or N

Do you have a pot of chicken soup for me and Aaron? Y or N

Afterwards, I grabbed my bag and headed out the backdoor.

I called out, "Be good and enjoy the day!"

I had thought about checking on my employee, Max, but decided against it. He rented the lone upstairs apartment from me. The outside stairs led to his apartment and he used the back door to the shop just like I do. His occupancy was helpful because he kept a close eye on the store, plus he could pick and choose his own hours. I really didn't see much of him, but always knew when he'd been in the store. He carved the dolls' heads and also took care of assembling all the houses. I depended on him and he was very trustworthy, but a bit of a rogue when it came to women—which wasn't my concern.

I locked up, headed over to the car, and climbed inside. As I turned onto the street and drove toward the entrance to the interstate, my thoughts went to the detectives and I wondered what questions they'd ask? Then my thoughts turned to Gina as I wondered how well I had really known her.

It didn't take too long before I crossed the Mississippi River and found my parking spot on the same level in the parking garage as yesterday. I locked up and hiked toward the hallway that would bring me to the main doors.

I showed my pass and slipped past security. I searched among the crowd of officers in the lobby, but didn't see Aaron. I continued walking, thinking. I thought about the woman who'd stopped by yesterday to see Gina. I couldn't immediately think of her name, then I saw a picture of a deer on one of the display walls, and remembered; it was Bambi. How could I have forgotten those lovely brown doe eyes and long brown braided hair? Her tiny features reminded me of a deer. Since it wasn't time for the exhibition to open, I headed toward the jingle dance area.

As I stood to the side of the entrance door, I realized that it wasn't just Native Americans in costume, many people of all races were dressing up. From the back, a woman resembled Gina so closely that it took my breath away. I didn't see Bambi, so I left, resolving to return later.

Maggie wasn't expected for another hour, and I stopped to get coffee and a muffin from Wrangler Jean's, before setting up my booth. I set my cup and muffin down and got to work arranging the mini houses to place on display. I noticed that they were slightly askew, but figured it was because of the late night cleaning crew.

After arranging everything, I began eating my muffin and relaxing. I'd barely taken a few sips when I noticed two men wearing suits approaching in the distance, and I presumed they were the detectives. I took another bite and sip, and tried to relax my rapidly beating heart as they neared. By the time they'd gotten within talking distance, I'd finished my muffin.

"Mrs. Reynolds?" He showed me his badge. "Detective Paulson."

"Liv."

"Detective Schmidt." The second detective also showed his badge. "Let's get down to business."

"Sure." I smiled and held my breath. These two guys looked prickly and worn-out. "Have a seat, if you want. There's one extra, you two can take turns."

"No, thank you," Detective Paulson stated. "Let's get started before it gets too harried around here."

"You could've contacted me at home." I raised a brow, cocking my head. "I'm in the phonebook."

"We're from St. Paul, not Minneapolis. Different jurisdictions."

"We're not sure what this is—call it a courtesy call." Detective Schmidt reached for his smokes, then slid the pack back into his pocket.

"What can you tell us about yesterday?"

"Not much. Gina took a few pain killers before coming here." My eyes opened wide. "Just a minute." I reached for the bottle and opened it. "This was her new bottle of aspirins."

"Count."

I emptied the bottle and did as told, coming up with twenty-three. "Sounds about right." I stared at the two men. "Now what?"

"How did she seem?" Paulson asked.

"Fine. A bit of a headache. A touch of out of sorts."

"Anyone stop by?"

"Her friend Bambi, and she's related to Sunflower and Ranger Harry from the TR park," I said.

"See anything suspicious looking or a little odd? Give it some thought Liv, because these details could be important," Schmidt said.

"I had overheard an argument, but thought nothing of it."

"Do you remember who the participants were?" Schmidt said.

"I believe it was between Sunflower and Harry. Brother and sister, nothing odd about that."

"Okay." He made note of it.

"I brought her purse and drink to security at the end of the day. I gave it to Officer Reynolds," I said.

"Your husband?" Paulson asked.

"Yes."

"We'll check that out."

"She was a very capable person. Not prone to excitement or taking chances. She worked hard. This was the first time that we'd ever done this-she as my employee, I mean."

"Know anything about Bambi?"

"She's a jingle dancer, that's all I know."

"That's all for now," Paulson said.

"We're not finished questioning," Schmidt said.

"Are you treating me like a suspect? I didn't do it?"

Schmidt barked a quick laugh. "You're jumping the gun. We havein't even detirmined if this is a homicide or not."

With that, the detective's left.

My heart pounded.

If it was murder, could they think I had something to do with it?

Chapter Three

I sat in the booth, drank my coffee and watched the hall slowly fill with attendees. *Had I missed something? Something important?* My thoughts went in circles and my heart pumped wildly. I told myself to breathe in and out, slowly. Eventually, my heartbeat slowed. My ears burned. I felt miserable, and gave Aaron a call.

"Honey? They made me feel like I was some kind of criminal."
"Just doing their job. It's probably going down as suspicious."
"Really?"
"Yep."

We disconnected, and I still didn't feel much better.

Since it was the Fourth of July weekend, many people wore the Stars and Stripes in various formats-shirts, pants, hats, shoes, and shorts. I liked the get-up of a guy wearing the Statue of Liberty for a hat and flag for a shirt. Little kids came dressed as Rangers, looking so cute. I hoped that someday they'd become a Ranger too, if they wanted. Anyone could become one.

The second day of the show brought the Rangers from their booths, out to take a look on their own. I watched as they criss-crossed the show and spoke to their opposite numbers from other parks. An impersonator playing Thomas Jefferson walked by. Why would someone impersonate him at a National Parks expo,

I wondered, then decided it was because he'd been a naturalist. He was a farmer, and someone who worked the land and would've supported the 'go green' trend of today.

I saw an older woman stop by the First Ladies booth, and ask a question. One of the women turned and pointed toward me. I smiled. Within minutes, she was before me.

"My name's Liv, how may I help you?" I held out my hand to shake but found hers was limp. She was about medium height and wore red capris and a blue and white tank top. I noted a distinct different line of coloration from her dark brown quarter-inch hair to the current shade of auburn she had. "I own the First Ladies White House Dollhouse Store in Minneapolis, and these are a few of my miniatures."

"Honey, I'm related to Gina." I saw tears in her eyes. "I have to speak to you. I feel like a big mess and I need help."

"Oh dear. You come on around here and have a seat." I scooted over for her to sit. The poor woman looked ready to drop. "How can I help?"

"The cops are probably checking for prints and everything so I don't want to barge in… but she'd borrowed some old books of mine. There's a ledger, you see…" She took a deep breath and looked away. "Name's Ida Gray. I'm her aunt. I was her closest relation. Sorry, should've said so right off the bat but I'm so nervous, honey."

"Not sure what you're after, books or a ledger?"

"Tell me how it happened. The poor thing." Tears streamed down her cheeks, and she removed a tissue from her pocket.

"She'd had a headache and took a prescription pill. She seemed fine when I went to listen to the opening ceremonies. I returned and saw that she was slumped over. I thought she was sleeping at first but found out otherwise. I called the police and medics right away." I reached around and pulled the hunched over lady into my arms. "I'm so sorry Ida. I wish I could be more helpful."

"I thought you might do me a favor?" She hesitated, grabbed my hand and leaned in closer. "I wondered if you might go through

the house and look for the ledger and books? I don't think that
I should."

"No. That's up to the police," I said, as I shook my head.

"Yes, but her death doesn't make sense. I thought, since your
husband is a policeman, that you would know more about the
investigation."

"Why would you think that?" I frowned. "I can't interfere with
an ongoing investigation. Besides, there's nothing that makes me
think it's connected to anything."

"Gina was a good girl. Hard working. She had her life ahead
of her. She'd planned for college but her mom got sick. My sister.
Both of Gina's parents are deceased. I have my family's inheritance
to think of. Just walk through and look for a book and ledger for
me, that's all."

"Tell me a good reason why I should snoop through Gina's
house." I could hardly believe the story Ida had to tell about Gina.
It seemed there was a missing deed to valuable family property,
maybe even with oil wells. Ida was convinced the deed hidden
was inside Gina's house, and wanted me to search for it. "I don't
know what to say." I frowned. "Why can't you ask the police for
permission to enter her house?"

"They don't want anyone entering the premises."

I wanted to pull my hair out from frustration as she took a
pen from her purse and ripped a corner from a sheet of paper.
She scribbled her phone number and handed it over to me. "Here,
Liv. If you find anything, please call."

"I'll think about it." I grabbed it and placed it into my pocket.
"Here, take one of my cards. Here's my home phone number and
you can send messages to my website. The number on the card
is for the business." I jotted the information down and handed
it to her.

"Thank you."

"Do you happen to have a key?"

"No, but I'm sure you could find a way in. I think there's
one hidden outside, just like what her mother always did—in the
planter or under a flowerpot." She stood, and stared down at me

through teary eyes. "She was also my goddaughter, you see. I loved her very much."

"I'll think about it."

After she'd faded into the crowd, I dug out the phone number and realized that the exchange was for St. Paul. I took out my cell phone and added her name and number to my contact list, then gave Aaron a call.

"Guess what?" I said when he answered. "You won't believe it." In my mind, I saw him raise a questioning brow.

"Let's have it."

"Gina's aunt was just here and she wants me to look for something in Gina's house."

"How odd. What else aren't you tellin' me?"

"She wants me to find either a ledger, land deed or old books." I pictured him narrowing his eyes and setting his jaw.

"Nope. Ain't gonna happen."

"I know. Oops! Gotta run!" I disconnected even though no one was beside me. I didn't care to hear him rant and rave about messing up police work or getting in the way. There was no police work going on, and he didn't see how sad and forlorn the poor woman looked. I no sooner tucked away my phone when Maggie appeared.

"Hey you!" she said, sliding in beside me. "You look a little bewildered."

"It's like this-." I went ahead and relayed to her what Aunt Ida had to say and ended with, "The key is probably hidden under the planter. What do you think I should do?"

"I take it she's gotten your curiosity up?" Maggie said, grinning.

"Is it a mystery or not?" I asked. I knew she was up for another adventure.

"Yes! So let's figure this one out. Was she murdered or not?" Maggie said.

"It's considered suspicious. I didn't see police tape outside of the doors," I said. "I'd like to know more about Ida Gray. Is there a husband, and if so, as Gina's uncle, where would he fit in?"

"Let's investigate." Maggie was engaged to Aaron's partner, Tim Dolquist. "Hmm—we won't tell our better-halves that we're snooping."

"It's not really considered a murder, at least not yet. Why have me go inside searching for books? Why doesn't she?" I cocked my head. "That's what doesn't make any sense." I told Maggie that the detectives had already questioned me, and what I told them. "I don't think they have enough to continue the investigation. My thoughts are that they'd like to but until something else develops, their hands are tied."

"I suspect you're correct." Maggie took out her cell phone and ran a web search for Gina Johnson. "You're not going to believe this, but there are two addresses listed, here and in Medora, North Dakota. How long has she been your neighbor?"

"Six to eight months." I hesitated a moment, and scratched the back of my head. "Search for Ida Gray."

A minute later, Maggie shook her head. "Nada. Zip."

"Do a reverse search." I showed the number to Maggie and she punched it into the pad. In about a second, Ida's address popped up. "She's not far from here."

"This has me wondering a whole lot," I said.

"I know what you're saying." Maggie took out a small container of cupcakes and handed one over. We ate them quickly, finishing by licking the frosting off our fingers.

"Ida said something about Gina's parents owning a ranch and how she's trying to keep it in the family."

"That only muddies the water, doesn't it?"

"You bet." I sighed. "The TR National Park Ranger, Harry, is her cousin and so is a jingle dancer named Sunflower. Harry and Sunflower are Ida's kids. Interesting, isn't it? I bet they're after the deed, too." Placing my hands on my hips, I looked out into the crowd. I thought about Bambi and wondered how she had taken the death of her friend. Glancing toward the TR display, I noticed the representative from yesterday standing behind the booth. The TR impersonator was busy shaking hands and working the crowd so much like a politician, it made me wonder if he wasn't one. The

John Muir impersonator was also nearby, talking with my friends at the First Lady booth. I decided to mingle.

"I'm going to stroll about to see what comes up. You okay sittin' alone?"

"Sure." Maggie grinned, still holding her phone.

I walked away knowing that she'd be happy checking her various accounts and playing a few games. I strolled right on over to introduce myself to the John Muir impersonator.

"You do a great job, sir."

"Ed Parsons is my name. Thank you," he said, shaking my hand. "I'm traveling the country, hoping to keep TR's vision and mine, alive." His scraggly beard was real, which didn't surprise me. His rugged skin reminded me of mountains and valleys.

"It's important to keep those memories alive," I replied. I had wanted to speak with the women, but with John and the TR impersonator near, I wasn't sure if I should. I went ahead and asked anyway, "Did any of you see anyone coming and talking for any length of time with my friend yesterday? She was at my booth for most of the day. Or maybe something out of the ordinary?" I studied each of them. "Her aunt is quite distressed."

"Nope, too busy stumpin' the crowds," the TR impersonator said.

"Didn't see anyone," said Ruby and the other ladies and Ed shook their heads.

"I heard rumors about something happening over here yesterday," Ed, or John Muir, as I still thought of him stated. "Everyone's taking turns walking about, makes it hard to put anyone in any one place at a given time."

"Yep. There are so many people too." I smiled and figured they didn't have anything else of importance to relay. "I'll be off. Talk to you later." I headed down the aisle toward the TR Park display. I hadn't any idea what to ask, and hoped for inspiration.

"Howdy, ma'am," the Ranger said. He smiled from ear to ear, and was just as good looking in person as from a distance. Reading his nametag, I realized he was Ida's son.

"I'm Liv. You're Gina's cousin Harry?"

"Yep, I'm Harry," he nodded.

"Do you have any clue as to how Gina died? Was she on other medications?"

"I really don't know much about her medical history. We haven't had a heart-to-heart in years." He rubbed his chin. "We're cousins, but not kissing cousins. Not close by any means."

"Oh, I see." I shrugged. "You from the Medora area? You must be if you're a Ranger for the park"

"Live not far away from the park, on the ranch with the family. Sunflower lives in town."

"If you think of anything, please let me know. Her death doesn't sit right with me."

"Me neither."

I started backing away. "Catch you later."

"Will do."

As I shuffled through the crowd, my mind wandered. Neither the John Muir nor the TR impersonators, had anything further to offer or the ladies. I erased them from the list.

I normally would've searched for my good-looking husband, but I was sure he had a lecture up his sleeve for me about not snooping or going into Gina's house. I didn't want to hear it so I passed quickly by the security station, and hiked over to the dancers.

Dozens of women and children stood in front of long mirrors, making sure their homemade beaded designs were straight and even across their bodice and shoulders. Over the years, the dancers and costume makers have kept to tradition and used healing colors such as red, yellow, green, and blue. Years ago, the traditional dancers always side-stepped, never in circles as the dance was used to help heal the unwell by dancing around the ill individual. Now the dancers interpret the beat, and dance to their own inner-rhythm. The rowed metal bells hung evenly and jingled as the dancer softly danced around the drum. The magnificent costumes took my breath away. Women wore their hair braided and down with a bead band or up with feathers.

The nearest woman turned toward me and asked, "Lookin' for someone?" Her bright red lips and stunning sunbeam design for a headband and across her blouse made me envious of her beauty.

"Yes. Do you know of someone named Bambi?" I took a breath. "Sorry, but your costumes are so beautiful, that it's left me speechless."

"Thanks. It's hard work." She massaged her chin. "I sure do know her, and she looks like a deer with the big doe eyes. My name's Sunflower. Notice all the sun beadwork?"

"I get it!" Chuckling I said, "Should I check back later?"

"Are you a vendor?"

"I'm at the First Ladies White House Dollhouse booth. Will you ask Bambi to come over? Mention Gina, and she should know." I hesitated, then plowed ahead. "I just found out that you were Gina's cousin. This has got to be hard to continue now with her passing."

"I manage."

"Yes of course. Your mother stopped by to see me earlier. She wondered about a deed or something hidden in Gina's house. Do you know anything about that?" I asked, and watched as her eyes glazed over.

"Nope."

"Please tell Bambi so I can tell her about Gina," I said. I began to walk away, when I heard my name called. I turned around. Sunflower faced me with a scowl on her face, and her hands on her hips. "What?" I asked.

"Keep your nose out of where it don't belong," Sunflower said.

"Got it," I said. As I continued on my way, I wondered what she was hiding? *Keep my nose out of what? Looking for the deed?*

As I walked from the room, the jingling in the background reminded me of windchimes in the summer breeze.

Before going back to the booth, I wanted to swing closer to the drummers and watch as they set everything up for the next performance. On the event calendar posted on a wall I noticed that a new attraction was added: The Wild West Show. I wondered how they'd be able to do that since Buffalo Bill Cody wasn't represented when out of the blue—from behind one of the walls—came his impersonator with Annie Oakley right beside him. I knew I was in for a treat if I could sneak away and watch their show. Peering closer at Annie, I realized physically how much she resembled me in stature. Annie wore an ankle length navy-blue dress—I figure she was under five feet since I barely made five foot-two inches. She carried the rifle like a marksman. I wanted to ask her any number of questions, such as 'do you really shoot as well as Annie did, or is that full head of brown hair all yours?' but she was immediately surrounded by people.

I had managed to talk with everyone I could think of who might be able to shed some light on Gina's death, but felt like I had gotten nowhere. I headed for my booth hoping the rest of the morning would be more productive.

Chapter Four

The exposition was a great hit. Maggie and I learned that next time, the organizers planned to send invitations to all the national parks in the country to send representatives. The enormous show would fill both the Xcel Center and the Minneapolis Convention Center across the river. I thought it'd be a great idea, having a convention between Minneapolis and St. Paul.

A few people came to my booth and asked questions about the first ladies, how they managed living in the White House and being under such scrutiny. My mind was kept running at full speed by all the questions. I thought I already knew everything there was to know about the first ladies, but I learned many things listening to the Theodore Roosevelt impersonator as he worked the crowds. TR had purchased land adjacent to the National Park in North Dakota and had given it to his daughter Alice. I hadn't known that. *Who owned the property now? Where is the deed?*

"Sunflower, Ida's daughter, just told me to keep my nose out of where it doesn't belong," I said. "Can you believe that?"

"I assume this has something to do with searching Gina's house?"

"Truthfully, I'm perplexed. I don't like being put in this position, but I'd like to know if there is a deed or something—

which explains what this puzzle is all about," I said, placing my hands on my hips. "It's annoying."

"If you searched Gina's house, the police would string you up and so would Aaron," Maggie said.

"I know, but what if the answer to the puzzle is there?"

"A quick walk through would tell you if there's anything missing or out of place," Maggie said. "Is there yellow tape on the door, telling you it's a crime scene?

"Nope. No cops around, no yellow tape anywhere that I can see," I said. "Gina was sweet, and I'd hate to have her house vandalized. Maybe it's a good idea for someone to walk through it so that if it did happen, then the police would know what it's supposed to be like."

"I get it, but you could get into trouble," Maggie said.

"I know. That's the rub. Aaron would lecture me until my next birthday." I frowned. "Let's refocus. We need to search land purchases around the Medora area," I suggested. "This search reminds me of schooldays when we had reports to write."

"I was thinking the same," Maggie said. "How far back will you search?"

"A hundred years." I punched in the letters and presto—a number of websites were visible. I selected the first one. "I wonder—you know? Is it possible that land still belongs to Alice? It makes me question why there aren't any distant relatives involved with the preservation or here at the expo."

"There might be, but we don't know it," Maggie said. She watched as I made the image larger so that she could see it. "No Roosevelt."

"Alice would've been living at home or married, I believe. How odd." I waited a few minutes before saying, "I'm going to search land ownership around Medora."

"Okay."

"Wow!" I peered closely as the two sites popped onto the screen. I knew that Maggie's eyes were lit up like fireworks, and that mine were a close second. "If I'm reading this right, Alice's name is on the deed." It showed that Alice Roosevelt owned property adjacent to her father's ranch. "I wonder if she even knew about the deed?"

"Good question." Maggie waited a moment before continuing, "Did Edith know?"

"We'll have to find out." Just as we started searching further, I looked up and noticed that Bambi was standing near. I nudged Maggie as I slipped the phone into my pocket. "Bambi, how good of you to come."

"Hi." Her big, brown doe-eyes looked so sad. I felt like crying just from her appearance. "I feel sick about all of this," she said, her voice trailing off.

"Me, too." I stood and went around the table to her. "Mind if we talk someplace quiet?" I glanced back at Maggie who nodded in agreement to watch the booth.

"Sure. I know of a place." Bambi led me to the back of the hall, an area where there were few people about. A stairwell loomed nearby. "I honestly don't know what else to tell you that the police don't already know."

"Bear with me, that's all I ask." I thought a moment. "How did you two become friends? How well did you two know each other?"

"We grew up together. Same schools, stuff like that. Gina inherited her, but no one lives on it right now." She wiped her moist eyes. "Nothing much else to tell."

"Can't you tell me anything?"

"Right now the oil companies are doing the 'fracking' for oil. It's a big mess and everyone wants their share." Bambi waited a beat, and then said, "There was something, not too long ago. Gina called me—it was completely out of the blue. She said that she thought someone was following her and worried about her safety."

"You're kidding," I said, my eyes opened wider. "Did you tell the police?"

"I didn't remember it at the time. I didn't think there was anything to it. Why would anyone stalk her?"

"Did she say, 'stalk' or 'follow'?"

"Hmm…," she rubbed her chin, "stalk." Nodding her head, she said, "Stalk."

"It could mean that there is something in the house that this stalker creep wants. You need tell the police about this," I said. "Do you know her aunt, Ida Gray?"

"I've met her, but that's about it. Why?"

"She asked me to search through Gina's house and look for either a deed, ledger or book. Anything that's out of place."

"Gina told me that her aunt bugged her at times, but she never said about what. I thought she was nice, but always asking questions. That's probably why Gina had trouble liking her aunt."

"Anything else? Can you tell me who was near when you were by the booth? Do you remember?"

"No, not really. Rangers were setting up and going around looking at displays just like everyone else."

"Speaking of Rangers--, do you happen to know Harry from the Theodore Roosevelt booth or Sunflower very well?"

"I've been friends for ages with them. Grade school, actually." She waited a moment. "Why?"

"Just wonderin', that's all." I hesitated. "Did they get along? Were the families close?" I asked.

"The families weren't close, but Ida did help Gina's mom when she got sick. They did care for each other even though they didn't seem to really get along because of the 'fracking'.

"That answers my question. It doesn't sound like their family is much different than everyone else's. Thank you." I smiled and gave her a hug. "Mind if I ask questions again if I need to?"

"Nope. I want to find out to what really happened." Bambi gazed upward and when she looked at me, her eyes were filled with tears once again. "She was careful. I don't understand what could have happened to my friend."

"It's considered questionable or suspicious. I haven't heard anything else."

After hugging again, we parted. On the way back to the booth, I shivered.

As I sat beside Maggie, I saw Harry nearby. "Hey, Harry!"
He glanced over and sort of scowled before smiling.

Maggie nudged me under the table. "Why did he scowl?" She raised a brow, and said, "Never mind. I get it. The police must've questioned him."

Harry gave a quick wave with his freehand and I watched him head back to his booth. "Any prospective customers?"

"Not yet. Still kind of early, but yet, look at all the people." Maggie eyes opened wider. "They're coming in droves."

"Next year, they'll split this with Minneapolis then the congestion won't be such a problem," I said.

"What did Bambi say?" Maggie leaned in closer. "Does she know anything about the death?"

"You're as much of a snoop as me," I said. "She is really upset over it. Neither of us are satisfied that Gina's death was accidental."

"What's the next move?"

"Not sure, but did she tell me that Gina had called her concerned because she thought someone was stalking her." Just then a young couple stepped from the crowd and looked over our booth. The woman wore flag earrings and the man wore matching USA Tee-shirts. *Very cute!* "How may I help you?"

"Well… you know… my mother still has her dollhouse from when she was a kid." Her brown eyes brightened, and a smile crossed her lips. "She loves it. Believe it or not, she set it out now that all of us kids have left home. I bet she'd love your shop."

"Where you located exactly?" the young man asked. His phone beeped a message. He removed his phone and took a quick glance, then put it back into his pocket.

"Right off from Hennepin Avenue Bridge and Main Street. Right across the river from the downtown shopping area in Minneapolis." I reached for the stack of cards and handed one to him. "Here's my website and it'll give directions if needed."

"First Ladies White House Dollhouse." He slid it into his pocket. "Thanks."

"Do you happen to have them in stock?" The young woman cocked her head, and the movement displayed a small tattoo in the shape of a butterfly near her collarbone.

"Yes. And we ship them. The prices include the pieces and dolls." I waited a moment before continuing, "Which First Lady are you interested in?"

"The rose garden First Lady." I noticed a long stem rose tattoo running up her right forearm. "Jackie Kennedy, I think."

"Yes, that's right. The store is open today. I have an employee working there while I'm here."

"Thank you, ma'am." The man took her arm, scooting her away.

I turned to Maggie, "Do you think?"

"Possibly. For her mom—most likely." Maggie glanced around the room, turning her sites back to me. "You haven't finished about Bambi."

"The call was out of the 'blue'. She forgot about it and didn't tell the police so I reminded her to. Do you know, I'm still bothered by Sunflower telling me to 'keep my nose out of where it don't belong'. What do you think?"

"I think this means that you need to take a walk through that house."

"Exactly. With or without Aaron."

"Tell me what else Bambi said."

"Something about oil fracking near the park, but that's happening all over the oil fields." I thought for a moment. "It may well have something to do with drilling."

"Adds a new twist, doesn't it? Have you spoken to Aaron about what you've learned?"

Frowning, I shook my head.

"Okay. It'll just be between us."

When Maggie got up and went for a walk-about, I decided to take a moment and do more research. I hoped for a decent connection on my phone and entered 'fracking into a search engine. I needed to understand what it meant before any further investigation. I found a site and read that it had something to do with drilling for oil. It's injecting water into rock at high pressure and forcing out the oil and natural gas by fracturing the rock. Thus, the term of 'fracking' made sense. I closed out the site and let my mind wander. What did I really know about Gina? She had red hair like myself, which drew me to her, and she had a wonderful personality. I wasn't sure about her personal life, but I knew that she was relatively new to the metro area and from Medora, North Dakota.

I didn't see how knowing these things helped to explain Gina's death, which haunted me. I turned my thoughts back to former conversations with Gina. I tried to remember every tidbit of what she had mentioned about herself, but came up empty. There just didn't seem to be anything memorable about her. She never spoke of her childhood, parents, or siblings, only about work and how much she enjoyed living in her house, but wished she'd earned a better living. I didn't care to scrounge around in her house without Aaron knowing what I was doing, but also knew that he'd disapprove and try to stop me. I resolved to not tell him until after, but would let I would Maggie know, just in case.

Looking up, I saw her in the distance—hand-in-hand with her fiancé, Tim Dolquist. I gave Grandma a quick call at the store.

I grinned as she answered with, "First Ladies White House Dollhouse, Marie speaking."

"Hi, Grandma! Busy today?"

"Just had a call. Someone asked about the 'Rose Garden' house." I heard her take a sip from her cup. Grandma is of true Scandinavian stock. She can't go long with coffee.

"A young person?'

"Sounded like it."

"It might be the couple that stopped by a short while ago." I glanced up as Annie Oakley came into view. "Annie Oakley's near. Gotta run!" I quickly disconnected and shoved my phone back into my pocket. My heart sank as the performer walked by without stopping. I'd hoped to ask her a number things, including how she learned to shoot so well.

The afternoon slipped past as fast as the morning. Maggie stayed until late afternoon so that we could each take turns watching the jingle-dance performances. I was impressed with the pretty dancers and beautiful dresses, as well as the drummers in their costumes and wanted to take advantage of all their performances.

Crowds thinned early on in the evening since it was the holiday weekend, so I decided to leave early. Aaron's shift wouldn't end until ten, which would give me time to walk around Gina's house after I got home.

As I passed the booths on the way to the main doors, I noticed the many people gathered around the Theodore Roosevelt booth, and most especially the actor himself. I wished they'd hired an actress to portray Mrs. Roosevelt's part, and resolved to drop a note to the man-in-charge of the event if ever asked for suggestions.

After unlocking and jumping into my car, I backed out and made my way down the winding ramps until at last paying at the street-level gate to exit. I turned left and kept going until finding my way to University Avenue and driving past the many buildings with made up the University of Minnesota. It took a little while to drive through St. Paul and enter the city limits of Minneapolis. But from there I was soon turning onto my street, and as I did I glanced over to Gina's house. Even though it felt good to drive into my garage, the sight of her empty home gave me a heavy heart.

The garage door was lowering as I entered into my kitchen. I set my bag down and gave Grandma another call just to make sure that all was well in the store. She reported, "No problem," and I went to stand in front of my front window and stare across the street at Gina's. I saw no lights or movement. Good!

My plan was to get in and get out just as fast as possible. I reached for the number of her Aunt Ida, and made a call. "This is Liv Reynolds, Gina's friend, and I'm going now to look around the house. Just thought you should know."

"Okay. Call me when you return or if you see anything suspicious."

"I will." Disconnecting, I wanted to ask what she meant by suspicious. It set my nerves on end. I picked up a small button flashlight and slipped it into my pocket beside my phone. I dropped my house key in my pocket too, before heading out the door.

Crossing the street, I hoped none of my neighbors saw me. I knew that in a small subdivision like this, it was entirely possible that someone would. I figured that since it was a holiday and summertime, backyard picnics would keep them from spotting me peeking through the windows of a neighbor's house. The key was right where I expected, under the planter where Ida said it'd be, and I left it there since I wasn't planning to enter the house. I made a mental note to relay the info to Aaron and tell the detectives the next time we met.

I stood outside the front window and I let my eyes focus on the dim interior. It was Gina's living room, and nothing appeared out of the ordinary. The sofa, table, and chairs all looked neat and the sofa pillows looked plumped. The television control lay on a table beside the one recliner, probably Gina's favorite chair. I cupped my hands against the glass for a better look, and decided that the living room looked fine, nothing out of place.

I went to the bedroom window and took a look. Gina's room appeared neat and clean. The spare room was much the same. Everything neat and tidy. From the kitchen patio door, I noticed a cup on the table and dirty knife. Nothing else. The floor gleamed from a recent mopping.

I shook my head and went around to the front door once again and turned the knob, where an envelope stuck between the front and screen doors slipped out.

The yellow envelope marked 'urgent' had a return address from an attorney firm in Medora. It was enough to make me question if I should take it or not? I decided to take it and turn it over to the authorities as soon as possible.

Before leaving, I looked up the street and down to make sure no one was out in their front yard to see me. I hurried home, and the phone rang just as I entered. It was Ida, which made me weary, because she immediately began firing questions.

"Nothing unusual. I only peered through the windows. I didn't see any books." I decided against giving her more information until speaking to the authorities.

After saying our 'goodbyes' and telling the other to 'keep in touch', I disconnected.

The sound of distant fireworks made me yearn for Aaron so we could go and watch the spectacle. Since he wasn't there, I took a quick shower and got into my pj's.

Curled up on the couch, watching the fireworks on TV. I no sooner finished deciding upon watching the movie, "Independence Day" with Will Smith as the main character when Aaron entered.

The evening was left for us to celebrate.

Chapter Five

A few things tickled my mind, causing me to lose a decent night's sleep. I chalked it up to all the commotion over the previous two days. To the best of my ability, I tried to make sense of Gina's death, but couldn't. By the time the morning sun streamed into the window, I was ready to get up. I glanced at Aaron who peeked open his right eye—then the left. "Mornin'." I kissed him.

"I have a few things to tell you, which I should've mentioned last night."

"I hope it isn't what I think it is, but go ahead," Aaron said.

"Well, I didn't enter Gina's house, I peeked in as many windows as I could."

"Good girl, no breaking and entering. Only invasion of privacy, they'd probably let you off on good behavior. Proceed."

"Gina's aunt, Ida Gray, wanted me to look for something suspicious," I said. I reached over to the bedside dresser for the envelope. "That set me on edge. I turned the front doorknob, and this envelope slipped out." I handed it over. "It might be important. I didn't tell Ida about it. Also, the key is under a flowerpot outside the door. Should I get it or not?"

"I'll contact the detectives, but they'll probably want to speak to you. If it turns into a murder investigation, then we're talking conflicting jurisdictions. My guess is that Minneapolis will take over since the home is located on this side of the river and any future evidence found in the home would fall into their jurisdiction."

"The authorities will work it out," I said. Aaron set the envelope beside him where his patrol bag was.

"I have a point of interest to tell you." He sat up with a grin. "Betcha can't guess."

"Hmm…," I pursed my lips, "tell me."

"Ed Parsons, the John Muir impersonator is from North Dakota."

"Really?" I questioned. "I would've thought he was from California because that's where John Muir lived when alive." I got up and reached for my outfit. Slipping into a short, flowered sundress I asked, "Want bacon and eggs, or a bowl of cereal?"

"I'm back at the precinct today. I'll pick up something."

"Okay. I'll do the same."

It didn't take long before my hair was brushed and red lipstick applied. I grabbed my things and headed for the door, kissing Aaron as I zipped by.

My favorite drive-thru was open, and I picked up a cup of coffee. By the time I'd made it to the Xcel Convention Center, the coffee was gone and I was hungry. Rather than go inside immediately, and risk eating a burger and fries for breakfast, I decided to go to the nearest diner and snag a muffin. People began pouring inside by the time I entered. I certainly hoped today would bring a peaceful and satisfying conclusion to Gina's death. I wasn't sure whether or not Maggie would join me. She may have made previous arrangements with her parents and Tim. I suspected he probably had to work today since Aaron did, and they were partners.

I stopped by the First Ladies booth and found them setting up.

"Hey you guys! Busy around here, isn't it?" I said.

"I thought we'd have more chances to get up and walk around," Alice stated, "but there's no time at all to do anything."

"I know. It's tough." I noted that all three still dressed similar, today in red and white flowered dress with a blue neck scarf.

"What about those impersonators? Aren't they terrific?" Belle asked. "I think Buffalo Bill looks like a whole lot of fun."

"And, in more ways than one." Ruby said.

"You got me on that one," I chuckled. "He is good looking." I smiled. "I must get to my booth. Have a great day." I waved and walked away.

I bought a small orange juice to drink with my muffin, and went to sit in my booth. Watching the crowds go by and eating my breakfast, my thoughts went to the furnishings in Gina's house. I tried to think of what Aaron always said to look for when entering a room. Something out of character, like two glasses when one person sat by the table. That was a clear indication that someone else may have been there. It also made me wonder about the envelope. I soon had myself convinced that I needed to return and take a closer look at Gina's house.

I looked up just as Ed Parsons approached. I grinned. "Hello, Mr. Muir. Glad that you could make it." I held out my hand, which he willingly shook.

"Thank you. Mighty fine to be invited." Ed crossed his arms and eyed me. "Tell me about your dollhouses."

"How boring do you want me to get?" I said.

He smiled. "Tell me the differences between the TR and the presidents before him. What innovations did he make to the White House?"

I proceeded to explain to him about the various first family changes and their need for privacy. The conversation continued for some time until at last I chanced asking him about the purchased land outside of the park. "Have you heard of a land deed purchased by Theodore Roosevelt next to the land that became the TR National Park?"

"Let me think." Ed scratched his head. "A separate parcel?"

"Yes."

"It's possible. He spoke of purchasing a parcel for his daughter."

"Yes, that could b it." My eyes opened wide.

"I guess so. But that's all I know, I'm afraid." Before he left, Ed asked, "Got anything that belonged to Alice Roosevelt?"

"I have one of her purses." I shrugged, wondering at his interest. "It's at my store."

"I'd like to see it. Bring it in tomorrow."

"I'll try to remember."

He gave me a nod then disappeared, leaving me wondering why he really stopped to visit. At that moment my cell phone chirped, and I responded. It was Aaron.

"Everything going good, baby girl?"

"Yep. Ed just left. He asked about the TR house and then mentioned something about seeing what I have from Alice Roosevelt. I'm not sure why he stopped by."

"He probably was just wondering about the White House and its preservation, that's all."

"Never thought of that." We both said 'goodbye', and disconnected. I knew he wouldn't be home until late again. I let out a long breath, and hoped the day would go by fast.

My thoughts went to Ida, and I wondered why she didn't go to the house and search it herself? *Why ask me to do it?* It didn't seem right. Who stood to inherit that ranch? How large was it? I didn't think Gina had a sibling or close relative besides her aunt and cousins. I took a deep breath and started to consider the notion that her death wasn't an accident. I needed more time to research.

I looked out across the vast room that was wall-to-wall people. A woman caught my eye, and we smiled. It didn't take long before she and I spoke.

"I love dollhouses," she gushed. Her perfume and sparkly eyelashes brought a smile to my lips. "Had a special one when I was a kid and Mother made me get rid of it when I got older. Never forgave her."

"Here." I handed her a card. "Come on over and take a look at them. A gal is never too big or too old to have a dollhouse. That's my motto."

"Thanks." She took the card. "I will."

I watched as she disappeared, and wondered which First Lady would be of interest to her?

I sat for another hour before Maggie joined me, carrying a bag from a fast-food place. As she ate her lunch, I told her about going to Gina's house. "I wonder if I should go back?" I glanced at the crowd. "I also would like to know if anything else has been learned about her and if they've questioned her aunt. I told Aaron that I peeked in the windows and gave him the envelope I found. It certainly seemed official-looking."

"I don't suppose you steamed it open?" She raised a brow, and I shook my head. "Shame on you." She picked up her phone to send a message to Tim. "Let's see if he knows anything else that we don't know."

"Thanks." I thought for a moment. "Don't we have a former classmate who is an attorney? I scratched my head. "Let's see—Brian Swain? Is that right?"

"Sounds right. Graduated with top honors and went to Harvard. Why?"

"He'd probably cost a bundle." I frowned. "I'm going to look up the courthouse for Medora and see if we can find out what property is owned by Gina." I began a search for the courthouse number just as Maggie's phone chirped.

"Hmm…." She looked at me. "It seems that the coroner decided to have a complete test of the blood samples from Gina."

"And?" I held my breath.

"Now it's officially being called 'a homicide'."

"Her death had to have been planned." I rubbed my chin. "Now what?"

"Not a clue." At that moment, Aaron called and I answered.

"Baby girl?" I could hear him taking a deep breath before continuing, "It's been declared a homicide. They're investigating further."

"Why?"

"Don't know all the facts."

"Thanks." We disconnected, and I looked at Maggie. "Now the stakes are higher." I turned to watch an approaching spectacle. Over the top of people's heads, I saw a man wearing a buffalo headpiece striding in front of us. Beside him were two young women dressed as Native American maidens. I loved their braids, their bright red painted cheeks and lone feather headdresses. I couldn't keep my eyes from watching as they passed by. I glanced at Maggie, her eyes were as wide as mine.

"Beautiful."

"We'll have to see the show," I said. "They're gorgeous."

Several Native American men dressed in costume led a procession of impersonators. TR, barely able to slow his pace, walked with Annie Oakley as if they were old friends, along with John Muir, Thomas Jefferson, and Buffalo Bill.

"I wonder who these people really are?" I studied them as they passed. The Jefferson impersonator I remembered from Colonial Williamsburg when Aaron and I were searching for the Star Spangled Banner manuscript. He didn't concern me for that reason. "I'm going to find out."

"Security should know, but why are you interested?" I noticed that Maggie's gaze still followed the procession. "They weren't around when Gina was poisoned."

"How do we know? Makeup can change someone's looks in a heartbeat." I began with running a search for John Muir impersonators in the region, and five names appeared on the screen. "Huh!" I pressed on the first link, which led me to a man who was retired. I did bookmark the site in case further scrutiny was needed. The next three images didn't match the looks of the man in question. Either the ears were too big, or the eyes were wrong, or else it was the height. I pressed on the site for the fifth man and knew I'd found the right person. The height, weight, and the bushy eyebrows fit the guy in question. I bookmarked the page and deleted the other. Maggie nudged me as I began reading his bio.

"I'm going for a walk-about while you do that." She stood and moved around me. "I won't be gone too long."

"Take your time and eavesdrop as much as possible."

"Will do."

I had the man's bio up and ready to begin reading it when a woman stepped up to my booth. I placed my phone inside my pocket after bookmarking the page.

"I love dollhouses. I love the First Ladies. What a neat idea." Her blond hair sparkled from the above lights and the blue bow in her hair reminded me of the flag because she wore a red heart on each cheek.

"Who's your favorite? Mine's Dolley Madison."

"She's the one that saved George Washington's picture isn't she? And bunches of other things, too. Right?"

"One and the same." I smiled. "Here's my card." I handed her one. "Come by the store anytime and take a look around."

Her smile brightened the room. "I loved Jackie because of her elegance, and Barbara Bush reminded me of my grandma." I saw a bit of wistfulness in her smile. "I will. Thanks."

"Anytime." I watched her walk away. My phone chirped, so I took a quick look and I'd received a message from Maggie. It read: brownies or cupcake? Want cheese or onion on your burger? I responded: brownie. Fried onions and cheese. Cola. Thanks.

I continued reading through the bio of the man known as John Muir, with the given name of Ed Parsons. He lived in a town between Medora, where he's a retired history teacher, and Minneapolis, Minnesota. *That stood to reason. This explains why he wanted to see Alice Roosevelt's purse.* I tapped from the site and slipped the phone back inside my pocket, deep in thought. The impersonators would have to know as much as possible about their character. John Muir's impersonator would be well-versed in the major historical characters of Muir's time. I made a note of his name and profession in the notepad app on my phone, once again tucking it back in my pocket.

I went ahead and did a quick search for Annie Oakley and ten sites appeared. I glanced quickly through them, and picked out two. They caught my eye because of the height and weight. They were near the same size, but I paid attention to the hairline to see if there was a growth of colored hair. One was a natural brown, the other was blond. I made a notation in my app about it. The impersonator must have hair growth, however, I figured that she'd probably just had it colored for the exposition. Fortunately, she was short so that made the find easier.

I was just about to look into the sites for TR when Maggie arrived with our burgers. I tucked my phone away and reached for my food. As we ate, I told her about John Muir, aka Ed Parsons. "Did you notice if Annie had root growth?"

"Nope. Want me to look? Between us, we should be able to figure that out easily."

"True. That's my next quest after TR now that John's figured out." I took a bite. After a minute, I said, "There's got to be tons of TR's. It could take a while."

The rest of the day and into the evening slipped by, with a few prospective clients dropping by and asking questions. It felt good to know that the dollhouses were well received. After closing the booth for the evening, we walked out to the parking lot together, said our goodbyes and went our separate ways. Aaron was working his regular shift, and I would be alone for the rest of the evening.

I started the car, and made my way down the exit ramp and out onto the street, following the signs to University Avenue. Once on the road toward Main Street and home, I let my thoughts roam. I thought of Gina and glanced at the clock. It was just after nine. It was my guess that no one from her family had arrived to clean out her house since she had few relatives.

I was unsatisfied with the reason behind Ida's request for me to search her house. Why didn't she do it herself? Could it be that she worried about leaving fingerprints and getting caught? As I drove to my development entrance, I glanced toward Gina's house and saw a flicker of light from the back bedroom. There wasn't a car in the driveway. Curious, I wondered if I shouldn't walk over and take a look or call the police. I pressed the button to raise the garage door and drove inside. I shut the car off after parking and climbed from the car. Before entering the house, I walked out onto the driveway and stared at the house. *Did I really see the light?* I glanced up and down the street and noticed that most driveways were bare of cars and the lights were on in the houses, but the lights shouldn't be on at Gina's.

I walked over to her house, and went around to the back where I'd noticed the unexplained light. I found the room dark, and wondered if I'd made it up in my mind. I decided to go ahead and enter. I circled back to the front and found the key, where it should be, under the planter. I unlocked the door and immediately replaced the key. Armed with only my phone and keys in my pockets, I went inside and closed the door behind me. There was still enough light from the street lamps that I maneuvered easily. I stopped by the mail and picked up two envelopes lying there and stuffed the them into my pocket. I went to the kitchen and opened the refrigerator and found nothing of consequence, but took several pictures. Something drew me back to the bathroom, where I stood with my hands on my hips and stared inside of the room. The bedroom floor creaked. Goose pimples raced up and down my spine.

Then someone threw a heavy shoe at me!

Chapter Six

By the time I'd got my wits about myself and raced out from the bathroom, I heard the backdoor slam. I hurried to look out the kitchen sink window, and only saw a flash of a figure dash between the neighboring houses. Was it a man? I couldn't be sure.

I went back into the bathroom and decided against picking up the shoe and replacing it where I thought it belonged. Glancing at the time, I realized that I must get home. Before I left, I walked through the house and made sure that all the doors and windows were closed and locked.

As I walked across the street, it felt as if there were eyes upon me. I glanced around but didn't see anyone suspicious, so I chalked it up to paranoia. Inside the garage, I quickly lowered the garage door, hustled into the kitchen, and leaned against the counter. I removed the envelopes from my pocket and read the return addresses. Both came from the Rose Oil Company. *You've come this far open it!*

The letters read: Ms. Johnson,

The Rose Oil Company will be drilling in your area and would like to make an offer for a land tract. Property on section: 345 mineral rights or outright purchase of tract of land.

Please contact me at your earliest convenience.

Sincerely,

Tracy Steward.

The rest was the address. I stuffed the letter back into the envelope, placing it into my bag on the counter. I wondered where to report it when several fireworks snap, crackled, and popped from the neighbors. I looked at the clock on the kitchen wall. Aaron was late.

The Minneapolis police station was busy, but I left a message for a detective that I knew to contact me. I headed to the shower, and jumped in.

I wondered about Aaron and why he wasn't home. As I climbed into bed, I checked my messages only to learn that he had to work overtime. That gave me ample time to think about what I'd learned.

Number one on my list was that I knew little if nothing about Gina. Also she'd never told me about her family or the land. Why would she work so hard, when money could be had by allowing the oil company to drill? Why live in Minneapolis when her home was in Medora? Nothing fit together and it left me puzzled.

Puzzled? I was more than puzzled as I wondered who the person was that had fled out the backdoor and what were they after? It hadn't appeared as if they searched very hard for anything. Nothing was out of place. I rolled over and thought of our conversations, but couldn't recall any concerning her family.

In spite of the more fireworks, and loud voices from backyard parties, I was able to fall asleep, thankful for air-conditioning muting the excess noise.

Aaron's loud snores woke me early. I kissed him on the cheek and watched him wiggle his nose, then pop open one eye. He groaned and rolled over.

"Hard night?"

Another groan.

"You workin' the 'X'?"

"Ten."

"Okay, but don't oversleep. I'm leavin'." I kissed him again on the cheek, ruffled his hair and left the room. "Poor man," I mumbled to myself. I'd wanted to sneak a peek around the rear of Gina's house before the neighborhood dogs began barking and the owners went walking.

I scooted quickly out to the garage and dropped my purse into the car before raising the door. I glanced out and since no one was around, I high-tailed it across the street, and around to the back of the house, retracing footprints in the dew covered grass. The few prints I found didn't lead far, evaporating on the backside of the adjoining fence line. I tried the backdoor to make sure that it was locked and walked the house's perimeter and tried the front door. Satisfied it was secure, I slipped back to my house and jumped into my car. Within minutes, I drove safely onto the main drag after picking up a needed muffin and coffee.

The incident at Gina's circled around in my mind as I drove and I had trouble keeping myself focused. Relieved to drive into the parking deck, I found a spot, climbed out, and locked the car.. I glanced at the flow of cars and felt lucky that I had my spot. As I walked toward the elevator, I noticed two people sitting in a car with a North Dakota license plate. I figured they were heading for the 'X'. The car's engine was shut off, and the windows were down as I passed near it. From the loud voices, I realized it was Harry and Sunflower having a heated discussion. I was tempted to circle back and listen, but noticed Sunflower catching my image in the side view mirror. I gave her a quick wave and continued ahead to the elevator, which brought me to street level.

TR was standing by my booth, holding his lapels and showing his big teeth as I approached.

"Mr. President, how nice of you to stop by."

"I'm surprised at all the interest in the First Ladies. It's wonderful, really." I watched him smooth out his walrus mustache. "Name's actually Bill. Bill Smith." He shot his arm out, and we shook hands.

"Liv. Olivia Reynolds." I grinned because his bulldog smile was infectious. "Nice to meet you."

"Tell me, Ms. Reynolds--."

"Liv, sir."

"What got you so interested in the good women?"

"Always had a strong interest. Went to Washington DC as a kid. The rest is history—since I'm a distant relative to Dolley Madison."

"Ask a stupid question. Wow!"

"I have a question for you." I cocked my head. "Did you own land near the ranch and give it to Alice?" I ran my fingers through my hair. "I have this purse, you see…"

"Hmm, interesting concept. It's been a few years to remember if there's a parcel of land, but it's entirely possible." He rubbed his chin. "I'd like to see the purse, though."

"I should've brought it in today, maybe tomorrow," I said.

"Bully!" I watched TR walk away.

I leaning back and watched the crowd strolling through the exhibits. I'd been sitting beside my display for three days and in that time, I'd lost a good friend to a suspicious death. I had trouble believing it, digesting that it'd happened. The concept scared me.

Naturally the police, including my husband, weren't saying much about it. I wondered who had been in the house and scared the life out of me by throwing that heavy shoe at me? Why not kill me too? I thought about it and realized that I must not be a threat. I hoped the danger wouldn't escalate. *Why haven't I heard from the detectives?*

Inga, the antique dealer two doors down from my store, was the person who'd sold me the Alice purse. There was a small pistol inside it. The lining seemed slightly unraveled, but it was old. I couldn't figure out why Princess Alice, as she was called, would want a pistol in her ready possession. Newspaper reporters weren't nearly as vicious back then, or were they? I took out my iPad and did a random search on Alice Roosevelt and got many, many hits.

I was reminded that Alice had fashioned the Gibson Girl look, and was featured on posters, in newspapers and ads. Her trademark huge hat was featured in a newspaper cartoon, and her photographs was everywhere. She was flocked by people at all her appearances, and the public adored her. She even graced the cover of Time Magazine. The President had her fill in for him when the need arose, and she was his right hand in politics. Few pictures were shown with her holding a purse, which caused a frown on my lips. I clicked from the site and began reading other, less bubly information about Alice. Her young years were troubled as TR paid her little attention until his marriage to Edith. With his first wife and mother dying, and the arrival of this little baby, at the same time, he was bereft with grief.

His grief brought him to the plains of North Dakota where he tried his hand in a variety of many things, most of all was ranching. And that information led me back to the same curious question - did he purchase land and give it to Alice?

If so, where was the deed?

My phone chirped and I found a message from Grandma. She and Grandpa were on their way down to the event to see what all the hoopla was about. I immediately straightened up the minis and made sure my collection of empty bags and cups were thrown away, and then continued my search while I waited for them.

Next on my search agenda was land ownership for the late 1800's in Billings County, North Dakota. I wasn't able to locate an old plat map of the area. My connection was slow and I wondered if I needed to take a different route to the answer. Just then, my grandparents arrived.

"What do you think?" I asked Grandma. "Busy isn't it?"

"It's fabulous."

I got up so that she could scoot around and sit.

"Thanks."

"Grandpa, here take my seat." I stood to the side so he could relax.

"Liv, this exposition will send plenty of customers to your store," Grandma said, looking at me. "Last weekend, was really busy, with the phone ringing off the hook. It was amazing. I almost couldn't handle it."

"You need two lines," Grandpa said. "I've talked to Aaron. He wasn't sure if it's necessary but I think it is. You know? Keep things separate."

"I'll give it some thought." I smiled. They were always giving me opinions. Mostly, they were appreciated. They had raised me since I was eleven, when my parents died in a car accident. I love them dearly.

"Here comes Aaron." Grandpa nodded toward the crowd.

I turned and greeted him with a kiss. "Missed you."

"I'm here until three, then it's time for my regular duty." He held my hand and greeted Grandma and Grandpa. "Are you working here?"

"Grandpa and I are here for the show. The Wild West will soon be on stage."

"Put your stuff away, Liv, and let's go see it."

I packed up my minis, leaving behind the pictures of my dollhouses for the public to look at plus a stack of calling cards. "Ready."

The four of us found seats in the back row, and felt lucky to have them. The room was full of spectators, and I tried to imagine what the crowds at the real Buffalo Bill shows around the United States and England. I scanned the crowd and didn't see many Rangers.

I watched as the Buffalo Bill impersonator came out front and introduced the cast of characters. The opening act were Native American dancers and drummers, which led to Native American men re-enacting a buffalo hunt. When finished, a large wading pool was brought to center stage and explorers pretended to catch beavers. Little Annie Oakley galloped in on her horse, cartwheeled off and picked up her rifle. Someone tossed disks and she shot, hitting all ten. The silence of the crowd deafened my ears as she shot an apple off the same person's shoulder and then another off her poor assistant's head.

After the show, Buffalo Bill spoke to the audience, imploring us to take care of our National Parks and of our environment. He talked about all the lakes, rivers, and streams that make up the roadmap of Minnesota, and asked us all to revere the land and be good stewards. The audience clapped and cheered.

All the participants paraded around the circle, and I looked for Sunflower and Harry but saw neither. Bambi danced, and she looked beautiful. We followed the crowd out of the room and made our way back to my booth. I was happy to return. The noise echo had been loud.

Grandma and Grandpa sat down on the two chairs while Aaron and I stood off to the side. I glanced at my phone for messages, but there weren't any.

"That was fun. Noisy though," Aaron said, massaging his temples.

"Yes, I agree. We're not used to all of that noise. Buffalo Bill did a great job, so did Annie Oakley," I said. "Know who she is?"

"Nope. Doesn't matter who she is, she'll soon be gone." He narrowed his eyes at me. "I don't want you asking questions, either."

"Anyone been over to Gina's house?" Grandpa asked.

I felt my face grow beet-red.

"Don't tell me you've been through it?" Grandpa asked.

"I left a message for Detective Erlandsen. I didn't get a chance to tell you, Aaron, but I saw a light inside the house last night, so I went inside. Someone threw a shoe me with a shoe and me and ran away. I brought two letters home from the house. They from the same return address and look identical."

"No more, Liv, and let me know when you've spoke to Erlandsen."

"I will."

Aaron's his pager beeped and he glanced at it. His mouth dropped open. "Something came up. I gotta run." He leaned over and kissed me. "We're picking up this conversation later."

Aaron no sooner left when so did my grandparents. I was not looking forward to going home and receiving a lecture about trespassing through Gina's house. Sometimes, the police need a little bit of help, I reasoned, but I should've been more cautious and contacted them.

My eye nervously twitched as I monitored the crowd. I tried to focus on what I knew about Gina, and still came up empty. Over at the First Lady site, I saw Ruby glance my way and waved. As soon as the crowd thinned in front of their booth, she hiked over to me.

"Hey there," Ruby said.

"I thought you guys would've gone to the Wild West Show?"

"Nah, maybe next time." Ruby glanced over her shoulder then looked back at me. "There's something I have to tell you."

"Yes? You're making me worried."

"A Ranger was at your booth for a while, and so was the John Muir impersonator, while you were gone. We couldn't see what they were doing though."

"Strange. How long were they here, do you know?"

"They pretended to have dropped something and looked on the floor."

"Pretended?"

"That's what it looked like. They both looked in different places."

"Separately?"

"Hold on. Let me look in my stuff." I dragged out my minis and everything seemed fine. I shook my head. "Doesn't make sense."

"Just lettin' you know. Gotta get back."

I watched her leave before looking through the mini houses. Everything was in order.

I must be missing something, but what?

I guessed it was time to do some more research. I opened my iPad and began a search on Buffalo Bill and his impersonators.

Chapter Seven

I tried several search engines, but came up empty. I found many sites that pertained to the Wild West Show and Buffalo Bill, but none gave names of impersonators. I found Buffalo Bill dolls for sale online, but that was about it. I was on my own with this one. I next searched impersonators of mountain men, scouts and explorers, and cowboys. It appeared as if I'd be stuck without a hit when the man's picture popped up along with a brief bio. Robert Coons. The description fit: six feet-two inches, brown hair and eyes. The image showed a man with shoulder length brown, naturally wavy hair and matching mustache and beard. The image and description fit the man. "Gotcha," I said to myself, and smiled as I wrote down his name and contact information.

Next I wondered who Annie Oakley was in real life. I'd bookmarked the websites that led me to Buffalo Bill, so I went back and noted the featured role-players. I was right in deciding that our featured Annie must have blonde roots. *How am I going to find that out?*

My phone rang, Detective Erlandsen. "Detective, I need to speak to you."

"Officer Reynolds filled me in a little. I can't speak about an ongoing investigation, especially when it's not one of our cases."

"Aaron gave you the yellow envelope?" When he admitted receiving it, I asked, "What about the recent one? What about being hit in the head by a shoe when I was inside the house?"

"Why were you there?" Erlandsen countered.

"I saw a light inside and was curious," I said.

"Next time, call the police," he instructed. "If you were anyone else, you'd be locked up. I'll relay the information to the correct people."

"Thank you," I said, and disconnected.

I glanced at the clock and realized that the evening had sped by faster than Annie Oakley's bullets. I packed up my minis and headed for the storage area near the rear of the main floor to store the items overnight. Before leaving the building, I gave Aaron a call.

"I'm just leaving." I waited a beat, and said, "I just spoke to Erlandsen. He'll be in touch with the lead investigator about the other envelope and the break-in."

"Good. I'm sure he told you that I spoke to him," Aaron said. "Drive careful. I'll be home at the usual time, midnight or later, depending."

I groaned. "Okay." I hesitated.

"What? You're not telling me something," Aaron said.

"Sunflower and Harry from the Roosevelt Park were first cousins with Gina. Gina owns property adjoining the park, and some oil companies want to drill."

"This is important because?"

"Gina is dead and they aren't." There—I said it and felt better, too. "Something's not right. Those two fight quite a bit too. I've seen it—twice!"

"You're telling me because?"

"Good night," I fumed, disconnecting. "Bone-head!" I grabbed my purse and hiked toward the main door and almost crashed into Annie Oakley.

"I know I'm short, but...," she growled. "Mind helping me pick up all of this stuff?"

"Of course not." I scooped up several disks, darts and targets. "How come you're bringing these things home? Don't you need them?" I placed them in the box and handed it to her. "Sorry."

"Mind your own business." She took a deep breath. "Good night."

"If you ever get a chance, come on around to my booth. I display the First Ladies Dollhouses. You might get a kick out of seeing the miniatures I brought along."

"Good night," she huffed.

I watched her hike out into the street, before turning toward the parking ramp. I wondered if she stayed in a nearby hotel and walked to and from the Convention Center. I realized that my shoulder slightly hurt, and wondered why, before realizing that it was the spot where I'd bumped into her. The woman might be short, be she certainly was strong.

It didn't take long until I'd found my car, jumped inside, and started it right up. Backing out, I realized how exhausted I truly was. I left the radio off. I needed silence after the noisy day. The number of spectators was dwindling, but the event still brought in record crowds, which was delightful. I wound down the exit ramp until reaching the street and turned toward home. It took almost thirty minutes until finally raising my garage door and driving inside. I closed up the garage with a sigh of relief.

My phone buzzed as I entered my house, and I answered.

"Liv? It's Ida, Gina's aunt."

"Oh. Yes. I'm just getting home."

"The Establishment, the restaurant where Gina worked, is having a small memorial at eleven tomorrow morning. I'm planning to attend."

"I didn't know about it. Thanks. I'll be there."

I realized that Erlandsen should probably know about Sunflower and Harry, so I sent him a text message.

It wasn't long until I'd dropped into bed.

I don't think I opened my eyes until morning. I know I never heard Aaron come home, and he was sound asleep when I woke. I tiptoed to the bathroom to shower, dress and get ready for the day.

As I fried bacon and an egg, I heard the floor creak and was pleased to see my man entering the room. His bright eyes and smile told me I was forgiven for snooping and I knew the day would be as bright as the sunshine.

"You're up. Thought you'd sleep in?"

"Nah…thought I'd check up on you since we haven't spent any time together since the exposition opened." He reached for two mugs and filled them, setting them on the table.

"One or two?" I held up the eggs. At his request, I fried two plus one for myself.

"I messaged Erlandsen about Sunflower and Harry."

"Did he reply yet?"

"Nope." I shook my head.

The meal went by quickly and soon we parted, he went to work at the 'X' and I headed to the memorial. I wasn't sure what to expect, and hoped to find two seats where Ida and I could be seated together. She'd been listed as next of kin, and I was sure glad that she'd contacted me. The Establishment was only three blocks away and I found a parking spot in the back lot. By the time I'd climbed out and locked the doors, Ida was parking. I waited for her.

"Morning." She waved. "Last minute, sorry about this."

"I'm glad that they're doing this, now the neighbors and friends can pay their respects to Gina. I wonder how many mourners will show?"

"Hard to say."

"Where will the funeral be held?"

"Medora." She took my arm. "I'm a little shaky."

I was about to ask if Sunflower and Harry would attend, when they appeared walking toward the door. I felt better for it. The thought of no other family was upsetting. I stood aside as they waited for us to meet them.

Harry held the door, and we entered. I followed the maître d' as he ushered us to the rear room, overflowing with mourners. The owner of the Establishment stood behind a podium, and he reminded me of someone, but I couldn't place him. The waitress/bartender sat beside an open chair, and I wondered if she'd saved it for him. The four of us found a seat near the middle, with me sitting on the outside. I took a moment to glance around the room and realized that there were several people I recognized, including the John Muir impersonator.

That struck me as odd since Gina never mentioned that she knew him, but, thinking back, I realized that she never had a chance—he arrived after her death. Glancing back at the owner, I noted the resemblance between him and John Muir. They had to be brothers or closely related. It warranted further questions. I turned my attention back to the memorial. The neighbors from either side of Gina's house got up and walked to the front.

"Gina was always kind. She'd help me out by walking my dog."

"Gina had beautiful flowers."

Ida squeezed my hand, and stood. She walked to the front and stood behind the podium. "She was a good person. Always helpful, even when she had her hands full taking care of the ranch, she could be depended upon."

Harry cleared his throat, and I glanced over at him. His complexion had taken a turn, from white to beet red. I noted that Sunflower's eyes were moist. I leaned into her, and whispered, "You two planning on attending the funeral?" Her eyes shifted from me to Harry and back. I decided not to press the issue. It was my turn to speak.

As Ida walked toward her seat, I made my way up front. Staring out at the crowd, I felt my heart leap into my throat. I cleared my throat. "Gina was a wonderful, kind, and generous person. She helped me occasionally in my store. I could depend upon her as an honest person. Gina's greatest talents were her flowers. They were gorgeous. Her rose bushes amazing and should be featured in a magazine." I smiled and left the area, going back to join Ida.

At the conclusion, I hurried to John Muir before he left. I caught his arm just as he walked out the door. "I never expected to meet you here."

"My brother's the owner. I've known Gina for a short while, and wanted to pay my respects."

"Do you happen to know anything about that parcel of land that they spoke of?" I wanted to see what kind of a reaction I'd get. His eyes glazed over, and just as quickly, he smiled down at me. "Ever been there?" I had an inkling that he had. It was like he knew more than he was saying. "Is it near the oil drilling?"

"Listen, missy, I don't know what you're driving at, but leave me out of it." He scowled. "Why not ask her family?" He turned on his heels and left.

His hurried gait brought him to his car quickly.

I wondered what he was hiding as I hiked around to my car. I saw Ida had left and so had Harry and Sunflower. I started up the engine and headed the few blocks to my store.

It felt good to park the car in the back lot and go into the store. I found Max carving a head in the workroom, and waved as I entered.

"Hey you!" Max looked up at me and grinned.

"Yo! Long time no see! How's the expo going?" He set his tools down and gently placed them into the kit. "It's too quiet without you. Just sayin--."

"I know. I miss this place." I heaved into a chair. "Just came from Gina's memorial. Sad deal."

"See anyone I know?" Max asked.

"Maybe. The John Muir impersonator was there, and it almost sounds as if he's from this area. Wouldn't talk to me, though. The owner and John Muir sure resembled each other. I bet they're brothers."

"Hmm." Max did the usual rubbing of his whiskers. "I'll check into it for you. What's aroused your curiosity?"

"I'm not really sure if I should tell you." I frowned. "It's a secret."

"Go ahead. Secret's safe." I watched him cross his heart just like a little kid. "Let's hear it."

Everything tumbled out of me beginning with the death, investigation, witnessing two spats between Harry and Sunflower, their reactions and behavior at the memorial, TR and John Muir inquiring about the Alice purse, and ending with the two searches of Gina's house. "One more thing." I held up my finger when he looked ready to interrupt. "Someone threw a shoe at me. I never did figure out who did it." I crossed my arms. "That's it. I feel better."

"What haven't you told Aaron?" Max asked.

"The memorial since it just happened."

"You really don't have much to tell him." When he pulled on his ear, I took it as a sign of thinking. "Yep. We'll keep it to ourselves."

"Any problem around here?" I stood and went to the doorway.

"Not that I'm aware of." He whisked his longish hair back from his shoulders. "Is Marie coming today?"

"Grandma took today off." I headed into the showroom to greet the dolls. "Hi Ladies!" I've missed each and every one of you. How was your birthday with the grandkids, Barbara? Laura, you're looking beautiful today. Dolley—smashing. Pretty soon I'll be back and it'll be just like normal around here. Hillary, enjoy your stay as First Lady but keep that husband of yours on a short leash. I'll say goodbye for now." I made a quick tour of the houses, stopping to straighten a few show items within certain houses. It really did make me smile, I was so proud of my houses. I stopped in front of the Penny dolls and readjusted a couple and realized that the Alice purse was moved from its usual spot, but chalked it up to customers looking at it. I placed it behind the check-out counter and inside a plastic bag. Something told me not to take it to the 'X'. I made sure that the statue of the jingle dancer figurine was secured behind the counter. I vowed to bring it, and the purse, home for safekeeping at the earliest convenience.

I walked back to Max, and said, "I'm off. Grandma will be here tomorrow and I'll be back the day after." I spread open my arms. "I'm ready to return."

"Yeah, I think Marie's getting kind of tired, too." He picked up a carving utensil. "Anything should come up, I'll call."

"By the way, do you know of anyone inquiring about the Alice purse?"

"Not right offhand. If I think of someone, I'll call." A frown crossed his brow and he stared at the dolls' head.

"Catch ya later!"

"Lock it."

I did as asked and bounded over to my car, jumping inside. I started the engine, put it in drive and headed out onto the street. It wasn't long before I crossed the Mississippi River and over to the I35-W entrance ramp. It took a few extra minutes to find a parking space for the 'X' Center because of the time of day but I eventually found one.

With my bag in hand, I locked up the car before walking to the elevator, which brought me down to the outside exit. I wanted a few extra minutes to think things over before going inside. It gave me time to process a few extra thoughts, such as last night's brush with Annie. I hadn't had time to give it a thought, and now realized that she had blonde roots. I placed it on my list of searches for the day if time allowed. Next on the agenda was another search on John Muir. I'd written his name someplace on my phone pad, and made a quick look. The notepad read: Ed Parsons. That meant the Establishment owner's name may be the same last name. I wondered if Gina had a will? A loudspeaker announced Buffalo Bill's Wild West Show.

I drew a deep breath and went inside.

Harry was at the TR booth, and I stopped.

"You beat me." He shoved his ranger hat back a little. "Didn't stand around and talk. Headed back right away."

"You're right! I did stand around."

I left and went to locate Sunflower, and found her back with the dancers. "Sunflower, I'm sorry I didn't get a chance to give you another hug and tell you how sorry I am for your loss." She burst into tears, the jingles on her dress jingled as I pulled her into my arms.

"My brother is so cruel."

"What is this all about?" I whispered. "Can we talk in private?" I pushed back and stared into her moist eyes. "You need to get whatever it is off your chest."

She nodded and guided me behind a large curtain. Before beginning, she tentatively glanced around. "It's like this…," she stopped, and looked down. "You won't tell anyone, will you?"

"Of course not. Gina was a good friend and I want to find out the truth." I dug in my bag and drew out a fresh tissue, and handed it to her. "Blow your nose and wipe your eyes, you'll feel better." She did as I suggested. "Better?"

Sunflower nodded, sniffled another time and blew her nose. "It's like this. Gina had herself in a fix with all sorts of things that most people don't even know about."

"Do you want to expound on that?" She shook her head.

"Can't." Sunflower shivered.

"Why?"

"I've got to get going—the show."

"Can we talk later?"

"No. It's not safe." She blew her nose.

"Who is scaring you?" Staring into her moist eyes, I asked, "Why are you so frightened?" She shook her head. "Sunflower, do you think someone killed Gina?" She shook so hard, that her bells began jingling. "Tell me."

She nodded.

"Why?"

Just as she opened her mouth, I watched Sunflower's eyes cloud over, and she rushed away. I turned around to see the back of the same figure who'd thrown the shoe at me. I dashed after him, but lost him in the crowd.

Chapter Eight

I slipped behind my chair just as two ladies approached the display. "Hi!" I set the mini houses out for them to peruse and straightened out the table items as they looked at them. "Fun, isn't it?"

"It is. I never knew I was interested in history until right this minute," the younger of the two women commented. "Look at all the furnishings from the Madison to the Lincoln, all the way through to the Roosevelt's."

"I loved Dolley. The cakes were named after her, or so I was told growing up." The other woman added. She appeared to be in her thirties, about my age.

"Are you two sisters?" I looked at them. "You two are so similar in looks."

"We are." She smiled. "Got a card? I'd like to see your store."

I handed them both a card. "Thanks."

They left, leaving me to my thoughts. I began the search for the name the owner of the Establishment, but found him under a different last name. His full name was Paul Vasek, which fit the area since the first settlers came from the Slovakian countries. John Muir's real name was Ed Parsons, which sounded more Scandinavian. *Name change or different father?* I wasn't sure if the search brought me any closer to revealing either men's biography. I clicked out of the site.

My next search was Annie Oakley, and I discovered her true name and origin. She lived near Look Out Mountain in Golden, Colorado, near the gravesite of Buffalo Bill. That could explain her interest in the Wild West Show. I didn't find much about her, but I learned her name, Sarah Page. I wrote her name on the phone's notepad for easy access, as well as the Establishment owner's name. I closed from the site, and let my mind drift.

I wondered about Max and if he'd be able to discover any information for me about the man. I took out my phone and sent him a question. Next, I turned my attention to the nearby line of hungry people. Wrangler Jean sure did one heck of a lot of business. I reached for my water bottle just as Aaron strode toward me.

"Hi hon." My eyes met his. "I missed you. Are you working here?"

"Yep. Undercover." He thrust his chest out. "Like my duds?"

"Of course." My eyes trailed from his smile to his patriotic Tee-shirt down to his blue khaki camp-shorts. "Every bit."

"You look perplexed. Let's hear it."

"Nothing, really, it's just that…." I went on to tell him about the connection and then names of the two men in question.

"Ahh, huh." Aaron nodded. "What else do you have to tell me?"

"Sunflower. She cried and was scared. Said something about someone watching and then she had to get in the queue for the dancers and the show. I also thought I saw the back of the man who threw the shoe at me, but didn't find out who it was." I shrugged. "Have you heard anything else about Gina?"

"It does seem a little more than suspicious, doesn't it?" I watched as he crossed his arms and stared into space before looking back at me. "I'll see what I can find out. I'll let you know. No more questions to anyone. Got that?" He narrowed his eyes and bore down on me. "I mean it! No snooping, either. I don't want any trouble."

"Promise." I watched him walk away as my heart pounded. Why didn't Bambi attend the memorial? Had she not been told or purposely excluded? It made me curious.

The day flew past. Just when I thought about going for a short walk to stretch my legs, someone stopped by and asked enough questions that I gave up on that idea. As I closed for the day, Aaron sent a message stating that he had a late shift for his regular police job. Sadly, I had to go home to an empty house again. I'd hoped that wouldn't happen.

After packing and locking up the houses for the night, I headed toward the elevators. A crowd formed ahead of me, so I decided to walk across the street. I didn't have to wait long for the light to change, and I walked across and entered the parking complex. I chose to ignore the elevator because I could see my car from a distance.

As I opened my car door, I happened to notice Annie Oakley climb into the car behind me. I did recognize the car from previously, so I stared closer at the person through my rearview mirror. Why was her hair down and swept back with a bow? Why had she worn spiked heels and a flowered dress? She'd certainly changed in a hurry because the final show had ended a half-hour before the public doors closed.

I waited as she backed from her spot, and then I followed her out onto the main drag. The interstate entrance wasn't far from the location, but, of course, I had to stop at every stoplight along the route. I entered the interstate and finally turned onto Main Street. It wasn't until I'd stopped at the light near the former Grain Belt Brewery, that I was again, right behind Annie Oakley. Curiosity got the best of me. I didn't want her to know that I followed, so I pulled into the other lane so a car could be between us. I was wondering where this tail would take me when she pulled around back of the Establishment and parked. I stopped at the end of the block and watched as she went inside.

If she was from Golden, Colorado, how did she know about this place? I really wanted to go inside to snoop but decided it was a bad decision. I drove a few more blocks until turning down my street and into my garage.

Aaron called the moment I stepped into the house. "I just walked in the house. Where are you?" I locked the door behind me and headed toward the refrigerator where I took out a bottle of soda and leftover spaghetti and meatballs to warm in the microwave.

"I'm working in the station for a while. Tim's wrapping up a case, then we'll go back out."

"Have you found out anything about Gina?"

"The lab testing is being done. This all takes time, and there's new drugs on the street all the time."

"Do me a favor?" I asked.

"I told you no more asking questions."

"I haven't. Please, just listen." I glared straight ahead. "I followed Annie Oakley's impersonator all the way to the Establishment where Gina worked. Isn't that odd?"

"No. Maybe she just knows the guy. Maybe she's related." I heard him sigh.

"Aaron? Can you look the guy up for me, and her?"

"Liv. One of these days you'll either get me in trouble, or you won't be able to get yourself out of a mess and then land in the hospital with something serious."

"Never mind," I grouched, ready to disconnect.

"Oh, okay. Give me the names."

I knew he sat poised with a pen and notepad in front of him. "Bill Smith and Sarah Page. I know she's from Golden, Colorado. I believe that he's related to Ed Parsons, the John Muir impersonator. See what you can find out please."

"I will." I heard him writing through the silence. "Love you."

"You too, and thanks." We disconnected.

I went ahead and heated my dinner, carrying it out to the living room where I turned on the TV and found an old movie to watch. Something told me it wasn't a coincidence that the movie, "Annie Oakley", with Doris Day was the featured network movie. I ate, lost in thought, as the background sound filled the void.

My phone rang, and I answered it. "Grandma, I'm home."

"You didn't call, dear. I was worried."

"Don't be. I'm tired. I went to Gina's memorial, then worked at the 'X'. Max wondered if you're working tomorrow, and I said you were. Right?"

"I'll be there," Grandma said. "By the way, I answered your note and circled that I don't have chicken soup made, but will when I have the chance to spend time in the kitchen."

"Thank you, Grandma, I've been so busy," I said. "To your knowledge, did anyone pick up Alice Roosevelt's purse or the Native American figurine? The jingle dancer?"

"Not that I'm aware of."

"Okay, Grandma."

"Good night."

We disconnected. My thoughts went back to the purse. Had someone moved it, or was I imagining it? I couldn't decide. I almost felt like going to the store and bringing the figurine home right then. I was tired, so I finished my meal and brought the dirty dishes to the kitchen and loaded the dishwasher.

In a few minutes, I was in and out of the shower, then jumping into bed.

My husband's snore woke me. The moonlight streamed in through the window, inviting me. I got up and took a look out. The stars lit the sky and were a backdrop to the multi-colored northern lights. Yawning, I went back to bed, curling up beside Aaron.

When the alarm woke me at seven, I felt ready for the day. I dressed quietly in a lightweight sundress, pushed back my unruly hair with a band, and brushed my teeth. In the kitchen I poured coffee and made myself a slice of toast. When finished, I grabbed my bag and headed over to the Xcel Convention Center for the last time. I smiled as I left. It'd been a good week, albeit, a busy one. By the sounds of it and the number of folks dropping by my booth, I reckoned that my sales would increase.

In just a few minutes, I was inside the building with a fresh cup of coffee in hand and heading toward my booth. With so few people around, I took a moment to speak to the three gals in the First Lady booth.

"Good morning. Are you happy the show is over today?"

"Oh my yes," Belle answered. "We're taking a flight back this evening."

"Yes, I'd like to spend another night and see your store, but it won't be possible." Ruby glanced at the other two women.

"Why not just change your reservations?" I asked.

"We'll come back another time."

"We can't be gone that long. We all have families," Alice replied.

"We'll keep in touch."

I nodded and went for my locked up minis, and then hurried to my booth. When the doors opened, my booth was ready for spectators to enjoy.

The morning sped by quickly and it was almost noon when my phone rang. It was Aaron. "Hi hon."

"Liv, I've got news that you'll want to hear." I pictured him smiling.

"Well?" I held the phone tight against my ear.

"Gina was poisoned. The lab results came in late last night."

"Oh my God," I whispered, my eyes opened wide. "What took so long?"

"The drug isn't well known in the U.S., and also, it's almost impossible to trace."

"What are you saying?"

"That's all I can tell you. I've got to run."

"That's incredible," I murmured, leaning back into my chair. My heart raced, and my thoughts were firing just as fast. I focused on the crowds and when that didn't slow my thoughts, I stared at the line for Wrangler Jean's. Finally, it subsided and I pulled my thoughts back to the present.

I thought over the past week. No one person stood out. Each person had a bothersome quirk, such as Harry and Sunflower. They definitely were hiding something, and Sunflower was scared. Was she scared of him? Both Ed Parsons and TR wished to see the Alice purse for unknown reasons. Who sneaked into Gina's house? Why hasn't it been cleaned out, and why hasn't anyone come around? Why did Annie go into the Establishment last night? I wondered if she knew how close I lived to it? My thoughts kept spinning, through to the end of the day.

Carefully I boxed up the minis and grabbed my purse. I'd hoped Aaron would help me with the chairs, and was just about to leave with a load of them when he walked toward me.

"Just in time," I said. He reached over and took the padded folding chairs from home. "Thanks." I picked up a box and followed him out the door. "I see you're still on duty?"

"I have a few hours left. It's my break," he said. I followed him out. "Where're you parked?"

"First level. It's easy to find," I said.

"We'll cross at the stoplight."

As we stood, someone came up from behind and before I realized what was happening, pushed me into off the sidewalk and out into the traffic.

Chapter Nine

I screamed, trying to keep my balance. Aaron dropped the chairs, and reached out to grab me before the lights turned. He enveloped me in his arms as people gathered and asked if I was all right. When the commotion settled down, I got my wits about me, and Aaron picked up the chairs. We were about to cross the street when someone nudged Aaron.

"Here's a picture. See?" He showed the image to Aaron. "I'll send it to you, if you want it? I think she was pushed."

"What am I looking at?"

"That guy, right there? See?"

"Yeah."

"He pushed her. I only got the back, of course."

"Sure. Send it to this account."

When Aaron confirmed he had received the photo we'd both said, "Thank you," and swiftly walked to the car. "I'm calling for a squad car to pick me up at home. I don't want you driving." He made the call.

"Thank you, hon." I no sooner had sat inside the car when I said, "I want to see it."

"Here." Aaron handed me his phone. "Tim's picking me up. He has the squad car, anyway."

"I'm sending it to myself." I took a quick glance, but the street lamp had just turned on plus all the headlights, made the image hard to see. I decided to wait until I got home to take a closer look.

"You hurt?" Aaron asked, driving from the lot. "It scared the life out of me."

"It didn't do much for me, either." I took a deep breath to calm myself. "What do you think? Was I pushed?"

"It's hard to say. It happened so quick." He drove toward the entrance, and yielded into the steady stream of traffic. "Let's wait until we're home. I'm frazzled over it."

"Why would anyone want me dead?"

"I think it was a warning, if that's what happened."

"Why?"

"You've been asking around haven't you?"

"Well..." I looked out the window and watched cars drive past. "I've been careful. I didn't ask one question today."

"That's good, but what about the day before?" He glanced at me. "You've got to leave the investigating to the professionals."

"We don't even know if I was pushed."

"True, but we're not going to forget it. It could've been deadly."

We soon exited and took the Hennepin Ave Bridge across and turned on Main Street. Driving past the Establishment, I said, "Don't forget that I saw Annie Oakley go in there last night on my way home."

"It's her life."

"You know what else?" I said as he turned onto our street. "I didn't see her today."

"Maybe she was just sick."

"She looked fine yesterday. I don't buy it."

We parked and I got out of the car, grabbing the box, and Aaron the chairs. We carried the items into the house. I set my box on the table because I planned to return the items in it to the store in the morning. Aaron set the chairs in the closet.

"I have to leave, but text once you've taken a closer look at that photo, especially if you recognize the guy," Aaron said.

"Will do." We kissed and Tim honked the horn. Aaron left the house, and I opened the refrigerator door.

With a full wine glass, I headed into the living room and sat down, turned on the TV, and decided on *Survivor* reruns. Glancing out across the street at Gina's house, I found it pitch-black. That made me happy because then I didn't have to worry about anyone sneaking around. I slipped my shoes off, and swung my feet up under me, and turned the small lamp light on beside me. I flipped open the phone and brought up the image, and studied it.

After reconfiguring it and tinting some of the light exposures, I almost dropped the phone. I saved the image and texted Aaron to call me as soon as possible

I no sooner sent the message, when my phone rang.

"Let's hear it," Aaron demanded.

"The picture is of the same man that was inside of Gina's house."

"Don't tell me this—Liv—you could be next!"

"I'm scared." I shivered. "First time, the aunt wanted me to look to make sure everything was fine and to look for the books, but I only peeked in the windows. That's when I found the large yellow envelope. This is the man I saw fleeing from the backyard."

"I'm reporting it to Erlandsen. Don't you dare go in that house ever again. You hear me?"

"Yes."

"Promise?"

"Promise." I disconnected before he started ranting and raving at me. Secretly I was happy because I wanted to know what was happening. Even though the murder happened in St. Paul, Gina lived in Minneapolis. I also hoped that the same detectives whom I'd previously worked with would be assigned onto the case.

It felt good to have that off my chest, and not have to worry about it. The question was, who is this mystery guy? I stared once again at the image, but now wasn't so sure. The image was of a normal height, white male who wore a baseball cap. Tall. Short cropped hair. I couldn't make out the color. The back of his Tee shirt was blank. Dark knee length shorts and sandals. I saw nothing unusual which led me to believe that it might not be the same person, but had to admit to myself that it could've been anyone.

I got up, shut off all the lights and walked down the hallway, and plugged my phone into the bedroom charger. Finally, I took a long, warm shower before crawling into bed. I wondered when Aaron would next be off duty as I turned off the light.

He surprised me by getting home shortly after I fell asleep and woke me up.

"Honey, Detective's Mergens and Erlandsen are assigned the case."

I sat up. "Really? I'm glad, though. I hoped those two would be on the case."

"To quote Mergens, 'No one else will ever believe her'. That's you, you know. This convoluted First Lady case that involves you, wouldn't happen to anyone else."

"I'm sure they're right." I yawned. "They'll call or come by the store in the morning?"

"I assume so."

Aaron gave me a kiss, and padded off to shower while I rolled over and went back to sleep. I didn't heard him crawl into bed or snore during the night.

I woke to the smell of fresh coffee brewing and bacon frying. My stomach grumbled with hunger as I got up. I snuggled into my robe and went down the hallway to the kitchen where Aaron stood cooking.

"This is a pleasure." I sat and watched as he poured me a cup. I smiled after taking a sip. "Thanks."

"We'll eat, and then I have to report in. There's several reports I must write regarding what you told me."

"Lots of work for both of us, I guess. I'm anxious to get to the store."

We quickly ate and I filled the dishwasher. I scooted down to the bedroom and dressed, combed my hair and put on some lipstick before grabbing my bag and heading out the door. I was eager to resume my normal, boring routine. The previous busy few days made me realize that boring wasn't so bad after all.

Barbara Schlichting

Once in the car, I raised the garage door and backed out, then turned onto the street. In a few minutes I was on Main Street and I thought how silly, I should've walked on such a beautiful day. I always tried to walk or run to work since it was located so close to home, but I'd gotten out of my routine.

Soon I was driving around to the back of the store and parking in the lot behind it, right beside Max's beat-up truck. Why hadn't he ever replaced it after all these years? The minis, I'd left at home. I was second-guessing my earlier plan to displayed them because the showroom seemed crowded. So many things, so much to do, and so much to remember. Running my own business took a lot of effort, but it was worth it. It felt good to punch in the back door code and enter my store.

"Max! You here?" I hollered at once on entering. I went to the workroom and found it empty. I dropped my bag onto the workbench and glanced around the room. I smiled at the new, unpainted heads on the stand . Painting the heads was my job. It took so much time and patience that I sometimes wondered if I shouldn't pay Max to do it. I also did the costume sewing. I'd pretty much made up my mind to hire Max to paint the dolls once I had more cash in the bank. Max came and went on his own accord. As long as he took care of the heads, I didn't mind. I knew better than to ring him. If he'd been busy all night carving, he wouldn't want to be disturbed from his sleep.

I strolled into the showroom, stood with my hands on my hips, and smiled.

"I'm back ladies," I said. I glanced around the room, taking in the sight of the beautiful dollhouses. I strolled to the historical house, and stopped. "Dolley, I'm back. I'll help you make ice cream. After all, we could use a bowl since it's so hot outside." I swore she winked. I moved to Michelle Obama. "You did a very nice job with school lunches. More children are eating fruit and vegetables because of you." She might have nodded. I continued to circle the room.

Grandma took good care of the houses. The houses were arranged as they should be. She'd had Max or Grandpa bring in a new item to replace a sold Historical White House, which meant that Dolley Madison was another person's favorite First Lady. I meandered around the houses and grinned as I rearranged a few items. Upon coming to the Lincoln Civil War house, I noticed that the bedroom was out of order in the Lincoln Civil War House, and I straightened it. At the TR White House, First Lady Edith Roosevelt looked stunning in her inaugural gown. I imagined the robin's egg blue color with the design of plumes and birds embedded into the fabric and laced bodice was lovely on her. I learned that she'd destroyed the pattern so it would not to be copied. It also was incredibly hard to piece together and make it authentic-looking.

The shop door unlocked, the sign turned from 'closed' to 'open', I went behind the sales counter. I sat behind the computer and it hummed while I opened the cash drawer and began making my deposit. After completing it, I hid it back in the workroom inside my bag, locking it in a cabinet. Back out front, I logged into my webmail and began reading new messages. There wasn't many. Most came from those who had met me at the exposition. I wrote a quick reply to each, thanking them for stopping by. One message grabbed me. It read: Mind your own business. *What did that mean?* I heard car doors from out front, and closed out of the webmail. I smiled as a new customer entered.

"Hello. I'm Liv, if you have any questions, just ask."

"Just taking a look."

"Go ahead." I turned my attention back to my webmail. I read through the message once again, and decided to move it to a new file titled: *ERoosevelt*. The last time I was caught up in a mysterious murder, the clues pertained to Mary Lincoln and an unknown speech her husband had written. The killer hacked into my account and successfully removed important information. Fortunately, the police, with my assistance, were able to apprehend him before I became the next victim.

"Liv?!" the young woman called from across the room.

"Yes?" I logged out and went over to her. "Can I help you?"

"I really like the Jackie Kennedy White House, but I think my grandma would like the Historical White House, you see? It's for her."

"Why not buy two? One for each of you. That would take care of the problem." I grinned. "Kidding. Why not wait and bring her in when you can for a look around? She might surprise you and like the same house."

"That's a good thought. I think I will."

"I've got a card. Let me fetch it." I went over to the sales counter and removed it, bringing it to her. "My website shows my store hours, also."

"Thanks!"

After she'd left, I gave my neighbor, Inga, a call. She owns the antique store on the corner, *Inga's Antiques*.

"Got time for a chat?"

"Be right there."

I knew there was plenty for me to do, but I wasn't ready to buckle down in front of the sewing machine or get busy painting the heads. Inga always had plenty of gossip to fill me in on and she was a good friend. She'd also landed in the hospital over that hidden speech of Abraham Lincoln, the Lost Speech, and was a longtime, dear family friend of my grandma's.

The bell jingled overhead and I glanced up as her smile lit the showroom. A long, silver-hair ponytail lay over her shoulder and her blue thick-framed glasses accentuated her green eyes. Did I mention, vivacious? She had more energy than a tadpole.

"Missed you." I got up and went around and gave the little lady a massive hug. "It's not the same around here without you."

I noticed tears in her eyes when I released her. "I missed you too," I said. She held onto a small grass basket. "What on earth do you have?"

"I should've brought the matching figurine to yours, but forgot it at home."

"Start from the top." I nodded to my chair and said, "Go ahead and sit. I'll bring out another."

"Nah, I'll wait," Inga said.

It took about a minute before I returned with a folding chair, and set it right beside her. "Have a seat."

"A deal came up on Amazon, which I couldn't pass on." She held up the basket. "This was woven by a Sioux woman. Isn't it gorgeous?"

I inspected the lovely woven grass basket. "It's quite old, I can tell by the brown sheaves, but in very good condition."

"I haven't had a chance to look up the bottom, center symbol meaning. Do you have any idea?"

"It's in the shape of a small cabin and these are teepee's. Okay, that would mean home and cozy," I said after studying the symbols lining the outside of it. studied the smaller woven symbols lining the outside perimeter. "Is that your conclusion?"

"I thought so too, but didn't want to say until I heard what you thought." She glanced outside, around the room, then reached out and grabbed my hand. "This came from a Teddy Roosevelt collection."

"Oh my…." I sank back in my chair. My head seemed to spin and I reached to give my temples a massage. "This can't be happening."

"Honey, you'd better hold on tight because the next thing I have to tell you is —the figurine is of TR wearing his cowboy outfit."

"Same size as the jingle doll figurine?"

"Exactly. We have to put them together and take a closer look."

"There should be one of a Native American man."

"But there isn't. I've checked in all of my books."

"Are you sure the basket is from the TR collection?"

"Yes. An auction house out of New York verified the items and the authenticity of all things presidential."

"Here we go again. Just what I didn't want."

"Yeah, well—honey—we're up to our eyeballs. Like it or not."

"I hope not. The police are coming sometime soon to talk to me about Gina. I just found out that she was poisoned. Another murder that I'm exposed to. It feels like the murders that circled around Dolley Madison or Mary Lincoln. I hope it doesn't involve

First Lady Edith Roosevelt." I shivered and continued, "Even though it happened in St. Paul, Gina's house is here and there've been a few things which don't add up. The same two detectives were assigned to the case since we have this history." I rolled my eyes. "We're like old friends by now."

"That sounds mighty suspicious. I'd be concerned for my own safety if another murder occurs involving people from the expo."

"Now I'm really getting scared. Let's change the subject," I said. "What were you going to say about the basket and figurine?"

"I'll leave the basket, and bring in the figurine tomorrow. You have yours here, don't you?" When I nodded, she said, "Okay. See you in the morn."

I began a search of Native American symbols and discovered that my idea about home and hearth was right. At least I had something concrete to tell the detectives should they ask. I reached down for the figurine and studied it closer. The figurine showed jingles along her waistline and the coloring of the belt and headband was familiar. I did another search and found it was from the Sioux tribe. I held it closer and very slowly turned it while studying the waistband design. It was different than the basket. This symbol was clearly of a blanket waved over a fire. *Burning a blanket?* Just as I began to search the site, the door opened and in walked the detectives.

"Detectives." I got up from my place and walked around the corner toward them. I thought they looked just as they did two years ago. Detective Erlandsen was still crumply like he'd slept in his clothes, and Detective Mergens' still had a sternness about him. I smiled.

"Mergens," he showed his badge and shook my hand.

"Erlandsen." He did the same.

"We meet again."

"Yes, I'm not sure if we're lucky or not, eh?" Detective Erlandsen winked. He took out his notepad, as did Mergens. "Let's start from the top."

"Are you alone?"

"Yes." I shrugged and drew in a deep breath. "Where should I begin?"

"The morning of the murder."

"It all started when we headed toward the 'X' Center. We stopped here first to pick up the boxes…" I continued by telling the whole entire story, which included my going into the house and being hit by a flying shoe. "Since then, I've tracked Annie Oakley, and found that she hangs out at the Establishment."

"Oh yeah? What else?"

"John Muir's impersonator, Ed Parsons, is the brother to the owner." I waited as they both wrote before finishing by saying, "And Gina, Sunflower, a jingle dancer, and Ranger Harry, are closely related. The family ranch is in Gina's name. Sunflower is scared. Gina had a friend named Bambi who is a jingle dancer from the same area. Both John Muir and the TR impersonator asked about seeing the Alice purse, which is here in the store. I never brought it to the expo."

"This is all interesting, but it doesn't make sense," Mergens stated.

"Just like the last two times." Erlandsen shook his head. "Topsy-turvy."

"There's something else. Not sure how it all fits."

"Let's hear it all."

I swallowed before proceeding, "It's this grass bowl that Inga just brought to my store." I held it up, handing it to Erlandsen. "It was in a TR collection and there's also a figurine of TR in his cowboy duds, which is the same size as my doll," I said. "I haven't seen that, but she's bringing it in the morning."

"The three items are from the collection?"

"I don't know about my doll, but she looked it all up and contacted the presidential historian who said that the two items, this bowl and the TR doll, came from the presidential collection and are authentic."

"Okay…," Mergens grumbled. "Back to this stuff again."

"It appears that way."

I watched them finish writing a few more words before looking up to me.

"What's your theory?" Mergens asked.

"No idea." I shook my head.

"Here we go again."

"When will I ever learn to mind my own business?" My eyes opened wide. "I almost forgot! I got an e-mail stating that same thing—to mind my own business."

"Let me see it."

I showed them, and then forwarded it to their phones so they had a copy of it before they left.

For the rest of the day, I straightened stuff and began painting the dolls heads, and wondered what First Lady Edith Roosevelt's past had to do with the murder of my friend.

Chapter Ten

While painting heads in the workroom, my thoughts went to Gina. I missed her, not that I saw a lot of her, but she'd become a friend. We were near the same age. I had hoped that I'd found someone nearby to chat with over a soda, sitting outside on lawn chairs or to call in the evening when Aaron worked, to come over and watch a late night movie with me. I sighed.

I wondered what information the detectives would find that could link the killer to TR? Once again the symbols entered my mind, and I wished that I'd taken the time to investigate further. I had heard the back door open, and knew it must be Max or Aaron.

"I'm in here." I swiveled the chair to see the visitor, and it was Max. "I wondered about you."

"I worked on heads into the night." Max yawned, and he had an unlit cigarette between his fingers. "Thought you'd stand outside and let me smoke, then we can talk."

"I need a break." I got up and followed him out. We propped the door open in case someone should enter from the front. "You do such a great job." He smelled of fresh soap and his longish brown hair was freshly shampooed. Those long eyelashes of his always made the girls swoon. "I'm glad that the expo is done. I'm worn out."

"There's been an awful lot of traffic on this corner lately." He lit his cigarette and took a drag, giving me time to think. "Something's up."

"What are you saying?" I looked up to him. "You don't think someone's going to try and break in, do you?"

"I'm just saying that it's more than normal. What that means, I don't know." He took a longer drag, then flicked the cigarette to the ground and snuffed it out. "I think we should have the lock people back to have a look. Make sure the place is secure."

"That's a good idea. It hasn't been done for two years." I ran my fingers through my hair, and pulled on a hair shaft that sprung back to normal once released. "I'll give Minnesota Nice Security a buzz. I'm glad you mentioned it."

"What do the cops have to say about the investigation?" Max asked.

"You're not going to like this." I watched his eyes narrow as I told him the long story which included the basket and figurine dolls.

"Let's get this straight—now it's Edith Roosevelt?" Max said. "Very good, zippy!"

"If I had any sense-, any sense at all-, I'd walk away. Quit!"

"But you won't, because you like your job," Max said.

"Right." I smiled up to him. "You're the best, Max. I couldn't do it without you, the business… you know?"

"Now that I'm up to speed, then it's a must."

"I'm going to give the security company a call right now." I took out my phone, found the contact number and called. I arranged from them to come out as soon as possible. "Done. They'll be here in the morning."

"Good. I wanted to touch bases with you about that." Max pulled on his beard for a moment. "I'm going to be gone for a few days. I've got to see to my mom, she's at her cabin up near Brainerd. I plan to leave once I get packed. Anything else you want me to do?"

"Nope. Take care and give her a big hug from me." We gave each other a hug, and Max went to the stairs leading up to his apartment. I went inside and continued painting the heads. My stomach began grumbling, and I checked the clock. It was already after two. I gave Aaron a call to find out his schedule, only to learn that he was on a pursuit and would have to get back to me.

I didn't like the sound of that. Car chases led to deadly accidents. My mind went back to something Max said, and I decided to give him a follow-up call."

"Max? I have a couple questions."

"Shoot."

"When you said more than the normal amount of people here, what time of day was that and when?"

"It may have been after the memorial." I could almost hear him stroke his beard as he thought. "Yep, it was. Also, there was one guy dressed older like and in a suit and bowtie plus…. let's see…what was it? Hmm…sure, it was someone with a walrus mustache, and I remember he reminded me of Teddy Roosevelt. Does that help?"

"A lot. What about women?" I asked.

"A real short woman with a long braid."

"No one dressed like a Ranger or Native American woman?" I asked.

"Not that I could tell. No Ranger that I saw, at least no one wearing the uniform."

"Okay, thanks." I disconnected and slipped my phone inside my pocket.

I no longer had the urge to keep painting, and hunger gnawed, so I closed up and headed to the corner café. The former owner had been convicted of two murders, hacking into my Internet connection, and breaking and entering. He and his wife were found guilty of all crimes and sentenced to life in prison. New owners had added their own spin on the café, augmenting the monthly schedule, with open mic nights. They also displayed art from local artisans. It's family oriented with a small room where the younger among us can play and move around. It's my favorite place for lunch. I ordered a turkey cranberry sandwich with a raspberry soda to go, and hurried back to the store.

While eating, I flipped through my notes where I'd written down the real names of the impersonators. I took a post-it, and copied them down, sticking it next to the keyboard, then went ahead and started a new search for Annie Oakley. It took quite a while because I wanted to be positive that I had the right person. Sarah Page. I found her website and read it completely. Same height, weight, and the blond roots gave her away. The rest spoke about her fondness for history. She was raised on a ranch and knew how to rope and ride, and her shot was almost as good as the lady she impersonated. The rest of the site had contact information and her schedule of events which did include the expo. There was something unusual about her features; I finally realized that she had a mole next to her right eye.

After finishing reading her bio, I renewed the search for Ed Parsons. His was a fascinating life story. He'd worked many jobs, including that of an engineer for the Santa Fe railroad. He'd also authored several nature books, but hadn't been successful. While growing up, he had a fondness for traveling. He'd lived in many places and now called Minneapolis/St. Paul home. He loved all the parks, rivers and lakes. I wondered what he did for a living?

Flustered, I quit researching, still wondering how semi-retired impersonators could make their living. They had to be involved in something else.

I went for a cloth and began dusting just as a customer entered the store. "Good afternoon."

"I have heard so much about your store. I'd like to take a look at the White House for the Eisenhower's," the woman said. She wore her blond hair was long, her skin looked stark white next to her black frame glasses. Wobbling as she walked, I noted that her feet were covered with spiked heels.

"Right over here." I circled back around and stopped. "Mamie and her pink fetish. Everything pink!"

"And, her funny looking bangs." She chuckled. "I liked her."

"She was a very gracious hostess. Did you know she suffered from Meniere's disease?"

"That's why everyone thought she was a bit tipsy at times, eh?"

"Yes, it affected her equilibrium. And that's why she valued her privacy. I held out the Mamie doll wearing her inaugural gown. "Wasn't she beautiful?" I said, continuing, "She was so elegant in the pink peau de soie gown. There were two thousand rhinestones embroidered into it. I only glued on a few. I didn't do it justice."

"And pink heels. Very feminine," she said.

"Just like her," I said.

"I'll take it."

"Oh my." I smiled at her. "Do you want all the furnishings?"

"Of course."

I went ahead and rang it all up and began the wrapping and boxing which took me quite a while, as I usually can count on Max's help. After carrying the purchase out to her van, I collapsed on my chair and smiled.

"I'll see you all in the morning," I called to the dolls.

I locked up for the day, and headed home.

The traffic was light, and I was soon home. My wish was for a nice meal with my husband, but I put that thought out of my mind. The air was fresh and the heat of the day subsided, so I was anxious for a nice jog up and down the walking path that ran near the river. Before long I was out the door and starting to run, my iPod earplugs in, water bottle attached to my belly-bag, and my house keys and phone zipped inside.

After reaching the main drag, Main Street, I began running toward the nearest footpath began. As I jogged along, my mind went in circles. I thought of Grandma and her circle of friends. Since we had the Dolley Madison connection, she'd taken it upon herself over the years to contact people who had worked in the White House at various times, such as secretaries, wait-staff, or cooks. A few people came to mind. There was a time when she'd been invited to a guest tea at the White House and become acquainted with the granddaughter of one of the many secretaries to First Lady Pat Nixon. As I wound my way up the footpath toward the Hennepin Avenue Bridge, I tried to think of her name but it eluded me. I'd have to ask Grandma if her friend still visited her summer home near Cross Lake. Is, Grandma would know how to contact her.

I kept jogging, but took after a while I took a short break and drank some water. I sat for a minute and looked across to the other side of the park, where possibly the string of Segway riders had stopped traffic as they maneuvered their way through the intersection. I could see my store from there, I was happy to discover. After another drink, I got up and began my journey across the historical Stone Arch Bridge, constructed by railroad baron, James J. Hill, and is now on the National Register of Historical Sites. I jogged onto the bridge, used only for walkers or bikers, and stopped midway to enjoy the sound of rushing water and the beauty of St. Anthony Falls, which was used to power the flourmills of the early century. Minneapolis was the home to Pillsbury Flour and General Mills. It was once known as the Mill City. During President McKinley's visit and tour of the Pillsbury Flour Mill, an attempt was made on his life, poor man

I ran over the bridge and headed toward home. I was running out of energy, so it took me longer on the run home. As I neared the Establishment where Gina had worked, I thought to take a quick tour around the parking lot before going home. Sure enough, there were two cars that I recognized, Annie Oakley's—Sarah Page and John Muir's—Ed Parsons. I needed to look closer into that and figure out the connection.

After reaching home, I headed down the hall to shower. The cool water felt good across my skin, so I stood a little longer than usual. Upon stepping out, I quickly dried and got ready for bed.

There wasn't much to watch on T.V., and I would've had trouble concentrating so I went to bed. I fell asleep instantly.

I never heard Aaron return during the night, but I knew he'd been home and slept because his pillow was dented in and the blankets on his side of the bed were ruffled.

Without Aaron, I felt lonely and not much like eating breakfast. I brewed a pot of coffee and toasted a slice of bread, before going to sit out on the shaded patio deck. After a sip of coffee, I gave Grandma a buzz.

"Hello, Dear, what are you up to?" she asked when she answered the phone.

"Hi Grandma. Not much. Aaron pulled an extra shift so I'm sitting on the deck, alone."

"No church? Shame on you. We taught you better than this, dear girl…." Grandma said. "We're just setting the table. A neighbor couple is coming for brunch. Do you want to come?"

"I thought you'd never ask." I smiled. "Be there in a minute. Can I bring anything?"

"Just you." I mouthed it while she said it, because that's what she always says.

"See you." We disconnected and I hopped up from my chair to go in and change. I slipped into a flowery, summer dress which had a matching short sweater in case the inside temperature was chilly.

I gave Aaron a ring. "Honey? I'm going to Grandma's. She's having dinner for some friends and I invited myself. When are you done with your shift?"

"At three, and then we'll have the rest of the day. No one else."

"Have the detectives said anything about the case?"

"No, not at all. They tried to find the link between the people, but all they found were people trying to sell some real estate."

"That might be the key, but so what?"

"Exactly. So what if they sell some land? It wouldn't matter."

"I'll see you when you get home."

I made sure all I needed was inside my bag before going out to the car. I punched the button, raising the garage door. Soon I'd backed up, the house was secure, and I drove in the opposite direction toward Lake-of-the-Isles, where they lived. It was a new subdivision for retired people, and they loved it. Grandma had a wonderful flower garden, and that's what I'll always remember her for. She was chair of the local chapter of Beautify the Lake.

The road wound up around the Calhoun Beach Manor and over hills, and beautiful green parks filled with walkers and sun seekers, until at last I reached the street to turn into. Grandma's Goldenrod lilies lit up the street boulevard, and I parked right beside them.

"Hi Grandpa." I entered and immediately saw him sitting in his chair in the living room, with a shot glass beside him. "Where's Grandma?" I kissed his sunken cheek.

"Kitchen. She kicked me out." His sheepish eyes looked at me.

"Didn't you pour her a glass of wine?" I asked.

"I didn't get the Riesling chilled."

"That's why. It's in the fridge now, right?"

"Will you go down and get the bottles?" Grandpa asked.

"Sure." I smiled and kissed him again. He did this to me constantly, but I didn't mind. He started me in business. I loved him with all of my heart. I fled downstairs to the wine and reached for three bottles and flew back upstairs. Grandma was in the kitchen cutting vegetables for the salad. I put the bottles in the fridge.

"Hi Grandma. You look great." My nifty grandma wore pink capris, and a matching flowered top and sparkly jewelry to match. I gave her a kiss. "Can I help?"

"I'm almost done, but you can set the table. They should be arriving any minute."

"Who's they?"

"I should've invited you and Aaron anyway. I apologize for not planning this better. Don't know what I was thinking." She looked at me and smiled, wiping her brow as she held the sharp knife. "It's Edna Blake. Do you remember her? She was a secretary for Pat Nixon."

"You're kidding? I was going to ask you about her, but couldn't remember her name."

"Hmmm, I really should ask you 'why' but I think it's better that I don't know. Last time, you almost got killed. And the same time before, too." I watched tears fill her eyes. "Never mind—go set the table." She wiped her eyes. "Wait! What president?"

"Teddy Roosevelt."

"Staying out of it."

Chapter Eleven

Edna Blake was just as I remembered her, and she answered all my numerous questions about Pat Nixon and other First Ladies. Questions about Alice or Edith Roosevelt stumped her, but she promised to send me the address to someone who would know about land sales in or around Medora, North Dakota. Even better, this person actually had ties to Edith Roosevelt.

Once I'd arrived home, I no sooner poured myself a glass of soda than Aaron returned home. I gave him my glass and poured another for myself. "Do you want to go sit outside right away, or shower?"

"Shower and change. I'll meet you in back."

He gave me a kiss, and I watched him go with the glass in hand. I turned and went out back to sit and think. Edna wasn't privy anymore to White House matters, and hadn't been invited for tea in a number of years. She'd now reached her late seventies, and didn't travel much, but she still summered in Cross Lake, and wintered in Florida. When up north, she lived in a small apartment in Minneapolis. Edna had told us that Mrs. Nixon was quiet and shy, and hated politics, as did most of the First Ladies. I thought of what she'd said about Alice, who was known for carrying her pistol, in her purse – the same purse I now owned. Unlike most women of her generation, she drove her own car. She also hosted many weekly parties attended by senators and congressmen and enjoyed the political talk in which then engaged. She rarely spoke during such conversations, but absorbed everything they said, and kept many secrets. Invitations to these gatherings were prized, in part because she made certain their glasses were filled and there was plenty to eat. I went back inside and fetched the purse and pistol, bringing it outside.

"What do you have there?" Aaron said.

I held Alice's Colt Pocket Pistol and admired the sleekness of it and how well it fit into the palm of my hand, like a glove. I looked up as he walked toward me.

"Alice Roosevelt's pistol. Remember? It was in the purse I'd purchased a while ago from Inga," I said, and handed it to him.

"You've got that look about you," he said, taking the gun in hand. Narrowing his eyes, he said, "You can't do any investigating, hon. There's nothing there to warrant an investigation at Gina's house."

"I know, but that doesn't stop my worries. Something's not right, and I don't know what it is." I gave him the pistol, handle first. "I'm sure it's not loaded, but take a good look at it."

Aaron clicked open the chamber and confirmed that it was empty.

"It's clean. Put it back in the purse and tell me what's eating you."

"There's quite a bit that doesn't make sense; everything that I've told you and then more." I took a deep breath and told him about Alice and how her interest lay in the area around Medora where her father ranched. The small cabin of his that had traveled the country until President Truman put a stop to it, and signed a bill stating that it belonged in the park. "Edna plans to send me the address to someone who can tell me more about land ownership back then."

"You think this all ties together somehow?"

"Yes, but there's more. The two impersonator's cars were parked outside of the Establishment this morning. Don't you find that odd? It's Sunday morning!"

"They're not breaking the law as long as no liquor is sold. I'll make sure that the beat patrol is aware of this, but that's all that can be done."

"No one has cleaned out her house, either. Makes me wonder…"

"You haven't seen any cars or lights, have you?"

"No." I sipped my soda and thought about what a beautiful day it is. "Should we go for a stroll over to the house?"

"We could, but can't enter. We can walk around it just to make sure that it's secure, but that's all."

"Okay. Let's put this stuff away." I brought the purse and pistol inside, placing it in a kitchen drawer. Aaron followed with the soda glasses and set them on the counter. "Ready?"

"Yep."

Aaron ushered me out the door and across the street. The neighborhood children scooted on their skateboards and bounced balls in the street. Smaller children ran around in swimming suits and jumped in wading pools. At the front of Gina's house, I said, "We should try her door to make sure that it's still locked." I glanced at my frowning husband but still reached for the doorknob. He brushed my hand down and turned it.

The door popped open exposing a room full of topsy-turvy furniture and papers strewn all over the floor.

My eyes opened wide as Aaron pulled me to the middle of the yard. Quickly he removed his phone and called it into the police station as a breaking and entering. Next he gave Detective Erlandsen a call.

"Gina's house has been ransacked." He hesitated a moment before continuing, "Liv hadn't seen anyone around and we thought we'd make sure it was secure. We haven't entered. I've reported it as a break-in." After another minute, he disconnected and looked at me. "Go home. I'm staying here until a team shows up."

"Nope." I saw him roll his eyes and stare upward.

"Can't you ever listen?" The flicker of lights became a police squad car with flashing lights. "Never mind."

I held my ground. I wanted to take a look inside. *What could they be after? What's missing?* I stood to the side, and watched as the officers went inside to secure the home and then return to speak to Aaron. During that time, the detectives arrived. They saw me, and Erlandsen crossed his arms and looked upward.

"I want inside."

"I bet you do."

"You're just going to have to wait it out," Mergens fired back.

"Shoot!" I knew then that I was sunk.

I went back home and plopped down on my front steps and watched from across the street. First after the patrolmen, the detectives entered. After a few minutes, they came back outside and talked for a while, all the time looking over at me. Aaron stayed with them for a while, and then found his way home, and sat on the steps beside me.

"Well?"

"The family's being notified."

"That all you're saying?"

"For now."

I growled, went inside for my soda, and brought it back out with me. "Bet you wanted yours too?"

"Yeah."

I handed him my glass and went back in for another, and resumed my watch. "Now what are they doing?"

"I think they've called forensics to check for prints. No one knows why this happened but since it's on record that the owner was murdered, the investigative team plans to come on board."

"St. Paul police?"

"Jurisdictions have to be worked out."

I continued staring across the street. By now it was getting hard to tell what was happening because of the spectators. It seemed like the whole neighborhood had turned out. I drank my soda in silence and thought about it. Why would someone break into her house and ransack it unless they were after something. What on earth would they be after? My phone buzzed with a message from Erlandsen. It read: get over here.

"He wants me over there." I got up and we left the glasses on the steps to be picked up later. Aaron walked beside me as we made our way through the gathering crowd. The patrolman guarding the main door ushered us inside where the detectives stood waiting.

"We meet again," Erlandsen said. "Since you were probably the last person inside here, how about helping us by telling us if you can tell if something is missing?"

"This is kind of getting a little ridiculous with you two, but let's get started," Mergens said.

"Sure." I smiled. I knew he spoke about the other two cases and didn't actually mean me. "Lead the way."

"You already know the way." Mergens looked at Aaron. "How about giving your statement while you wait?"

"Okay." Aaron walked away.

"Follow me."

The detectives began the walk-through with me in tow. First we stepped into the living room which was a mess with the papers scattered across the cushions and ripped magazines. We walked down the hallway and I stopped at the bathroom. "You've already taken the shoe?" I looked around quickly. Gina's mattresses were overturned, and all the dresser drawers dumped out. I gasped. "Why would they do that?"

"They were after something in particular." Erlandsen looked at me. "Anything missing or unusually placed, that you can see?"

"From what I recall, the jewelry is as it was except slightly spilled out. That bottom drawer of the chest, of course, is overturned." I glanced down at the small chest beside the bed. "She had papers on top, but they're scattered all over."

"Let's go downstairs."

I followed them to the kitchen, and then down the basement stairs. I noted that the drawers were overturned in the kitchen, too. "Definitely looking for something, but what?"

The basement had very little in it besides an old bookcase, laundry room, and an old furnace. However, the bookcase was empty, and all the books were piled on the floor. "What on earth?" I bent over to have a look. Most of them were quite old.

"Any books catch your attention?"

"This is what Ida wanted me to find, but I never went downstairs."

"Did she mention one in particular?"

"A ledger." I started reading the covers and picking through the pile.

"Right here." He picked it up. "I think I'll keep this with me."

"I'd like to look through this old family Bible. There's two or three other books I'd be interested in taking a look inside of. This one here about how Medora started, it tells more than the plat book, and this old school ledger. Maybe this one about the old church." I picked them up, and looked at the detectives. "Maybe I can find some clues inside these?"

"Okay. We'll let the family know."

We went back up the stairs and I continued out the door. I held the books with one arm, while the other swatted some horrible mosquitoes that had arrived with the sunset. I raced right across the street and into our living room, where I found the TV blasting and Aaron watching it. "Look at what I brought home." I placed them carefully on the coffee table. Old books can be fragile.

"Oh." He glanced at the titles, clearly not impressed.

"Amazing, isn't it?" I smiled over at him. "The house was sure a big mess. Yikes." I shook my head. "I didn't see anything missing, nothing that I knew about."

"That's good. I'm sure the family will be around soon. I'm anxious now to meet them."

"Me, more than you. Why leave the house for so long? Wouldn't the police let them start packing up since it's not the crime scene?"

"It is now," he said. "I also wonder who will take over the murder investigation. I suspect, we'll know tomorrow."

"Make sure you let me know." I said, looking at him. "We're in this together."

"Yeah, if only we knew what we were going after—it would help."

I picked up the plat book and tried to figure out where the farms were located and the proximity to each other plus the Roosevelt property. It was difficult because of not knowing the counties and the pages were filled with complicated diagrams presumably because of the farmland ownership. I decided to put it off until later. I reached for the small church history book and found it interesting. St. Mary's Catholic Church in Medora was built by the De Mores family. I glanced through the pages enjoying all the pictures of the tiny church, but nothing popped out and caught my attention. I set it aside, also. The family Bible was huge and the print was of old English style, so it was hard to follow. *I must not be in the mood.* I placed it on the table with the other books, and leaned back to sip my drink.

"What on earth would Gina have that someone else might want?"

"That's up to the detectives to figure out." He caught the pillow I threw at him. "What's that for?"

"You're sounding too much like a cop." I stood in front of the window. "How crazy, really. I thought I knew Gina pretty well."

"How well do you really know someone, though, until you've lived with them?"

"That's true." I shifted over for Aaron to join me at the window. "I don't see anyone I recognize besides neighbors, but it's getting dark."

"None of her jewelry or expensive things were stolen, were they?"

"Nope." I shook my head. "It's getting late." I sighed. "I'm going to get ready for bed."

Aaron yawned. "Me, too."

I glanced outside one last time to find that the number of spectators had dwindled to almost none. "Do you think any of our leading suspects were in the crowd?"

Aaron crossed his arms and said, "You've been watching too much TV."

It didn't take long for the both of us to jump into bed and fall fast asleep. I woke about an hour later and glanced once more outside toward the street, and didn't see the squad car. Back in bed, my mind kept going over the messed up rooms. What were they after? The intended find eluded me, and I finally fell asleep.

Rain pounded the windows and lightning crashed, which woke us to a grey day. "So much for walking to work," I grumbled, and sat up.

"I can take you." Aaron kissed me. "I'll be there at lunch time, too. I'm going to hang-out with you as much as possible."

"You're worried?" I leaned over him and kissed him softly.

"You bet I am. The crimes are getting closer. They're creeping in on us."

"Hmm…." I got up and headed toward the shower. I heard Aaron's phone chirp as I closed the bathroom door. I hoped he wouldn't be called back to work another shift. When I'd finished toweling off and entered the bedroom, I found it empty. Aaron must be fixing breakfast, I guessed, as I pulled on a Tee-shirt and red capris. I ran a comb through my unruly, springy red hair, put a bow on the side to hold it back, slipped into a pair of black wedges, and headed to the kitchen.

Fried bacon was already on a plate and Aaron stood cracking an egg over a small frying pan as I entered. "Who was on the phone?" I sat in my usual spot and waited for our meal. Aaron loved to cook. I was getting better at it, but still burned eggs quite regularly so I cleaned up after he cooked. It seemed to work better that way. I sipped my apple juice.

"It's like this." Aaron poured a mug of coffee, and I had apple juice. He leaned against the counter and took a sip of his before clearing his throat.

I braced myself. Whenever he took this tactic, I knew it wouldn't have a good outcome. The grave look in his eyes made me tremble. "Well?" I set my glass down to wait.

"Inga's been burglarized." He set his mug down and stared at me.

"Was she there when it happened?" I had trouble catching my breath. The last time this happened, I'd found her and called the ambulance. She'd been hospitalized for a concussion and had to stay a few days.

"Fortunately it happened before she arrived."

"I was supposed to meet her this morning. She had something for me."

"What?"

"A figurine of Teddy Roosevelt that went with my jingle dancer figurine to make a matching set."

"Well, my dear, I do believe that the detectives will be around sometime today."

"We best get moving."

Aaron dished up the fried eggs, and we both ate. Each of us deep in our own thoughts. I wondered what the day would bring when my phone buzzed. It was Grandma, so I thought I'd better answer it.

"What's this I hear about a break-in across the street? That Gina's house?" Actually, it was Grandpa using her phone.

"Yes, Grandpa. Aaron and I found it open so he called it in."

"You okay? No one hit you over the head, did they?"

"Nope."

"He's going to be with you all day, isn't he?"

"Yes. I don't need a bodyguard, I have Aaron."

"Okay. Grandma says we're to come anyway."

"We're fine. Don't worry." He disconnected in mid-sentence. I looked at Aaron and let out a long breath.

"Don't tell me, I already know—they'll be at the store by the time we get there."

"How'd you guess?"

Chapter Twelve

Lightning and thunder struck again as we backed from the garage. I looked over toward Gina's. I breathed a sigh of relief thankful for my husband, and reached over to squeeze his hand. He smiled at me. "We need the rain." He drove out onto Main Street.

"What was taken?"

"I'm not really sure, but it sounds like most of the presidential items."

"By that, you mean Teddy Roosevelt?"

"Inga will have to tell you."

"That poor woman."

Passing the old Grain Belt Brewery, I thought of the many uses for the park and now the building had been turned into a library, and realized I needed to visit it more often. Perhaps it held clues to mysteries yet to come. Once across the small bridge, we soon drove through the intersection of University and Hennepin, and circling in back of our store and parking. I reached for my umbrella and bag, and we raced through the rain to the back door. As Aaron punched in the code, I glanced toward the antique store, but couldn't see anyone. We went into my store.

"I wish I'd worn a sweater." I shivered. "It's cold in here." I turned the thermostat to a more comfortable degree.

"It's been so hot, that's why you're cold." Aaron sat on a stool in the workroom and glanced at his phone for the time. "Let's see, ten more minutes?"

"I say fifteen." I knew he meant my grandparents. "They drive about twenty."

"The bet's still lunch?"

"You got it."

"Good morning, ladies." I busied myself by walking through the store and turning on the lights. "Mrs. Ford, you didn't dance on the desk last night, I hope?" I rearranged the doll's locations. "Much better. Now you can peak into the oval office better to see your honey." I continued circling the tables.

"The security guys from Minnesota Nice should be coming this morning," I said. I turned the sign around and unlocked the door. It was raining so hard I could barely see the cars going by. I stopped by the check-out counter and sat down in front of the computer. The lights flickered as I went to start the computer so I decided to let it go for the time being. I picked up the store phone and gave Inga a call.

"Inga, I'm here at my store now. Would you like me to come over?"

"Please do, when the police leave. Thanks!" Inga said.

"Okay," I said.

We no sooner disconnected then the two security guys from Minnesota Nice entered.

"Hi," I greeted them. "I'm Liv Reynolds, the owner."

"We're the new team. I'm Thor." He reached out his hand and I shook it.

"I'm Helmer." I wondered if it hadn't been a vise that I'd shook instead of a hand.

"Follow me." I brought them to the back and introduced the men to Aaron. "He'll show you the lay of the store, and you can decide if we're up to date, or not?"

"You betcha," Thor said.

Grinning, I sat behind the sewing machine and began studying some patterns I planned to use. Aaron left the room with the two men and I heard their voices in the distance. The back door opened, and I wondered who it was, when Grandma poked her nose into the room. "Hello, Dear."

"Hi," I chirped and read the time on my phone. Fourteen minutes. Close enough. Aaron had to buy lunch.

"Let's hear it." Grandpa barreled into the room, found an empty stool and sat next to Grandma.

She looked at me with expectant eyes. "We're ready."

"What do you know?" I said.

"Just start at the begining," Grandpa implored.

"From Gina's death?" When he nodded, I began. I went through the whole bit—everything including seeing the two historical impersonators at the Establishment. I ended with adventure from last night, taking the books home, and Inga's burglary. "I don't know what all's missing from Inga's store, but I'm afraid it may have been a clue."

"We're not leaving until we find out what's going on." Grandpa narrowed his eyes. "The jerks are getting closer. You need protection."

"Aaron's here. Don't worry," I said.

"Honey, you're not getting rid of us that easily." Grandma smiled, and her eyes twinkled. "Your mother would never forgive us if something happened to you."

Aaron entered just in time to save me. "August." He shook his hand. "Marie." He kissed Grandma on the cheek. "I'm glad you're here. We've got to keep tabs on Liv."

I narrowed my eyes and watched as Grandma leaned closer to him. "Oh no, you two." I glared at them. "You guys aren't setting up guard watch. I can manage just fine, thank you." I crossed my arms, and huffed, "I'm going into the showroom."

"Liv," Aaron caught my arm. "The security team just left and will send a bill. They said that all doors are secure, including the outside door that leads to the basement. Max's door is also secure. He won't have to worry about a break-in either."

"That's good. He'll be happy to hear that." I took a deep breath to calm my temper. "No bodyguards?"

"Okay, but if anything else should develop, you're going to get them—young lady." Grandma pointed her finger at me.

"We mean it," added Grandpa.

"I'm fine," I said. I thought of telling them to leave me alone, but didn't. They must've sensed that I wanted just that, because in an instant we said, 'goodbye', and they walked out the door. "Yikes. The wrath of Grandma." I blew out a long breath. "I'm walking down to Inga's to see how she is."

"No, you're not, I am," Aaron said. "The store security is up to date."

I clenched my jaw and sat down behind the sewing table and watched him walk out the door, knowing that the doors were locked. Sometimes I just wanted to scream, and now was one of those times. I searched through patterns and found the inaugural gown for Jackie Kennedy. I almost drew blood a number of times cutting the light, pink chiffon fabric used for her bodice. Earlier I'd pieced together the skirt, now the top needed assembling. I turned the radio to my favorite station, working for quite a while without noticing the time pass.

An hour later, Aaron and the two detectives entered. "We're back." Aaron grinned. "I brought your two pals."

"I see that." I nodded to each. "Let me finish this one thing." I tied a knot, cut the thread, and set the piece aside. "Okay, ready."

"Ma'am," the detectives stated in unison.

I pushed my chair back and stood. "Where should we go?"

"Right here is fine." Mergens glanced to his partner and then to Aaron.

"I'll leave." Aaron walked out, shutting the door behind.

"Liv, can you tell us what happened in your words?" Erlandsen said.

Both detectives sat perched on a nearby stool and had a notepad and pencil in hand. "What did you and Aaron do after you left with the books? Did you look outside and see anything or anyone different?"

"You're not accusing me? Us? Of doing this to Inga?"

"Nope." Erlandsen shook his head. "We're trying to find a connection no matter how thin it is."

"I wondered the same thing myself." I twirled a few strands of hair between my fingers. "I said that to Aaron, that I didn't see anyone familiar besides the neighbors. They left eventually."

"Find anything that 'hits' you as odd in the books?"

"I didn't look close enough." I looked from one to the other. "Want me to keep an eye out for anything in particular?"

"No," Mergens said. "We want you to tell us, without any influence from us."

"I'll go through them carefully tonight."

"That's all we can ask for." Erlandsen stood, looking more crumply than usual. "Now for the computer." They followed me over to the counter where Aaron sat behind the computer.

"Have you checked your e-mail lately?" asked Mergans.

"Have you checked my mail, yet?" I asked Aaron

"Just going to do it," Aaron said.

"Let me." I scooted in and sat once Aaron moved aside. It took about a minute before I had the few messages loaded. "I haven't posted a thing about Teddy Roosevelt on my website. Not like what I did with Mary Lincoln or Dolley Madison to help flush out the killer. Want me to do something like that?"

"We aren't really certain if this is about him or not, though." Mergens glanced at Erlandsen. "What do you think?"

He shrugged. "The connection is so vague. Not sure if any good will come from it." He ran his fingers through his hair. "Heck. Let's do it, but what?"

"How about asking the public if there's anyone alive who knew Alice?" I questioned. "It's bound to bring some kind of a discussion."

"What if this person doesn't know about your website, hon?" Aaron asked. "Never mind, dumb question. The killer would know."

I watched as the detectives each scratched their heads. "What should I say?"

"Go ahead and ask the simple question. It'll generate answers, and we should get some good results from it."

"This is about real estate, isn't it?" I cocked my head and stared at them. "Right?"

"It's a slim thread. We don't know for sure but all of the historical impersonators involved are real estate agents. They are usually licensed by their state of residency and Gina held the property title. That's all I can give you."

"And there's the oil companies and drilling." When they didn't respond, I knew for certain that I was on the right track. "I'll post it right now." I typed in the question, 'Any available land for sale near the TR national park?' and saved it on the website. "I'll let you know when I have responses."

"We'll want to see all of them. Not just the odd, questionable ones. We're not taking any chances. This guy seems to be more aggressive than the other two."

"All right." They wrote a few things down before heading out the door. I looked over to Aaron who appeared slightly pale. "What is it?"

"Something about the way that they talked about this guy makes we worried," Aaron said. "I'm sticking with you as much as possible."

"I'm glad you're my bodyguard." I was about to kiss him when the door opened and in walked a customer. "Can I help you?"

"Just looking. It's almost my daughter's birthday." She strolled around and occasionally stopped to look at one of the houses. I noticed she reached into the house and kept her hand inside of it a little longer than usual. I loudly cleared my throat. I glanced at Aaron who strolled in her direction.

"You must like the early White House designs?" He held his hand out to shake hers. "I'm Aaron, the husband of that spectacular woman and part owner."

"Look. The dolls are missing from this house. Are they supposed to be?"

"Liv?"

Curious, I walked over and looked inside of it. "It's the McKinley house. They should be inside of it. They were here earlier today." I looked inside, then back at her. "Sorry. I can have a new set ready by tomorrow if you're interested?"

"As a matter of fact, I'm interested in Mamie Eisenhower." She smiled at us. "I'll return another time. I need to think about it."

"McKinley wasn't that popular, was he?" Aaron asked, leaning over the counter, after the customer left.

"He was president when TR was vice. That's the connection." I took a deep breath. "We'd better call the detectives."

Aaron listened while I gave them a play-by-play report of the incident. When I disconnected, I said, "They told me to keep them posted."

"If they have anything of value to report, they'll let us know."

"I wonder if there's a connection between the thief and the killer?"

"The police will figure it out." I gritted my teeth when Aaron gave me a forced smile. I knew that as a signal to cheer-up and step-back, and let them do their job. "It'll work out, just wait and see."

"In the meantime, I could be the next victim. They're getting bolder." I turned my eyes away from him and stared at the computer. It wasn't long before I thought of Bambi and wondered if she'd mind a phone call. I was just about to reach for the phone when Inga walked in. "Hi Inga. I wondered about you."

"I'll bring us both out a chair," Aaron said.

Aaron walked away to fetch them, and I got up and gave my good friend a bear hug. "I've worried about you. You didn't get hurt did you?"

"No. Thank goodness. Not like last time when I landed in the hospital." Inga sighed. "That figurine of Teddy Roosevelt was stolen. Do you believe it?"

"Why would anyone steal that? Anything else?" I studied her, and decided that her brown eyes were clear and she didn't look any worse for wear. She looked good and I breathed a sigh of relief.

"The other presidential items weren't taken, just messed up. It was as if they had trouble deciphering between Teddy and Franklin." Aaron brought in the chairs and opened one for her, and she sat. "Thanks."

"Anytime." Aaron opened his and sat down. "Did I hear correctly that only Teddy's items were stolen?"

"Yes. That's crazy, isn't it?"

"Maybe and maybe not." I decided to go ahead and tell her about the unresolved questions surrounding Gina's death including the break-in of her house and my suspicions about the impersonators. "I hope nothing else happens."

Inga glanced at Aaron and then back to me. "That's why you're here. Just like the other two times. Bodyguard." She crossed her arms and must've seen the veil come over my eyes because she said, "I was right."

"We don't really know what this is all about. No real clear suspicions, that is." I shrugged. "I'm not sure of the connections. It might be as simple as real estate."

"Nothing is simple. Never simple with Teddy Roosevelt, that's for sure." She shook her head. "Maybe the mystery lies with the Rough Riders and San Juan Hill?"

"No. I don't think so. It might have to do with either the TR National Park or Yellowstone. I think it has to do with sellable land and the oil drilling or ownership of the mineral rights on a piece of land, which vary by state."

"Yes, but any park land is unsellable," Inga stated.

"I know, that's why it's confusing," Aaron said.

"I wonder if he didn't squirrel away something of importance and set it aside for Alice? Right after his first wife died—he took off—handing her over to his sister." I knew that I was on to something, but unsure what. "What else is missing?"

"Campaign items—pins and buttons—that sort of thing." Inga glanced around the room. "His tennis racket. A small map of Cuba and a framed picture of him as Police Commissioner of New York City. Miscellaneous items."

"Do you know if there was anything hidden inside the frames of either of them?"

"Not that I'm aware of. I never removed the frame to look." Her eyes opened wider. "You think there was a letter or something?"

"I don't have any idea of what I'm thinking, really." I shrugged. "I find this all a bit peculiar, that's all."

"How does it all tie together?" Inga frowned. "That's the rub of it all, isn't it?"

"My jingle dancer figurine might hold a relevant clue," I said. "Then we have that grass bowl with the symbols. That wasn't stolen, was it?"

"Nope. That's going into a safe-deposit box until this is settled." Inga hesitated, "I had it set in the front display cabinet. Unless you knew it came from TR's collection, no one would suspect its importance."

"Good. Aaron can take you to the bank right now so you can lock it up." I looked at him. "You should do that with the figurine. It's at home on my dresser."

"Let's do it." To Inga, he said, "We can go now."

"Are there symbols on the TR figurine?" I said.

"I don't remember," I said, shaking my head. "Aaron, take lots of pictures of it before you go and send them to me. I want to look at them. Take some close-ups of my dancing figurine, too." I smiled. "We might be on to something here."

Chapter Thirteen

As soon as Aaron and Inga left for their bank errand, I turned my thoughts to research. I began my search with Alice Roosevelt. For some reason, I kept going back to her. I was certain Alice held center stage, but how or why? A number of sites appeared and I weeded through several without luck.

While police commissioner for New York City, he'd disguise himself, ride a bike along with a reporter late at night to catch 'beat cops' who were either sleeping on the job, or conducting themselves shamefully such as accepting bribes or drinking liquor while on the job. How did he end up in North Dakota? A conservationist. It brought me full circle to land. I reached for my phone to locate Bambi's number and called her.

She didn't answer, so I left a message before disconnecting, asking her to call me back.

I held a tiny, naked doll to the light. "Mrs. McKinley," I said. "I'll be really careful dressing you. We don't want another epileptic seizure. I'll also rearrange the chairs so you'll be seated right beside your husband. He looks after you like such a loving man, softly placing the handkerchief over your face before a seizure, and gently removing it. You must really love him." I smiled while dressing her in a beautiful white gown with lace overlay and a scalloped hem. The long-sleeves with the laced cuff were gorgeous, and the matching laced shoulder enchanting. The high collar embroidered with pearls took my breath away. "Mrs. McKinley, you're stunning. All eyes will be centered on you."

Did I hear her say, 'thank you, dear'?

While I waited for a return call, I got busy and cleaned. I no sooner placed my feather duster back on the hook and straightened out a few display sets when Aaron returned.

"How did it go?" I asked. "Get a lot of pictures?"

"Yes. Sorry for not sending them earlier but will do so now." I watched as he did the deed. "Now you can inspect them closer."

"Thanks." I studied him and said, "You look like there's something on your mind. Am I right?"

"There is, but not sure if it's significant."

The serious look on his face caused me to worry, and I curled a few strands of hair around my finger. "Let's hear it. Did you hear from the detectives?"

"It's not that, but I think I was followed."

My phone rang and I looked at the caller ID and held up my finger saying, "Hold that thought." and answered my call. "Bambi, thanks for returning the call."

"Oh sure, anytime. I assume this is about Gina?"

"Yes, but first how was the funeral? I'm still really sorry about it."

"It was huge because she's from here, you know?"

"Any impersonators show up?"

"You're wondering who from the expo, right?" Without waiting for me to answer, she continued, "Harry and Sunflower. They were at arm's length, and clearly not speaking."

"Do you know why they weren't speaking?"

"Not really. Ida Gray was there of course. She was the cheeriest of the three."

"Anything odd happen?"

"I don't think this is odd because it's right after a death, but my uncle owns a law firm and told me that he met with them right afterwards."

"It's a start. May I ask his name?"

"Gunnar Whitehorse."

"Thanks. Let's keep in touch."

"I'll call if there's anything else that I can find out."

"I don't want you digging around and getting yourself injured or worse."

"Don't worry. I want to find out who killed my friend just as much as you, if not more." We disconnected, and I slipped my phone back into my pocket. To Aaron, I said, "You were saying?"

"I was tailed," he said. My eyes opened wide as he continued, "when we left Inga's and went home for me to pick up the figurine."

I stared at him. "Then what?"

"He must've realized that I had spotted him, because I didn't see the car again." Aaron crossed his arms and looked outside before turning back to me. "We have to be careful."

"Did you tell the detectives?" When he shook his head, I asked, "Why not?"

"It could've been a fluke. I could be mistaken." Aaron stared down at me and said, "Don't worry, everything will work out."

"It always does. Did you recognize him or the vehicle?"

"He seemed average, and no to the car." We stared at each other for another minute until he walked away, calling, "I'll get us a couple of sandwiches. Be right back."

I decided that another Internet search wouldn't help my muddled thoughts. I needed to focus on trying to fit the puzzle pieces together. All these clues didn't add up to any singular idea, which brought me back to Gina and the ranch. I took out my phone and made a note about checking to see if it was on the market and if so, the realtor's name.

My phone chirped and it was a message from Grandma inquiring about me. I replied, 'I'm fine. I'll call later'. Aaron returned with chicken salad sandwiches just as I entered the workroom and sat in front of the work bench.

As we ate, we discussed the same old thing—why was he followed—who is behind this—and nothing made sense. We opened our respective phones and studied the photos.

"Do you see anything along the base of my figurine? I don't." I flipped from one photo to the other. "I don't recall seeing anything on it except the painted bells."

"Maybe each bell has a symbol? Ever think of that?"

"But, they're asymmetrical. All silver." I stared at one in particular and flipped to another image. "I suppose it's entirely possible but nothing appears on the image."

"We'll keep it right in the bank where it's secure. If we want another look, we can go one afternoon over there to look at it."

"That's a good idea."

As I began sewing a new inaugural gown for Mrs. Taylor, while Aaron busied himself by reading a sports magazine. "Let's find out what hunts TR went on, it might be helpful."

"Okay. I'll get right on it," Aaron said.

I went back to sewing. As I finished cutting the fabric for two dresses for the First Lady, I heard the front doorbell chime. I got up and went out to the storefront when the bell rung indicating the entrance of someone.

"Hello. I'm Liv. If you have any questions, let me know."

"You betcha." She smiled a toothless grin. "Yust lookin' around."

Her thick Scandinavian accent, plus her short, heavyset stature reminded me of a lady who used to come in whenever there was a cleaning emergency. Her short gray hair looked in need of a good combing and her worn clothes could use a good wash. I wondered if she had a flask inside a pocket?

"Ya know anyting about Bess Truman?"

"She didn't like living so much in the White House because she thought it'd fall down around her, and it nearly did!" I smiled. "After his re-election, the White House went through massive renovations."

"You betcha. What about Nancy Reagan?"

"The comeback kid as Margaret Truman coined Mrs. Reagan in her First Ladies book. Just say 'no'."

"You betcha." I watched the lady reach into a house, then change her mind and not touch a thing. In just a few seconds, she headed for the door saying, "Bye," over her shoulder as she walked out the door.

"Weird," I said.

Aaron entered the room, "I'll say so."

"Go follow her."

"Why?"

My glare must've propelled him, because he immediately left. I stayed near the window and kept my gaze on the outside street and watched the walkers and Segway riders come and go. The bright sunshine brought an unexpected smile to my lips. It wasn't long before Aaron returned.

"She drove away alone." He massaged his chin. "Better?"

"Thank you." I gave him a kiss. "I must be getting paranoid."

"I have to admit, the woman was different."

I glanced at the clock. "We have another hour before closing."

"I thought we could eat supper at the Establishment." He cocked his head at me. "We need to eat, don't we?"

"Sounds like a plan."

While Aaron read his magazine, I finished out the afternoon by sewing together the gowns for Mrs. Taylor. It didn't take long to do, but it was tedious work. Sewing all the tiny buttons on by hand made my eyes water from the strain. I decided to spend the money and purchase a strong magnifying angle poise lamp for the workroom. I carefully pressed the pieces and lay them aside for dressing the doll in the morning.

I dug out the two wigs in preparation for gluing tomorrow. Satisfied, I walked out to the showroom and found Aaron researching Teddy Roosevelt's African safaris.

"Did you know that his first safari was commissioned in 1909 as a scientific expedition from the Smithsonian Institute? He was a fascinating man," Aaron said.

"I think it's impossible to learn all there is to know about that man," I said. "Ready to leave?"

"Yep."

I locked up the front door, turned around the sign, and left through the back door, which automatically locked itself upon closing. For safety measures, I walked to the corner door that led to the basement. It was huge, covering the length of my store, Mikal's palmistry room, a restaurant, and Inga's. At one time it was used as a gangster hideout during Prohibition. Originally there were stairs leading up to my showroom, but have since been knocked out and the hatch leading down, sealed. Satisfied, I strolled to the car and jumped in beside Aaron.

"I'll feel better once Max returns," I stated, buckling up.

"Me, too." Aaron had the car running and the air-conditioning going. "It's about ninety degrees outside."

"Let's try and eat on the patio if there's shade."

"Oh, all right. I suppose you'd like me to shut the air off, too?" He glanced at me, and immediately turned it off and rolled down the windows.

"Ahh, fresh air." He drove from the lot and we started up the main drag toward the Establishment. After a minute I asked, "Do you think we'll know anyone?"

"Hard to say." He stopped for a red light on Lowry Avenue.

My thoughts went to that old lady who had earlier entered the store. Something about her bugged me, but I couldn't put my finger on it. Was it because she did remind me of the former cleaning lady?

Aaron turned the corner and we parked behind the building and stepped from the car. After locking it up, arm in arm, we strolled toward the main door. Unfortunately, the outdoor eating area was filled, and we headed indoors. Once inside the dark interior, it took a moment for our eyes to adjust after the bright sunshine.

"Let's find a corner booth." I let Aaron steer me toward the nearest one, and we sat opposite each other.

"I wonder if they serve anything other than burgers?" Aaron asked.

"We'll see…." At that moment, I glanced over toward the bar and my eyes flashed open. "Look at that woman sitting by the bar." I touched Aaron's hand and whispered, "Don't let her see you look."

"Huh? Who is it?" Fortunately, Aaron followed my instructions and didn't turn. "Annie Oakley?"

"Shush! Yes, and no. Annie Oakley is over at the bar, talking to a woman bartender. And guess who she is?" I looked up and smiled at the waitress. "I'd like a glass of your house white wine. Nice and cold, please."

She turned to Aaron who said, "I'd like a tap beer. Bring menus please."

"Coming right up." She reached over to a nearby table and handed us greasy menus. "Here."

After she was out of whispering range I said, "You can look now." Aaron cranked his head around and shrugged. "Doesn't she look familiar?"

"Sort of, but also different. It can't be who you're thinking of."

"Yes, I'm certain it was the old woman who entered the store. There is such a thing as makeup, you know? And costuming."

"But why? Why would she go through all that trouble?"

"They needed to know what was in the store, to see if it was worthwhile to break-in or not. Don't you see?" To my chagrin, he got up and walked toward the person in question and stopped to speak for a minute. My irritation grew. The waitress returned with the two drinks, and I told her to come back for our orders. I watched as Aaron pointed toward the restroom sign and headed for it. I opened the menu and tried to look interested but had a terrible time keeping my eyes from the woman bartender. *Can it really be her? The size is right.* No doubt was left in my mind.

I resumed reading the menu. Since there were four burgers mentioned and deep-fried chicken fingers it didn't take me long to decide what I wanted. When Aaron returned, I readied myself for what he had to report.

"Yes, it's her." Aaron smiled that big grin of his, and I almost burst. "I've already contacted the detectives."

"Jeez!" He raised a brow and cocked his head. "This place is beginning to give me the creeps."

"Look at the menu. She's returning for our order."

Aaron sipped his drink and cast his eyes on the page and was ready when she stood before us. "I'll have the Lumberjack burger with fries." When she asked about another beer, he shook his head.

When my turn, I said, "I'll have the Lumberjill burger with coleslaw. A glass of water, please."

"Me too."

"Okay. Be back with the water."

I watched as she marched away, stopping at another table before taking the orders to the kitchen. "It is the old lady who came this afternoon, isn't it?" I tried hard to not look in her direction. "I knew there was something fishy about her."

"The question is - what on earth could we possibly have?" Aaron asked.

"You're certain it was a man that followed you earlier when you two went to the bank?" I asked.

"I'm positive," Aaron said.

I frowned. "That means that they probably put this woman up to spying on us. They followed you, realized that whatever it was that we have is safe—then they wanted to know if there's anything of consequence left behind." I looked over at the small crowd and thought for a minute. "Can you think of a better reason?"

"Not really. But, who's 'they'? By the way, the owner's in the backroom."

"Who's they, is right. That's what we need to know." I glanced around the room. "I wonder if this barmaid person plays a role in any of this or is she just a dupe used to carry out their wishes?"

"I tried to spot a name badge each time I walked past, but she doesn't seem to have one."

I took out my phone and made a quick notation to myself to search the employee names of this establishment.

"I'll send a message to the detectives." He quickly punched in the message and took a distant headshot of the person and sent the message. "We'll get results."

"I know-, I'll be patient."

We ate our meal as fast as possible and headed home. We didn't want to be there when the police showed up or they might realize we were the ones who called the cops. By the time we watched a movie and headed to bed, we still hadn't received a verification of the barmaid's identity. I tried to think about her, but sleep overtook my thoughts. During the night, I woke and saw the northern lights dancing across the sky. I looked closer and wondered if I really saw lights on at Gina's or was it the stars?

Chapter Fourteen

I woke early in the morning and looked out across the back yard and smiled. Flowers bloomed, my rosebush looked marvelous. Grandma did wonders with my garden, and I wondered what I'd ever do without her. Glancing at the clock, I decided that there was plenty of time for a run before work. I gave Aaron a peck on the cheek. "I'm going for a run. It's only six. Go back to sleep." I slipped into my jogging shorts and top, and out in the kitchen I did a few stretching exercises before grabbing a water bottle and dashing out the door.

The early morning freshness cleared my mind as I jogged. I let my thoughts wander. I thought about my parents who'd been killed in a car accident and realized once again, that the driver was never found. *Time to talk to Grandpa.* I turned the corner and headed in the opposite direction of the store. I hoped that the identity of the barmaid would soon be discovered. I didn't like the idea of that woman coming into the store in costume. It struck me as duplicitous and dangerous. I questioned the friendships between the others in the case, and wondered again about the motive behind the camaraderie. I headed back home after jogging two miles, and that's when I noticed the car inching along behind me. When I glanced over my shoulder, the driver wove into the outer lane and turned a corner. I couldn't be sure if this person was following me, but it certainly felt like it. It gave me goose-bumps.

I felt relieved as I entered our little development. And, once inside the house, I didn't want to leave again.

"How was your run?"

"Not sure, but I think I was followed." I plopped into a kitchen chair and let Aaron place a full glass of orange juice in front of me. I nearly drank it all down.

"How so?" He held up two eggs, and I held up one finger while finishing my juice. "What did the car look like?"

"Small and dark blue."

"It's not conclusive by any means, but it does sound like the car that I think was following me. We'll have to pay closer attention to who is behind us at all times."

"I wish I had gotten a better look, but I just didn't expect it."

"You better drive to work from now on. When will Max return?"

"Hopefully today."

Aaron dished up the fried egg and I ate my breakfast. After that, I took a shower and prepared for work. As I brushed my hair, I asked, "What shift today?"

"Afternoon."

"Good. You can stay with me at work." I set down my brush and applied lipstick. "I'm off. When will you come?"

"After I mow the lawn."

I kissed him goodbye, and headed out to the car. I tossed my bag inside, and started the engine. As I backed from the garage, my cell phone chirped and I stopped to answer it. "Hi Bambi." I heard sniffles and said, "What's wrong? What happened?" More sniffles. "Bambi? Tell me."

"My...my...uncle....," she sniffled and blew her nose. "I'm sorry, Liv, but this is really tough."

"Take your time, honey." I put the car in park to wait. "Want to call me back?"

"No...I...have...to tell someone. Someone who can help."

"Did something happen to you?"

"No," she whispered. "Worse."

"Bambi, what happened?

"It's my uncle Gunnar."

The lawyer uncle who was in charge of Gina's ranch property. I was afraid to ask but went ahead with the question, "What happened?"

"He's dead."

"That's awful. What happened?"

"No one knows yet. The police aren't saying anything, except that it's considered a suspicious death."

"Oh my God!" I said. "Sit tight. Don't do anything. Let the cops do their job. I'll see what I can find out and will get back to you if I learn anything." She disconnected and I sunk deep into my car seat. After a couple of minutes, I shut off the engine and climbed out of the car. Once inside, I marched straight to Aaron.

"Uh-oh. Let's hear it," he pulled me down beside him on the bed. He'd been dressing. "You look dreadful."

"Bambi just called. Her uncle, the lawyer overseeing Gina's ranch property, has been found dead. It's considered suspicious."

"Oh dear God." He pulled me close. "Bodyguards?"

"No, I can manage. No one's after me, anyway." I sighed.

"I'm putting the mowing aside and taking you to work." Aaron smiled down at me, and then reached out to fluff one of my curls. "Nothing is going to happen to my baby girl."

"No way. The lawn needs mowing. Let me go, big guy." We kissed.

"I'm taking you," Aaron said. He stood by the door waiting as I approached. "You're looking good, girl."

"Thanks." He held the door for me, and I swept past, going right into the garage. "I'd hoped to start back into walking," I grumbled, "guess that isn't going to happen for a while." I climbed into the car beside Aaron and buckled up.

"It'll all be over with soon, just be patient." Aaron started the engine and backed out of the garage, then pressed the button to lower it.

"That's what you always say. I wonder when--?" I glanced toward Gina's house. "Hey, pull over for a minute. I want to take a quick look at Gina's house. I just remembered that I thought I saw a light on in there last night. We should really take a look."

"Good grief. I'm calling it in and reporting it. There's no stopping you." Aaron parked in the driveway and shut off the engine. He found his phone, and spoke to the dispatcher.

In unison, got out of the car and strolled together across the street. It'd been a week since Gina died, and I realized I'd totally forgotten about the books. I made a mental note to thoroughly look through them tonight. As we approached the front sidewalk, I took Aaron's hand and he squeezed mine.

"I'm sure everything's fine." Aaron tried the front door, and found it locked. "Let's circle around the back." I kept my eyes peeled as we walked for inside shadows or broken glass shards from basement windows but found everything as it should be.

"How about the back door?" I waited on the steps as Aaron tried the back door and also found it locked. "This is all good news. The house seems secure, right?"

"You did see a light?"

"Yes, I think I did, but I was mostly asleep, and can't be positive."

He took my hand and we briskly walked toward out car. I climbed in and got ready to leave as Aaron answered his phone. "Someone's going to check it out," he told me after hanging up.

We drove silently to the store, lost in our thoughts. I couldn't help but wonder if I hadn't seen a light in Gina's house, and if so, which light it might have been. As I thought about it, I realized that there was one light I couldn't see if it was on when we walked around her house, as I was too short for that window. "Aaron, I just realized, that the light had to have come from the bathroom."

"The detectives will look into it. Any questions, they'll stop by and ask." Aaron waited a beat. "I'll also tell them about someone possibly following both of us."

I turned to look out the car window. I didn't want him figure out what I was thinking. I wanted back in that house. I wondered if the spare key had been removed, figuring that it must have been. Then I got to thinking, if Aaron hadn't told them about the key—maybe it'd still be in the hiding spot. I resolved to go back later this evening when he was on shift at work to see for myself. What could the killer want or hope to find? There had to be something we overlooked. I turned my thoughts back to the last conversation with Gina and play-by-played-the conversation and previous conversations, but nothing struck a chord. Perhaps the aunt warranted another phone call?

"You're awfully quiet." Aaron glanced at me while waiting for a light to change.

"I'm curious about the house and if I should speak to the aunt. When will her house be emptied? Someone should've come for her things by now." Truthfully, I wondered who would come, Sunflower—Harry? Someone I didn't know?

"I expect they were going to wait until after the will was read. It can take time to settle her estate, after all."

"Yeah, well, that isn't going to happen for awhile now that the lawyer is dead." I shook my head. "Don't you find that suspicious?" I snapped my fingers. "Just like that? And, there may be a huge amount of money involved, too."

"It's not for us to say." The light turned and he drove ahead, soon parking in back of the store. "We need more information, but because the lawyer's death happened in North Dakota, way out of my jurisdiction, that may be hard to come by."

Disappointed, I didn't speak as I climbed from the car and went to the building with him following. It bothered me when he played the cop routine of not discussing stuff with me or saying that it's up to the police. It was as if I don't have a brain of my own.

"Everything look good?" Aaron went first into the workroom, turning on the light. "Nothing's out of order here."

"Good." He stepped aside for me to enter the room. I noticed that the work I had set aside for myself the day before was still in place. "Let's go through the showroom." I placed down my bag, and took out my cell phone, slipping it into my pocket. I held my breath and shut my eyes as the remembered the horror of finding Jackie Newell's body leaning into the corner dollhouse. "This is going to give me nightmares."

Aaron pulled me into his arms, and said, "It'll be fine. Don't worry." He held me tight for a few minutes until my breathing became regular once again. "Better?"

I nodded, pulling back. "Thanks." I wiped tears from my eyes. "I'm glad you're here even though I don't think anything will happen, but you never know."

Aaron went to open the front door and turn the sign around as I sat in front of the computer, and started it humming to life. It wasn't long before I logged into my account. "I'm going to check to see if anyone answered my question about land ownership near the national park.

Aaron came around in back of me and watched as the computer loaded twenty replies that had arrived overnight. "Wow."

"I know." I weeded through the many good-hearted people who heard timeless stories around their great-grandparents tables about his kindness and how he'd hunt down thieves and riff-raff. A close friend of Allice's reported that he was known to never drink anything stronger than a cup of coffee. How he loved hunting and exploring. Another guy mentioned that he became his great-great-grandson's godfather. Everyone speaks highly of him except one. "Read this." I leaned over for Aaron to see.

"He swindled my family out of my ranch, Wrangler Pete's," Aaron read.

"Do you think the ranch is still in operation?" I asked. Maybe this was the break we needed.

Aaron's phone buzzed with an incoming message. "I just got word." Aaron slipped his phone out of his pocket and checked it. "Here's something. The bar maid's name is Pam Simons. Ever heard of her before?"

"No." I shook my head. "I wonder how she's connected?"

"I think they wanted someone to look around. Simple as that."

"That's probably it." I scrolled through the rest of the mail, deleting a number of junk messages. Aaron's phone buzzed again.

"They checked the house," he reported.

"And?"

"Nothing. They think the light was left on in the bathroom accidentally. I told them about the spare key, and they have the it, so you can now put that thought out of your mind." He smiled.

"How did you know?" I stared at him. "It's like you can read my mind."

"Because you are my Baby Girl, and I love you." He gave me a hug. "I'm going after coffee. Be right back."

I didn't know if I was irked or pleased that he could read my thoughts so easily.

I gave Inga a call. "Inga, how's it going?"

"Not bad. The police called about some items they found, wondering if they were among the things stolen. I made a list for them, but—well—the police—they're always asking questions." She sighed. "What can I say?"

"Gina's lawyer is dead. I spoke to Bambi, a friend of hers, who says the police are regarding it as a suspicious death."

"Hmmm, let me call some of my old contacts, maybe I can find out more."

"Thanks." I hoped she could. The woman had contacts all over the US, I wasn't sure how, and I wondered if she hadn't been a CIA agent in a former life. I knew she has a daughter, but she never spoke of a husband, and didn't invite questions.

I logged out of the account and got up once again to stretch my legs.

"Good morning, ladies. Sorry for ignoring you a few moments ago." As I circled the houses, I took more time than usual to rearrange the tiny furnishings within each. I stopped at the Eisenhower house and studied the pictures on the wall, especially those hung in the master bedroom. I removed a tiny picture and held it closer and smiled. The picture was of President Eisenhower's boyhood home in Abilene, Kansas. "Mrs. Eisenhower, you're a peach. I love your bangs. I've searched high and low for the material to have a dress sewn similar to what the women wore during your husband's final campaign." President Eisenhower was born in Texas, but lived most of his life in Kansas near the Presidential

Library in Abilene. No, the White House isn't in Kansas. I replaced the small picture just as Aaron returned with the two coffees.

"Here." He handed me my cup. "When's Max due back?"

"Anytime, why?"

"My sergeant needs me to fill out some paperwork. I wouldn't be long." He eyed me over the cup ridge. "I can call Marie."

"Go ahead, I'm fine. Grandma's busy." I gave him a kiss, and watched him walk out the back.

The morning sped by pretty fast; I made two sales, one of the historical White House with Dolley Madison and the other of Edith Roosevelt's newly remodeled family rooms. After the buyers left with their purchases, I wiped down the display table and placed a new house on it. The task took most of the afternoon since I had to deal with another prospective customer who spent a great deal of time perusing my entire stock and asking questions, and then left without buying anything. By mid-afternoon I was wondering why Aaron hadn't returned yet, when a pounding on the back door startled me.

"Aaron?" I called as I marched toward the back room. "Aaron?" *Why didn't he answer?* I opened the door, but there was not one there. My heart pounded as I slammed it shut, and leaned against it.

Chapter Fifteen

After pulling myself together, I went out to the showroom, telling myself that it'd been neighborhood pranksters.

I checked for new messages, and scrolled down and found Grandma's. She couldn't make it because Grandpa's car broke down. I responded by telling her that everything is fine.

"Girls! I'll be rearranging the houses, so don't be worried. You'll be fine. Mrs. Kennedy? Mr. Kennedy loves you completely. He adores that pillbox hat style."

I started for the back room to begin carrying out new dollhouse sections for display when the front door opened.

"Ida?" My eyes opened wider since I hadn't expected to see Gina's aunt. "Is that really you? I didn't expect to see you so soon after the gathering at the Establishment. I thought you'd be in North Dakota helping to close up Gina's estate."

"There's still plenty to take care of here in town," Ida said. We met half-way across the floor.

"What brings you here?" We sized each other up and down. "Would you like a tour of the houses?"

"I sure would." She glanced toward the stool behind the counter.

"I'll bring one out for you. Hold on a sec." I hurried into the back room and returned with a folding chair. I set it up in front of the sales counter. "Here. I'm afraid I don't have anything to offer to drink, though there's a café just down the street."

"I'm fine." I went behind the counter to get comfortable while she sat on the offered chair.

"A lot of people attended the funeral. It made me feel good." Her phone rang, but she let it go to voice mail, and then put it on vibrate.

"Who attended? I assume that Harry and Sunflower were there. Do you suppose Gina left her estate to them?"

"Neither my son nor my daughter would murder anyone, if that's what you're insinuating?" She huffed, and stood.

"No, no, I was just making conversation. I'm sorry." Why was she so touchy about it? "I'm still trying to understand what happened. Sit back down and relax." I smiled. "Tell me, were any of the expo impersonators there? Annie Oakley or John Muir, for instance?"

"They all pretty much were." She shrugged, sitting down. "I mean the few from the Teddy Roosevelt time. Even Buffalo Bill showed up." She smiled. "It was nice of them to show their respects like that."

"It certainly was," I agreed, though inside I was wondering why.

"Especially, since I know that she wasn't one of them. She was a simple girl who worked hard. She was just tired of the ranch life."

"Why not sell it?"

"She didn't want the oil companies exploiting the land."

"Oh."

"Did you ever find that ledger book? Any books?"

I didn't want to lie to her, but also didn't want to admit I had them. "If any were there, the police would probably have them."

"Possibly." She glanced around the room. "Nice store."

"Thanks, but can you tell me whether or not there's a land deed that Teddy Roosevelt may have given to either Alice or First Lady Edith? I'm curious, actually," I asked. The look on Ida's face made me want to seek shelter, it frightened me so. Obviously, there was more to the story than she was letting on.

"I don't know anything about such things," Ida said. Her eyes looked like fireballs. She stood. "I'll stop back sometime and you can show them all to me. I just wanted to know where you're located." She stared at me. "I'll invite you out one of these days."

"Sure." I watched her leave, and shivered, before removing my phone and typing in the information I'd just learned onto my notepad. At least now I had confirmation of the location of all known suspects.

Afterwards, I sat down and did an Internet search on favorite recipes of Edith Roosevelt. I found two in the Timeline site and printed a copy of each. One recipe was called Fat Rascals, which were a type of hot biscuits, and the other Sagamore Hill Sand Tarts. I read that President Roosevelt, TR, not Franklin, gobbled cookies like there was no end to them. Maybe I'd give the recipe a try. Since learning to make a Mary Lincoln cake, I'd become braver in the kitchen.

Aaron arrived just as I was about to close the store down for the day. "Hey you."

I greeted him with a big kiss. "Guess who just left?"

"No clue."

"Gina's aunt."

"Did she say anything about the attorney?" Aaron asked.

"Nope." I shook my head. "I didn't ask, either. I still don't know why she stopped by."

"Snooping around, most likely." He hesitated before continuing, "We discovered the drug that killed Gina. It's brand new to our knowledge."

"Tell me more."

"It's an odd one. It's almost unknown in this country."

"Oh my gosh." I glanced at the clock. "It's five. Closing time."

It didn't take long for us to lock the store and jump into our car. On the way home, I told him about the found recipes and we decided that on Sunday, we'd bake the biscuits and invite my grandparents over for a meal. I enjoyed surprising Grandma with my culinary feats.

"I thought you worked tonight?" I asked while we drove into the garage.

"I took it off. That's why I'm late. A few extra things to do." He finished parking the car and we climbed out as the garage door lowered.

No sooner had we walked into the kitchen than both our phones jingled. It was our friends Tim and Maggie. We invited them to drop by for a visit. They quickly agreed and told us they would bring a pizza. Talk about great friends.

Aaron went to take care of a few things, while we waited fro Maggie and Tim to arrive. I used the time to made another notation on my cell phone pad to check out unknown killer drugs. I also made notations next to the suspects as to whether or not they had traveled recently, and put in a bold question mark. I slipped it back into my pocket.

I filled the wine glasses for the ladies and set out the beer mugs for the guys, and took mine with me down the hall to the bedroom. They arrived soon after I changed into more comfortable clothes. Soon, the four of us were sitting out in the cool air and enjoying good pizza and conversations with best friends. All-in-all, it was a lovely evening.

As soon as we'd gobbled up the pizza and had a few drinks, it was time for them to leave. All four of us had places to go in the morning so they said their early 'good-byes', and left.

"I'm hitting the sack," I said yawning, right after they'd left. Aaron followed me to bed, where I spent quite awhile thinking about the few pieces of information I'd obtained during the day, and wondered what it all meant, before finally drifting off to sleep.

The sun shone through the windows, promising another pleasant summer day. It didn't take long before I'd dressed and met Aaron down in the kitchen.

Aaron had to leave for a morning shift, so couldn't go with me to the store. Instead, Grandma planned to stay with me throughout the day. I wished Max would get back soon, because at least he wouldn't stay inside the store the entire time. He left me alone to do his thing, working on various projects.

I grabbed the Alice purse and the small pistol before leaving for the store, driving rather than walking. I'd wanted to go for another run but because of the circumstances, I felt it unwise. It wasn't long before I entered the main drag and was soon at work, parking behind in the small lot. As I approached the back door I realized that the garbage company had already taken care of emptying the dumpster. I recalled finding the young woman inside of it during the middle of winter, half-frozen. I shivered at the thought. It took a couple tries before the door opened, which didn't make sense since the company had just gone through the security system. I chalked it up to the heat causing trouble.

The door closed behind me, and I entered the workroom. I set my bag down and removed the purse and pistol. I took them out to the showroom and turned the computer on.

"Morning ladies!" I grinned. "Mrs. Clinton, I'd like a batch of homemade chocolate chip cookies to devour, if you don't mind." I chuckled remembering her remark about staying home and baking cookies.

It didn't take long for the computer to boot up, and I logged into my website. I took a few photographs of the purse and pistol, but only placed shots of the purse on the website. I added a note to them, explaining that it once belonged to Alice Roosevelt, and would be on display for two weeks. Maybe that would draw out the killer. I checked my email but was disappointed when there wasn't a reply from the person who'd written before about Teddy Roosevelt stealing a ranch from his family.

"Weird," I murmured. "Doesn't make sense." *Maybe it's not suppose to?* My response was: *Too bad you feel that way.* I moved the message to another file. I shook off the shivers, and logged out from the webmail.

There was a sudden, loud sound, a sort of screech, which seemed to come from the basement. As fast as it came, it went away.

After opening the front door for business, I began my daily stroll around the houses to make sure that they were ready to face the day. "Mrs. Hoover, you must look your best even though you'd rather be outside." I smoothed her gown out because somehow, it'd become wrinkled. "Did the Mister chase you around the house?" As soon as I'd finished walking around and straightening things, I heard the back door open, and walked toward it.

"Max, it's so good to see you," I told Max as he entered the room.

"Good to see you, too." He smiled, and his eyes twinkled. "It's great to be back. What's been happening?"

"Well--," I continued filling him in about the Establishment barmaid who visited the shop wearing a costume. I also told him about Gina's uncle being found dead. "Gina's aunt stopped in yesterday." I crossed my arms. "The poor guy may have been murdered, and Aaron said the drug used to kill Gina is unknown in this country."

"What's your thoughts on all of this?" Max asked.

"I believe it's connected to Teddy Roosevelt. From what I've lately discovered, it has to do with land, and possibly the oil companies."

"The family may be fighting over rights." He reached for his smokes, and flicked one out, holding it between his fingers. "But can this have anything to do with them?"

I placed my hands on my hips. "I believe it's actually about Alice or something that maybe Edith hid for her. Teddy, as an attorney, would've made sure that all 't's' were crossed and all the 'i's dotted." I shrugged. "I haven't searched drugs yet, I just found out that she was poisoned."

"Now that I'm up-to-date," he scratched his head, "I don't know what to say. You've left me speechless. Costumed people, impersonators, another murder and probably by the same hand,

Inga broken into—and I'm sure there's more but they've slipped your mind."

"I'm glad you're home." I smiled. "I've sold a few houses and figures, so I need more heads, and I've got sewing to do. Oh, and Grandma's coming soon to be my bodyguard."

I sat down by the computer once more after Max left for the workroom. I heard the back door open, and knew he was having his smoke, and would soon carry his bag upstairs. I felt safer knowing he was nearby.

I wanted to research drug trafficking before starting my sewing. I clicked into a search engine and placed a request for new drugs entering the U.S., and only a few sites popped up. The most likely was a drug that caused muscles to twitch and stopped the victim's breathing. I bookmarked it, even though I wasn't sure if it was the right one. Reaction to this drug was rapid, unlike the other two possibilities, and that gave me some confidence. I closed out of my computer and started for the workroom, when the front door opened and a customer entered.

"Hello. How may I help you?" She looked familiar.

"Just looking," the older woman responded. "I was at the expo and loved looking at the miniature houses you had displayed." Bingo. That was where I had seen her. She continued, "It made me start thinking that I should invest in a dollhouse. I mean, why not? Right?"

"Right!" I smiled, loving this woman already because of her zest. "Why not? Life's too short to not enjoy it while you can."

"I've always wanted a dollhouse." She looked at me through watery eyes. "I can always leave it to my granddaughter." "They all thought I was silly when I mentioned buying one of these." She looked around her before continuing in a more quiet voice. "I don't think they want me spending their inheritance."

"Well," I shot back. "You deserve to enjoy yourself." A notion struck, and I asked, "Did you go to Roosevelt High School?"

"Yes, as a matter-of-fact."

"Then let me show you the Edith Roosevelt White House," I said. "It's right over here. Edith remodeled the White House living quarters. She added a kitchen, and so forth. I'm sure she needed to do that because the children were younger. Did you know that the children roller skated and bicycled all over the house?" We stopped next to the house. "She did a remarkable job. It's beautiful, isn't it?"

"They sure were active, just liked their father. I love this house," she said. "You're right. Wrap it up." She winked. "My grandson's right outside waiting. I'll go out and get him."

After she left the store, I sent Max a message asking him for some much needed help. The number of pieces that came with the Roosevelt house was amazing—well they all were—and it was always nice to have help boxing them up.

Max came straight away.

I said, "TR house."

"Should I use the boxes in back or do I need to fetch some from down below?"

"There should be enough in the store room."

I busied myself bringing the dolls—Mr. and Mrs. President—from the workroom, and then pulled out the inventory list for that particular house, and began checking all the pieces. Wrapping each piece individually and placing them inside the box took a little while. I went to the front with the box and found my customer and a young man waiting by the counter.

"Max, my woodworker is boxing the house. Instructions are in the box if you have trouble. I also placed a small list in the box that explains where the furnishings belong. If you happen to be short anything, let me know. I'll either send it or deliver it in person." I loved this woman, she reminded me of grandmotherhood personified.

"Thank you, dear."

"Don't worry, I'll put it together for her." The grandson's smile covered his face and his face was lit like a two hundred watt bulb.

Max and the grandson carried the boxes with the grandma and me following out the door, and to a car parked near the door.

My bodyguards arrived as they drove away from the curb. Max waved goodby and hiked up the outside stairs to his room.

"Hey Grandma, Grandpa," after giving each a squeeze. "Thanks for coming. I hope that it wasn't too much of a bother."

"I'm sure we can manage." Grandpa grinned.

"We're gonna clean this place up for you." I had wondered why Grandma wasn't dressed in a snazzier outfit. "Okay?"

"Sure. I have work to do. If anyone happens in and I don't hear the bell, come and get me."

I checked out a few things on the computer, including my personal e-mail account and the website's webmail. As yet, no one responded about the purse image. I took the pistol back with me and placed it inside the drawer where I hid valuables and extra keys. I put away the boxes and went out to the showroom to make clear and make ready a table for the next dollhouse.

Chapter Sixteen

"We can only stay for an hour," Grandma said. Grandma and Grandpa finished cleaning the showroom and then decided it was time for them to go home and take a rest—I knew it meant a late afternoon nap.

A customer arrived after they left. She walked the length of my showroom floor and asked plenty of questions while pulling on her ear, Carol Burnett, I thought. She asked a few questions and then left, leaving me alone once again. Fortunately, the rest of the afternoon sped by quickly and I'd just finished logging out from my accounts when Inga came in, wearing a huge smile.

"Let's hear it." I got up and said, "I'll get a chair. You should have come by earlier. Grandma and Grandpa were here."

"Nahh. They stopped in a few minutes ago, so they already know."

"Know what?" I unfolded the chair for her and then went around the counter to my chair and did the same.

"A pawn shop contacted the police and told them they've found the TR figurine." She took a deep breath. "It's funny. I never expected to take such an interest the items stolen from my store. To think that they sent out notices for it."

"True. There's been a lot of strange happenings around that darn thing. Did you go down to the station to identify it?"

"Yes, and it's the right one. They'll call when I can have it back."

"Do you have any pictures of it?"

"No."

"Hmmm. I wonder if I could ask Aaron to take some down in the evidence room?" Inga shook her head. "Darn it. I wonder if I can get Aaron to do that?"

"Probably not. It may not be the right thing for him to do."

"Shoot! You're right." I reached for the purse and set it on the counter. "I put a photo of this purse and the pistol that was inside it. I've put the purse's picture on my website, and I plan to put it in the bank with the figurine."

"Good plan." She nodded to the purse. "Ever take a good look inside?"

"No." I reached for it and opened it. I carefully ran my fingertips along all seams and frayed edges of the inside nylon lining. "There's a little catch right here." I showed it to her. "What do you think?"

"I wouldn't rip it open."

Peering closer at it, I said, "It appears to be the same thread color. I think it's from the manufacturer." I set the purse back inside of the sales counter display. "Here I thought I was onto something."

"I know—it's all a mystery. I asked my contacts about the lawyer who died, and they hadn't heard if it's a murder or not. They are waiting on the autopsy results." She shook her head. "It makes me wonder if this is connected to TR? Are both deaths because of something that happened over a century ago?"

"I wondered about that." I shook my head. "I think it's a land deed we're after, but I'm not sure. I think the symbols from the grass bowl and my jingle dancer figurine hold clues as to its whereabouts."

"My figurine must also have a relevant symbol somewhere on it." Inga raised a brow. "I wish I could remember."

"Me, too."

"I'll let you know when I get it back or if something else happens." Inga stood. "Time for me to go. I'm beat."

After Inga left, my thoughts went back to the purse, so I brought it out for a closer look, but again, I saw nothing that really stood out or seemed odd. I placed it back inside the cabinet, and glanced at the clock. It was time to close up shop. I got up to close and lock the front door. As I did, the store phone rang. I answered, "First Ladies White House Dollhouse Store, how may I help you?" No one answered, and so I hung up. An eerie feeling crept up inside of me and made me anxious to leave and go home.

As I walked toward the back rooms, I heard a noise again from down below. I hurried to leave. With the lights shut off, I grabbed my bag and opened the backdoor. Suddenly, someone caught my arm, and muscled me inside. They moved so fast, that I never caught a glimpse of him. Or was it a woman?

I started to scream, but in an instant a ski mask covered my head, backwards so that I couldn't see anything. I felt what I guessed was a pistol against my forehead, right between my eyes. I fought to speak through the ski mask. "You'll never get away with this."

"Where's the deed?"

"Deed for what?"

"I'm not playing games."

The voice seemed familiar, but I couldn't be sure.

"Better run fast! I'm married to cop," I said.

A crack on my head was all I got in return.

It knocked me out for a short while. Fortunately, I wasn't tied up and I was able to pull the mask up and over my head. My headache worsened when I looked around the room. Splattered paint and tipped over boxes holding small items were scattered all over. I pulled out my phone and called my Aaron. Within a few minutes, I heard sirens outside my door.

"Liv?" Aaron raced inside with Tim right behind him. "My God what happened?" Tim called it in to the precinct as I sobbed in Aaron's embrace.

"I..." I gasped. "Just leaving... and... this person came from out of nowhere... and..." I collapsed into a chair. "I need water."

"Okay." Tim found a fresh water bottle and opened it for me.

"Thanks." I took a long drink. "Something horrible happened.

"Like what?"

"One person, a woman walked through, then left without buying anything." I blew my nose. "I didn't recognize her, but she seemed legit. Oh, and there was a phone call a little while ago, but there was no one on the other end."

"Anything else?" Tim asked with his pad and pencil out.

"There's been noises coming from down below, the basement, that is, lately."

"We'll check into that." Aaron kneeled before me. "Honey, don't worry. Where are Marie and August?"

"They left after cleaning the shop. Inga was here for a short while and then I was going home right afterwards." My head throbbed and I held the cool bottle on the knot on my forehead. "Good grief."

"The detectives are on their way." Aaron reached to help me stand. "Let's move to the showroom. This is a crime scene now."

"Ahh jeez." I sighed and let him help walk me out where I sat behind the counter. "I'd like to go home."

"It'll be a few, but I'll ask them to let you leave as soon as they can."

It seemed to take forever for the to arrive, but it really took only about five or ten minutes for the two detectives to appear. By that time, I still had moist eyes, but was through sobbing. "Here we go again," I said to Detectives Erlandsen and Mergens. "Now I'm the target."

"I see that. Your forehead is getting pinker by the minute."

"This has to end." I held the cool bottle against my forehead.

"What did they want? What did they say?"

"Something about a deed. The threat that my husband is a cop and he should run must have scared him."

"Sure it's a 'him'?"

"Nope." I started to shake my head but the throbbing stopped me. "Please. I want to lie down and get ice on my head."

"Can you think of anything else?"

"Not at the moment." I looked down, and my eyes flashed open. "The purse is gone. This can't be for real." I jumped up and sat right back down again. "Oh, no. the pistol!"

"What?" Detective Mergens asked sharply. "Purse? Pistol?"

"I was just going to bring Alice Roosevelt's pistol into the station. Her purse was right here, and now it's missing. I must check if the pistol is still where I left it," Aaron said. "I'll be right back."

"It's hidden in the work room," I said, as we watched him walk away. Every slight movement made my head pound. All I could think of doing was lying down with a bag of ice on my noggin after taking a couple aspirin.

"It's gone," Aaron said when he returned. "Tim's taking over. I'll drive you home and stay with you." I noticed my bag. "I need my bag. It's right there."

Another squad car parked, and two uniformed officers entered.

"Okay, we'll make a note of that. Aaron, we want all that you have on it," Mergens said.

"Will do."

"Oh for the love--." Holding on to Aaron, we walked out to the car and he opened the side door for me to sit, and then shut the door.

We drove home silently. I held my head and tears streamed down my cheeks.

"We're going to the doctor to get you checked out," Aaron said.

"I'm fine. I need ice for the noggin and blankets to curl up under."

"We'll get you comfy on the sofa and then I'll call Marie to let them know what's happened." Aaron stated as he drove down the main drag. "You can't be alone. Why did they leave early?"

"They'd been cleaning and the day was almost finished."

"What about Max?"

"He'd just been with me putting together a new house since I'd just sold one." I blew my nose. "I don't think it could've been prevented."

"Yes, it could've." Aaron frowned. "It's happened once, so now we have to be more careful." He put on the blinker for our street. "The detectives will be over later. They'll have more questions, and I'm sure they'll want to discuss the purse and pistol some more with you."

"Oh yes. That, I am sure of." We parked in the garage and Aaron came around and helped me from the car and walked me inside of the house.

"I'm going to the sofa," I told him.

"I'll get ice and aspirin."

"Thank you. Bring the bottle." I and covered myself with the nearest throw, very slowly, and sunk onto the sofa pillow, which gave me a crick in my neck. Aaron came downstairs a minute later and swapped it out with my bed pillow, and I sighed. The aspirins, I hoped, would soon shoo-away my pounding headache. The ice on my forehead seemed to numb the bump. I hunkered down and reached for the remote, and switched on *Are you a Good Dancer?*. I was just drifting off to sleep when my arm was nudged. I opened my eyes and saw rumpled pant legs. I looked up and saw Detective Mergens. "You're back."

"Yep, Liv." He half-grinned. "Can't be helped."

"I know. Where's your side-kick?"

"He's got plenty to do." He shrugged. "Now, about the purse and pistol?"

"Tell Aaron to get me my phone. Where is he anyway?"

"Right here, honey." Aaron entered bearing a water bottle and handed it to the detective. "What?"

"Please get my phone. The images of the purse and pistol are on it."

"Right."

"Start from the top."

"From today?" I sat up and stared at him.

"Today."

I gave him a brief outline of how my day went, and who came into the store. He asked about my late afternoon browser.

"What'd this person look like?"

"Nothing spectacular, but she reminded me of Carol Burnett because she was pulling her ear all the time. Sort of medium height, medium age."

"And the person who assaulted you?" He took the offered phone from Aaron and glanced at the images. "Send them to me."

Aaron took the phone and started pressing buttons.

"He seemed like a male. Tall—course anyone is taller than me—but his arms were strong. Immediately he swung me around and I had the ski mask covering my head and eyes. I warned him that I was married to a cop. He hit me on the head right after with, I guess, the pistol butt."

"You think that scared him?"

"It seemed like it. I don't think I was out more than a couple of minutes. The store was quiet when I woke up. Then I pulled off the ski mask and dialed Aaron. I didn't touch anything."

"The purse and pistol?"

"I purchased the set from Inga—you know who I'm talking about—and they once belonged to Alice Roosevelt. It was under the sales counter. As for the pistol, I'd put it in a special drawer for safe-keeping. I had planned to take it home but had forgotten to place it in my bag as I left."

"He caught you as you stepped out and the door was still open?"

"I was midway. We have had the building checked for security." I waited a moment. "Something else. You might want to go down below again. I keep hearing noises."

"It's sealed. Not possible. Must be mice."

"If you say so—but I'm not so sure. They can get in via the restaurant on the other end. Their trap door still is open."

"We'll check it out." He folded his notepad and placed it inside his pocket. "Thank you, you've been a big help."

Aaron opened the door for him and then sat on the opposite end of the sofa, placing my feet on his lap. He massaged my feet while we watched television, and I drifted off to sleep.

Chapter Seventeen

Television laughter jerked me awake. I glanced at the set to find Lucy and Ethel stuffing their mouths with chocolate. Aaron chuckled. Grandma and Grandpa sat to the side. "I didn't know you guys were here."

"Didn't want to wake you," Grandpa mumbled. "Grandma brought chicken soup."

"I'll get you a bowl."

Grandma left the room, and I forced myself to sit. Still groggy, I yawned, which made my head pound. "How long was I out?"

"About an hour." Aaron tickled my toes. "Need a couple more?"

"Not yet." I knew he meant aspirins. I expected the soup to cure all my ailments. Grandma set a steaming full bowl in front of me, and I said, "Thanks." I slurped and listened as they talked about what had happened. When finished, I crawled back under the blanket. "We need to figure this out."

"Where do we start?" Grandma asked. She picked up my empty bowl and stood looking down at me. "There's no beginning."

"True, but we can write everything down." I glanced at Aaron. "Mind getting a notepad and pen?"

"Sure."

"There's also three books that need looking into." I turned to Grandpa. "They're on the chest in the back bedroom. Would you mind going and getting them?" Gently, I touched the bump and winced. *Darn it.* I didn't want to freeze my head anymore. The swelling would have to go down on its own. I sat back up, and hoped that the evening wouldn't go too late.

"I'll keep notes for you." Aaron sat beside me.

"Thank you."

Grandpa set the books on the coffee table while Grandma returned with a tray of coffee and cookies. She set it on the table, also.

"Thanks." Aaron set a cup right in front of me with a cookie.

"Cheers!" We said in unison.

"Let the discussion begin." I sipped from my cup. "We have symbols from a grass bowl and my jingle dancer figurine. We should each have copies of the images."

"Check." Aaron wrote it down. "We'll see what else needs printing."

"The symbol in the bowl center is a waving blanket which means--,"

"Which means writing or other message," Grandpa said. "Is there more than that?"

"The figurine--, Aaron, can you go and print them?"

Aaron jumped up and went to the back room to take care of that task. After he had left, I picked up the first of the three books. It was the grammar book. "I've flipped through these pages but haven't found anything that catches my eye. Who wants to take a stab at it?"

Grandma held out her hand. "I was always good in grammar. Best subject, ever." She turned the nearby lamp on and began searching the pages.

"This one is a plat book, a description of properties in that area a hundred years ago. Grandpa?" I gave it to him, and then I opened the old, huge, family Bible.

We perused the books in silence until Aaron returned a few minutes later with the print outs and handed them around. He sat beside me and I showed him the handwritten entries in the Bible.

He studied them for a moment, and then shook his head. "Nothing strikes me as unusual."

I pointed where the more recent entries had been written. "Look. Here's Gina's name, and her parents, plus her siblings. And, here is Ida Gray, who is Harry and Sunflower's mother. There's Native blood scattered throughout the family tree. I wonder if that figures into this in some way."

"Problem is, all we're going on is pure hunch."

Grandma sipped her coffee, and swirled the remaining while staring into her cup. "Nothing is written by hand in this book."

"Shoot. Take a look at the photos," I suggested. "There has to be clues someplace, or we're stuck." I placed the Bible into Aaron's lap. "Grandpa, what about you?"

"Not sure, but I may be onto something here." He passed me the platbook. "Take a look right here." He pointed at a page. "This has to be what we're looking for. Take a look."

I stared at the page. "Oh my goodness. Aaron…"

He took a look and nodded. "Theodore Roosevelt. Section number twenty-four. That could be it. Let's look it up."

"The laptop will work better." He went to fetch it. "Grandpa, you're a genius." He blushed.

I had time to take a bite from the last cookie before Aaron hurried back. He logged in right away and began searching.

While Aaron searched, I filled Grandma and Grandpa in on the days' events and who everyone is.

"The family must have issues, but so what?" Grandma asked. She shrugged. "Someone wants to sell the land and someone doesn't. It must be the oil company that they're all mad about."

"I get that, but there's something deeper to it. I'm sure-." I thought for a minute. "Aaron? Did you find anything worthwhile in your search?"

"Wait a sec." I watched him flip from one site to another and back again. "You're not going to believe this, but TR purchased land back in 1895 and it's right outside of the Medora town limits. It's almost butt against the park," Grandpa said.

"That's wonderful news." Grandma smiled.

"What aren't you telling us?" Liv asked.

"The land beside it shows Gina as a part owner," Aaron said.

"Who owns the land on the other side?" Grandma asked.

"Ida Gray," Aaron said.

"That makes sense. Gina stands between the park and Ida," Grandma said.

"It still shows Theodore Roosevelt on the deed with Gina." Aaron scratched his head. "That can't be right." He looked at me and then my grandparents. "Can it?"

"There must be some kind of glitch."

"The legal deed must be lost," Aaron said. "I wonder why the Roosevelt family never claimed it?"

"Could it be that Edith hid the deed?" I asked. "It's very possible. She may have set it inside of something and later forgot about it. Now there's few descendants, and they probably don't know about it."

"Would she have saved it for Alice?" Grandma asked. "I may have if I was her. Alice deserved to have a piece of land since her mother died right after her birth."

"True," I agreed. "Let's get back to facts. This is all speculation."

"What else?" Aaron stated, and picked up the pen and notepad and wrote it down.

"Write down the two major symbols. The blanket and the cabin from on my figurine." I watched him do that. "I think that's it for now. We've started pulling our loosely fitted clues together."

Grandma yawned. "I think it's time for us to leave."

"My thoughts, entirely." Grandpa stood. I held back my grin because Grandma did also as if on cue.

"Thanks for coming." They retrieved the pot and I knew the leftover soup was already in the refrigerator.

"Grandma? Are you going to be in the store tomorrow?" I stood, but sat right back down. "Sheesh! I moved too fast."

"I'll go if you need me." They left, and I was already sorry to have them gone. "Bedtime?"

Aaron walked me to the bedroom and helped tuck me into bed. Sleep came almost immediately, but I couldn't stay asleep for any length of time. Several times I had to get up. Once when I glanced out, I noticed several different cars parked outside that weren't there before. The next time I woke, the cars were gone. I didn't think anything of it because the next-door neighbors' light was on outside and I saw lights within.

Morning came with bright sunlight coming in, and I immediately rose and went for a shower. First I looked in the mirror and found the bump bruised, raw and painful to touch. I showered and dressed. When I styled my hair, I brought it down over my forehead, and the look reminded me of Little Orphan Annie. I went back to the bedroom and found Aaron still sleeping. I leaned over and gave him a kiss.

Down in the kitchen, I poured myself a cup of coffee and went out the front door to pick up the newspaper. I looked across the street as a small car parked in Gina's driveway. I threw the paper into the house and went across the street. The person climbing out of the car was Sunflower.

"Sunflower." I waved and went over to her. "Remember me?"

"Oh yes. But, what's your name again? You're the lady with the dollhouses, right?" She grinned, and pushed back her long brown hair from her shoulders.

"Liv." I looked around her to the house. "I'm glad that it's finally being wrapped up. I hate to see Gina's house vacant. I miss her."

"We were friends and cousins. That's the best kind of friendship, isn't it? Like sisters?" She started for the house and I followed. Where she got the key from, I hadn't a clue but she opened the door and I kept in step. "I'm going to pack her things up."

"Anyone helping?" We stood at the door, with her inside, and me on the outside, trying to finagle a way to go in with her.

"I can manage. Mom might be out later."

"Your mom is Ida Gray, right?"

"Yes." She nodded.

"I understand your family has some land over the state line near Medora. Is that true? I love that part of the country."

"Why do you need to know?"

"Curious."

"It's none of your business, is it? I've got work to do."

I took her sudden hostility as a sign to leave, and said, "Goodbye. If you need anything just let me know." As I walked away, I wondered if the police knew that this was happening?

I heard kitchen noise as I entered the house and went in to greet my husband. I told him about running into Sunflower at Gina's house across the street. Next, I called the precinct and asked to speak to one of the detectives. When finished, I said, "Sunflower notified them yesterday that this was going to happen."

"So it's okay?"

"Yep." I asked, "Any news about the murder in Medora?"

"Nope." He set two toasted bagels on the counter and we each had one. "What'd Sunflower have to say?"

"Talk about hostile. She wasn't at first, but then I asked who owned the land right beside her, and she got mad."

"That's odd. Why not just say?"

"That's what I thought." I shrugged and finished eating. "Let's go separate in case you get called. "

"Right."

I placed my empty cup in the dishwasher, grabbed my bag and made sure that I had aspirins and my phone before heading out the door. Aaron was right behind me, allowing me to back out first from the garage. Soon we were both driving down the street and heading toward the store. As I passed the Establishment, a few questions came to mind, such as what was the role of the barmaid? Are the impersonators back to working their regular jobs, and just exactly, what were they? Where did they work? And finally, how could I contact someone who sells real estate in North Dakota?

I also wondered about the drug. Was the lawyer poisoned? It sure sounded possible. If the drug was unknown in this country, then who may have traveled to buy it? How was it possible to enter the US without customs spotting it? Maybe someone had an inside person who allowed them to slip through at the airport. I needed sit down and do some more research.

Parking side by side, we climbed from our cars.

"I'll go to the cafe and get us a cup of coffee," Aaron said.

"Okay."

I watched him walk toward the restaurant at the end of the block. I trembled as I opened the back door and entered. I hesitated at the workroom doorway because of the huge mess. Anger swept through me. I was sick and tired of being afraid. I tip-toed around the floor mess and brushed aside a mess on the counter in order to set my bag down. The mess wasn't as bad as it could have been, much to my relief. Only a small amount of paint had spilled so it hadn't touched the fabric. *Thank heavens!* The costly fabric didn't need replacing. Small items such as furniture needed sorting but the perpetrator had dumped only a few boxes. I left the mess as it was, putting off straightening things out until after I went out to the show room.

"Morning ladies," I called. Slowly I circled the tables, straightening items here and there. "Mrs. Lincoln, how are you? Thank you for sitting and writing letters for our soldiers during the Civil War. It was very kind of you." I finished walking around and then turned my attention to the days' business.

The computer began humming right after starting and didn't take long before I logged into accounts. To my chagrin, there were no new messages in the webmail. I weeded through my personal email and then logged out. Aaron entered with the two cups of coffee and brought one of them to me.

"Thanks." I took a sip. "Do you have anything in particular that you plan to do today?" I looked up to him. After all the hours he had been working, it was nice that he had a full day off.

"No," he shook his head, "nothing that comes to mind."

"I thought about the drug and it being new to the U.S. Can you find out more about it? I'd like to know if it's the same drug that poisoned Gina and the solicitor in Medora. I think it has to be."

"I'll do what I can, but I can't compromise an ongoing investigation." He took a sip of coffee and leaned back. "What I can do is research as much as I can about the drug and see if anyone working the case will tell me anything."

"There had to have been someone who allowed this person entrance into the country without going through customs."

"I'll see what I can dig up."

"I'm going to the workroom in a few minutes to begin the cleanup. What a mess."

I circled the showroom again, taking time to stop here and there beside different houses to make sure that all was as it should be. I spent a little more time checking the new Roosevelt house, because the furnishings were out of order. This was odd, as I'd just set them where they belonged the day before. At one point, I had to refer back to a photograph of the original, before setting down the bear rug and a bookcase where Edith kept her recipe books. She did like to make special meals for her family. She was such a busy woman, and even hosted weekly musicales for her family and special guests.

I thought of Mrs. Obama, our recent First Lady, and how she strived to make sure that the school lunch programs were healthier. Almost every First Lady since Dolley Madison had a special cause. Dolley had founded an orphanage for the children left without parents during the War of 1812. With the burning of Washington and the fighting, the smallest of survivors needed care, and she ensured that it happened.

I made it to the workroom where I began the arduous job of sorting through the mess. Fortunately, it took less time than expected. I went out to the store to see how Aaron had faired with the assignment.

"Any luck finding out anything about the drug?"

"It was the same drug. Succinylcholine, which originally appeared in Dubai." He glanced up to me. "Guess what the nickname is? Sux'."

"Well, this whole thing sucks."

Chapter Eighteen

A customer and her granddaughter walked through the store in the mid-afternoon, and before you knew it, we'd sold another house. We knew Max was home because his truck was in the parking lot, but Aaron helped box and carry the house out instead my asking for Max's assistance. I knew he had a lot of doll heads to finish. Afterwards, we no sooner cleaned the table for another display than we sold our next house of the day. Both models were of the historical White House. One sale featured Dolley Madison and the other President Monroe's wife. Dolley was a better choice, in my opinion. Mrs. Monroe, who followed Dolley in residence, had redecorated the White House in French style rather than American.

We cleared the tables and Aaron helped me carry the new houses out to the respective tables for setting up. "I'm going to have to do this the other way around," I told him. "They all say, 'I want this one', and I should have boxed houses ready for them."

"Maybe Max could help with that?"

"Well, he is pretty busy carving, but that would certainly help."

The remaining few hours were spent putting houses together and preparing the showroom for the following day. We were about ready to leave for the day when Aaron got a message asking him to work that evening.

"I'll leave from here for work. I have a spare uniform in my locker."

"I'm on my own?" I thought of the leftover chicken soup, and grinned. "More soup for me. I can taste it already."

I had a few spare moments and went to sort through the furniture in preparation for the following day. I would have to dress the dolls tomorrow, as well. I was sure thankful that I'd spent the morning cleaning up and could concentrate on store work.

Aaron locked the front door, while I took care of the lights and then followed him out the back door. We kissed each other goodbye, and I jumped into my car. We first drove in the same direction, then waved at each other as he turned toward police headquarters. I kept driving toward home, but at the last minute decided to take a quick tour of the Establishment parking lot. Out of curiosity, I wondered if I would recognize any of the cars parked there. I slowly circled the lot, and was about to give up, I noticed Ed Parsons, the John Muir impersonator, leave the building with the barmaid on his arm.. I noted which car they entered, and recognized it as his. I hadn't noticed it before, because it was parked down the block. As they drove from the curb, I decided to follow.

I waited for them to drive by, then pulled out. I kept one car between us. , They turned at the corner and I followed, keeping my eyes peeled for their next turn. They were heading toward University Avenue, in the direction of the suburbs of Blaine and Spring Lake Park. I tried to kept up with them, but had trouble because of all the traffic and stop lights. Soon they got two blocks ahead and though I sped up, I lost them. Frustrated, I tried turning up and down a few streets with hopes of discovering their parked car, but didn't spot it. I parked in an open lot and pulled out my phone to do a search for John Muir or Ed Parsons, but, of course, no sites appeared except for his website, which wasn't of much use. However, I did a reverse search using his name in the white page directory and found an address near where I was parked. I drove toward it and saw the car parked outside. I could movement in the house through the front window. I circled around and parked down the block. On my phone's notepad, I wrote down the address and his name. I wanted to take a close-up shot of the house but the more prudent choice was to remain down the street. It was a good choice, too, because soon he emerged, dressed in a jogging outfit, and headed up the street. I considered driving past the house to take a picture. Just as I was about to signal and drive away from the curb, I caught sight of a person in my rearview mirror. It was Ed. He had just stood up from behind my car and then jogged away.

I decided it was time to leave and pulled away from the curb. I got about a block down the street when a back tire became completely flat. "Doggonit!" I shouted, after stopping and getting out of the car. It was flat as a pancake . I looked closer and found the little cap missing from the stem. Ed! "The dirty bugger!" I took a deep breath and stared back down the street toward his house and noticed the garage door quietly closing. I guess he had seen me.

I didn't want to alert Aaron about my stupidity so I called Grandpa and asked him what to do. It took him close to an hour to come, because he brought a neighbor to help change the tire. Once it was changed, and he'd loaded the flat one in the trunk, I headed home. During the drive, I scolded myself for being so stupid as to be caught. I should've skipped it all and gone home.

The place that needed my snooping services was at Gina's. It took a little while driving on the temporary tire, as I couldn't drive very fast and seemed to hit every stoplight on University Avenue, but I finally reached home.

It was already close to seven and I was starved. I heated a bowl of soup, got a cold glass of milk, and went to sit out on the steps and stare across the street. I saw a shadow cast by the light in Gina's hallway. I knew it wasn't Sunflower at the house, as the driveway was empty. I decided to find out who was there. I quickly finished and took my bowl and cup inside, grabbed my keys and cellphone, and slipped out my house by the back door

Not wanting to be seen, I crossed a little way down the street, and then circled back, hoping not to be seen. Slowly I crept along the side of the house, mindful not to step in the flowerbed, and cupped my eyes against the window. I winced when the bump touched the glass.,I didn't see any movement or a light in the kitchen. I climbed the deck in the back and walked quietly over toward a bedroom window. The back door squeaked open, and I froze, holding my breath and praying that whoever was there wouldn't look in my direction.

My heart pounded and palms became sweaty as I held my breath. A woman stepped out, but never glanced in my direction as she pulled the door shut, and then fled down the stairs and across the backyard lawn. Something was familiar about her, but I couldn't lay my finger on it. I waited until my breath evened out before going to the backdoor. It was locked.

This was enough excitement for the evening. I went home and filled a glass of wine and sunk into the sofa. I turned on the TV, and flipped through the stations, settling on the old movie, *The Sound of Music*. Aaron hated watching musicals, so I was happy.

I didn't remember falling asleep or going to bed, but I woke with him beside me and the sun shining. I had slept in the nude. "Hmm." I wondered what else had happened in the night. I rolled over and gave Aaron a kiss and watched him grin. It took but a few minutes before I'd jumped into the shower and got ready for the day.

A note on the table read: "*Wrap up meeting at the 'X' at three. Get Max to watch the store. Pick you up at two.*" I wrote back, "*Okay.*" I grabbed my bag from the kitchen and headed out to the car. In a matter of minutes, I was on Main Street and turning toward the neighborhood car fix-it shop. Bill was already working on an engine, but when he saw me, he came right over.

"What's up?" He glanced down at where I pointed. "Ahh. A tire."

"Yep. Someone let out the air. The cap is missing." I opened the trunk. "Can you fix it right away?"

"Sure. Almost done here." Checking the coffeepot, he offered, "Help yourself, little lady."

"Got it." I'd known Bill for ages. My grandpa went to him with all car troubles and now, I did, too. With a Styrofoam cup filled with steaming coffee, I sat down and made a call. "Max?"

"What's up?" I heard crunching. Max was probably having his morning cereal.

"I'm getting my tire fixed. Long story."

"Want me downstairs?" He chewed. I covered my other ear because of the noise of the car shop.

"Please. Oh. Aaron's picking me up at two for a meeting. Can you watch the store this afternoon?"

"Sure." We disconnected. Max was of few words on the phone, which I liked, as I finding texting more efficient. I watched Bill as he backed the other car from the inside of the garage and drove mine in. He hefted my tire out of the trunk with his meaty arms and soon had it pumped with the correct air poundage, then raised my car on the lift. Within minutes the tire was mounted and tested. He checked the other three tires before lowering the car and backing it out of the repair bay.

"All set."

"What's the charge?"

"Forget it. I'll charge your grandpa extra next time." He chuckled. "Now, tell me why someone'd do this to you?"

"Sorry, but it's a secret. If I told you--."

"I know." He laughed. "Get on with you!"

"Thanks!" I laughed, and jumped into my car.

The parking lot for the restaurant next door to my store was filled with cars, but it seemed too early in the day for that to happen. So, instead of going right inside after parking, I went into the restaurant via the rear entrance. To my surprise, I found the place was full of knitting women.

"My gosh. I wondered why all the cars."

"We're knitting baby blankets for local charities." A woman smiled at me. "Pretty clever, eh?"

"And, they're quilting down below. Cutting fabric and sewing baby quilts." She cocked her head, and said, "The owner is my brother-in-law. Neat, eh?"

"Excellent idea." I grinned. This answered my question about all the noise I'd heard from below. I wondered if the detectives already knew, or if they had even gotten around to looking into it. "I thought I'd heard noise. Keep up the good work." I started to back out, then stopped. "I'm the owner of the dollhouse store next door. If you need a donation for yarn or thread, let me know."

"Okay." I exited and walked to my store. Round and round the words, 'brother-in-law' went in my head. I knew that I was missing something, but wasn't sure what it was as I entered my store.

"Hey you!" I called out. I looked in the workroom, leaving my purse behind and strolled out to the show room. Max was busy talking to a customer.

"Here she is. Just in time." Max smiled at me. "She's interested in Laura Bush."

"Wasn't she beautiful? And so serene looking? She was such a nice First Lady. So steady during a time of crisis in our country. She was wonderful." I smiled. "How can I help you?"

We chatted some more about Laura Bush, and about the White House models before she decided. "You just convinced me. I'd like to buy this house. This one not another one out in the back boxed up."

"No problem at all," I assured her. Max was already going toward the backroom, presumably to get the needed tools for disassembling it. By now, we knew the exact steps and it wouldn't take long. "Let me begin to remove the furnishings and dolls to the counter," I asked her. "And then we'll ring the sale."

Max and I worked in tandem, getting the house ready for removal, and the items wrapped and boxed. The woman was parked in front, so it was easy to carry the items out to her car. Less than an hour later, we'd finished carrying the last box to her car. I was sure happy to have Max around.

"Thanks." I said to the woman and handed her a business card. "If you need help with assembly, call." I watched her drive away before going back inside.

The morning was spent setting up more houses for display. "Max. We really must have more houses boxed up and ready. I keep having to take models from the showroom."

"I know. I've just been so busy and find it hard to keep up."

"You saying we need to hire someone?"

"Maybe—if you can afford it." He looked my way. "It'd be helpful."

"I'll consider it." I'd been reluctant to hire anyone since the last employee's husband had tried to murder me, more incredibly she had been an old classmate. I could see that I needed to have someone else around to at least watch the store so I could get my other work completed in a timely manner.

"Ladies, I hope your night went well. It looks like it did," I said. I meandered among the tables. I smiled at each before walking to the sales counter.

I got the computer humming and soon logged in, going right to the local paper website and placed a help wanted ad, to appear next week. At the moment, I didn't want to take the time to check my accounts, so I shut down the computer and went to help Max assemble new houses and carry pieces out to the display tables.

The morning went by quickly.

Aaron called instead of messaging. "Hey baby," I answered.

"Liv. August called and asked about the tire. You're busted. It's time to fess up. What on earth were you doing in that neighborhood when you should've been at home slurping soup?"

"I'm busted by Grandpa? It's like this-," I went ahead and told him the whole story. "Bill fixed it this morning. No charge."

"Nice guy." Aaron hesitated. "The two left together?"

"See? I'm not the only one who thought it odd." I smiled.

"Doesn't make it right, though."

"I know." I knew he wouldn't yell at.

"I'll be there in a little while. I just woke. Max is there?"

"Yep. Just sold a house, too."

"I'll be there soon." We disconnected and I glanced over to Max. "He'll be here in a jiffy."

I went back out to the showroom after all my extra chores were completed, and sat behind the computer. I had to wait while ten new messages were loaded. My heart pounded in anticipation of another cruel answer from Bunny, or maybe from someone unknown.

The first email seemed innocent enough, and from a local grocery chain. The second was from an upcoming ice-cream social, but the third... Someone unknown did leave a message, and it too, was cruel.

She's dead. Join her.

I saved the message to a folder to show Aaron later.

The next message wasn't menacing, but it was certainly perplexing.

It's safe, and where it belongs.

I sent this message to the same folder. I logged out of the store's webmail, and sorted through my personal messages, responding to a few. Earlier in the day I had invited Maggie to swing by that evening so I could fill her in on what had been happening. I also mentioned the soup, knowing that for sure she'd come by. She loved Grandma's soup.

After tending to the messages, I started another search on each impersonator, trying to cast a wider net for information about them. I didn't want to leave anything to chance. With my phone notepad handy, I jotted down names I found for each of them. The next search was for any addresses associated with those names, never an easy task, made worse if the subject of the search was avoiding attention. I immersed myself in an online world of search engines, switching quickly from one to another to find them. Time had flown during my search, and my eyes were tired from staring at the screen. I started to shut the computer down, when a thought made me sit upright. A moment later I continued my search.

Chapter Nineteen

At least I knew that Ed Parsons or the barmaid, or both, lived in that house. I wondered if they would be at the afternoon's meeting at the X. I applied fresh lipstick and made sure that my forehead bruise was amply covered with makeup. My hair sprang up in all directions, but figured that no one would care.

"The store will be fine," Max reassured me. "Don't worry about a thing."

"I'm know. You know how to handle sales? The inventory for each house is still pinned on the inside cabinet or else there's the binder."

"Got it."

I was nervous for some reason. Who was the woman last night, fleeing Gina's? So familiar looking. I stepped outside to wait, and checked the street. Then I checked the locks twice. Aaron should've been here by now, so where was he? I walked to the end of the alley and looked toward home but didn't see the car. I scratched my head, hiked to the corner, and looked in all directions. Not in sight. I turned on my heels and went behind the store, where I stood next to my car, wondering what to do. Finally, my phone rang, and I thought for sure it'd be him. It was Grandma. I hesitated, then answered.

"Grandma? What's up?"

"Aaron took a run over here because I needed help. He's on his way. Just giving you a heads up."

"Why?"

"Grandpa fell, and but he's fine."

"Good grief. What happened?"

"He tripped while climbing the stairs. He's fine."

"Okay. Put him to bed." I heard a car and saw Aaron approaching. "He's here. I'll get back to you."

As soon as he stopped, I opened the door and climbed inside. "Just hung up from Grandma. How's Grandpa?"

"It was nothing. He's fine. A little bump on the noggin."

I touched my forehead and said, "Must be going around."

Within a few minutes, we were entering onto Interstate 35-W and heading east into St. Paul. We crossed the Mississippi Bridge, and it wasn't long before we drove into the lot and parked.

"Do you think the impersonators will be here?"

"As in Ed Parsons? Better known as John Muir? Probably." Aaron grinned.

"You read my mind."

Hand in hand we hiked across the entry way and inside of the building, and followed the signs to the meeting room. I recognized several people in the room, other venders and organizations who had booths at the Expo. The speaker was up front, checking his microphone and making sure the projector was on and her laptop working. There was a large number of rangers, and I recognized a few.

"Let's get started," the speaker said, and cleared her throat. "I'm Dot Nelson, and welcome." She glanced around the room. "I see there's a few impersonators here. Sarah Page as Annie Oakley, Ed Parsons as John Muir, in the back, and Robert Coons as Buffalo Bill. Thank you for coming."

Aaron nudged me. "Don't even think about talking to Parsons."

"I won't," I scowled. I couldn't help but to glance over to where he sat and realized that Pam Simons, barmaid, was beside him. I had learned her name only that afternoon, during my online search.

Dot Nelson's talk was about event security and how to improve it, and also for us to give our feedback on how the exposition turned out. Most of us thought everything went well, and that sharing the event with Minneapolis had been a good idea. Ideas for next year's expo were explored. When the topic turned to splitting up the parks by sections of the country, I sneaked a trip to the bathroom.

Pam Simons, the barmaid, was washing her hands at a sink as I left the stall. , I ignored her went to another sink. I thought she was ignoring me, as well, but as I dried my hands, she said in a low voice, "If you ever follow me again, you'll regret it."

"I won't." I caught sight of her face in the mirror. Her eyes burned like fire, frightening me. "I promise."

"I know people who can take care of snoops like you." She opened the door with a flourish and marched out.

I stared after her. "Good grief." I waited a minute, then left and went back to join Aaron., I immediately leaned, trembling, into his shoulder where he placed his arm around me. I was happy when the meeting wrapped up soon after and we left.

"What's up?" Aaron asked as we left the building. "You're like a scared rabbit."

"Pam Simons threatened me in the ladies room," I said. He pulled back and stared at me. "She told me to never follow her again,- or else."

"Liv, you could easily be the next victim. Don't speak to anyone. Don't make eye contact. Period! Understood?"

"Yep." I wiped my eyes.

"I'm getting you home," he said. He took hold of my arm. "We'll throw in a movie and finish that chicken soup."

"Okay, but what about Grandpa?"

"Give him a buzz on the way home, but I'm sure he's fine."

Aaron steered me toward the car, and opened the side door for me and closed it once I'd positioned myself. He walked around, opened his and climbed in, and turned on the engine. I gave Grandma a quick call as he drove from the lot and out into the street.

"He's fine," she assured me. "Just a slight headache, and he just woke from a nap."

"Good." Fortunately, we were exiting soon because it was rush hour traffic time. "I forgot to tell you, last night I saw a light on at Gina's and went over to check it out. I was in the backyard and a woman rushed out of the backdoor and ran off. She didn't see me."

"Recognize her?"

I shook my head.

"I thought the doors were locked," Aaron mused.

"Me too. Odd, isn't it?"

"I better call it in."

Once we were home, he stayed in the kitchen to report the news to the detectives, while I went to log into my laptop. I brought it into the living room, settled myself, and turned on the TV. I heard Aaron's footsteps, and turned toward him.

"What's up?"

"Someone's going to take a look, and then stop over."

"Okay." I opened my laptop and punched in the website address for each of the impersonators and searched through their event calendars. Every last one of them had an event in Medora or nearby at the time of that attorney's death. Satisfied, I logged out, poured myself a glass of ice tea, and joined Aaron outside on the patio.

"They all were nearby at time the lawyer was murdered. I'm sunk. Now what?"

"You leave it to the cops."

"In the meantime, I need a bodyguard." I sighed, and took a sip. "Tastes good."

"Supper?"

"Sure."

We finished our drink and were ready to fire up the grill when Aaron's phone buzzed.

"It's a couple of patrol officers. They're out front. I told them to come on back."

As if on cue, two uniformed men walked around the side of the house, and introduced themselves.

"Officer Polski." He showed his badge.

"Officer Newby." She did the same.

"Was anything out of the ordinary?" Aaron asked. "Have a seat."

"Want a glass of ice tea?" I asked.

They declined.

"We found this," Officer Polski flicked a card from his pocket. It was sealed inside a small plastic bag. "It's got your store name on the front."

"It's one of my cards." My eyes opened wider. "Now I recognize her. I remember handing her that card. It was Ida Gray, Gina's aunt, that I saw!" I crossed my arms. "Okay, I'm angry about it, but why was she there lurking about? Where did the key come from? She told me that she didn't have one."

"Some people lie to fit their needs, ma'am."

"That's for sure," I agreed. I stared at the card. "Anything written on it?"

"Nope. Only what's printed on the card."

"It must've fallen from her pocket." Officer Polski stated, and slid it back into his breast pocket. "We'll turn it over to the detectives. Someone will be in touch."

We watched as they walked back around the side of the house. "Why would she do that? Sneak into the house like a common thief?" I asked.

"She's after something."

"What, though? Do you think the ledger book is what she's after?" I said. "I bet she's in search of the lost land deed from TR."

"Possibly. What about our figurine?"

"I'm taking a look at it soon. There must be a clue on it, leading to the deed."

We had our easy meal of burgers before retiring for the night. I woke many times, always checking on Gina's house. My thoughts circled between the two symbols, and the plat book stating where TR owned property. Eventually I fell asleep and woke to rain showers. Birds chirped approvingly.

I was happy that it was Saturday morning, and I didn't have to rush so much. The store opened at eleven instead of ten, which gave me more time to plan my day, and it also closed earlier, at three. I hoped we'd be able to visit my grandparents after closing.

"Going to be my bodyguard today?"

"Nope. Marie's going to sit with you." Aaron kissed the top of my head. "I have to report in and probably work overtime."

"Grandma? I was wondering how they were doing."

I went to dress for the day. The clouds were breaking apart, and the sun peeking through, so I decided to walk. Aaron and I kissed goodbye, and I headed out the door. As I walked, my thoughts returned to the card. I should've known it was Ida fleeing from the house, but the question is, why?

I kept walking, past the Establishment and further until at last waiting for the final light for me to safely cross.

Max's truck was parked out back, which relieved me. I hadn't realized how much I didn't want to be alone. I texted him the moment I opened the back door and entered to let him know that I was there. I dropped my bag and went out to the shop in front.

"Hi, ladies." I stopped near Eleanor Roosevelt's doll. "How are you today? Have you written your column, My Day?" She wrote it everyday between nineteen thirty-five and nineteen six-ty-two, except the four days after your husband died. It must've been hard to keep it up.

The counter looked empty without the purse and pistol taking center stage. I wondered if I'd ever see them again? I got the computer humming and logged into my website. The person who'd left the nasty comments, hadn't taken my bait, and no more had been left. I posted a message that I hoped would help flush out the killer. It read: *Come and look at our dollhouse of the White House during the Teddy Roosevelt era. See what new arrangements First Lady Edith Roosevelt added.* I closed out, hoping for a quick response.

The next part of my plan was to begin to dig deeper in my search. I had just logged into a site when Max entered.

"Glad you're here." I smiled at him. "I don't like being alone."

"No problem." He grinned. "I'm going to box up a few extra houses, plus get the inside furnishings together and boxed. That'll keep me busy for most of the day."

"Thank you," I answered and was reminded again of Max's suggestion for another employee. The phone rang and I answered. "First Lady White House Dollhouse Store, how may I help you?"

"Ida here. I'm calling to say thanks for looking after Gina's house. How about coming out for a cup of tea or coffee or a soda? Then I can pay you back for all of your kind work?"

I was stunned, and stammered out a replay. "Sure. Sounds like fun." Well, it certainly would be would be interesting. Business was slow, anyway. Plus, it would give me a chance to discover the reason behind her entering Gina's house the other night. "I need your address and what time?" I jotted it down, and told her I'd be at her house at three. It'd take me about twenty minutes to get to her place, I reckoned, since it was near the Xcel Convention Center. I sent a message to Aaron so that he'd know my afternoon schedule. I got up and went to locate Max. I peeked inside the workroom and saw two boxes stacked as well as the counter loaded with miniature furniture, but no Max, as he was having a smoke outside

"I hope the person who applies will be a history nut," I said. I looked up at him, and had to hold my hand up to block the sun's rays. "I bet it'll be slow today because people will be out walking and having picnics." I started gathering my things together for home.

"Leaving early?" He dropped the finished cigarette to the ground and crushed it out with his sandal sole.

"Yeah. I'm going to visit Gina's aunt. She invited me to come around."

"Be careful. Sounds suspicious," Max said.

"What's the harm in a cup of tea or coffee?"

"Poison. That's the harm."

I laughed. "See you later." I turned on my heels and left. I pushed the thought out of my mind as I hiked back home. Poison? Good grief! Why would anyone try to poison me? After reaching home. I walked through the house to make sure that all was well at the Reynolds' household, and then jumped into my car. I keyed the address into the GPS and drove from the driveway.

I became more anxious as I drove about the what Max had said about poison, and that made my throat dry up. I stopped at a small store and bought a bottle of raspberry flavored water before continuing toward Ida's. I cursed Max for putting the notion in my head.

She'd told me that the bright yellow house on the corner was hers, so I easily found it and parked on the side street. She was sitting out back, on the patio. "Hi, Ida." I waved with one hand, holding the water bottle in the other. "Got some ice?" I figured ice cubes would be safe in my drink.

"Good to see you. But, put that away, I've already made refreshments." She nodded toward the pitcher and empty glass displayed on the patio table. Wow. If I was the paranoid sort, I'd really be worried.

"I already opened it, sorry. I was really thirsty since I'd walked home from work before I could get the car." I sat in an opposite chair and reached for the filled Northwest Airline glass of ice cubes. "I'll have a drink of your ice-tea when I've finished this." I smiled and hoped that appeased her. "What a lovely day, isn't it?"

"Are you busy in the store?" She crossed her arms and cocked her head. "I bet everyone's outside and it's slow. That's too bad."

"It's been busy. Ebbs and flows." I shrugged. "Tell me, how are things going with the house and the will? Anything new about the solicitor's death?"

"Everything's in the air. The police have interviewed Harry, Sunflower and me. As if I'd want to murder him." She shivered.

"Your property is right beside Gina's, isn't it?"

"Yes, it's been in the family for over a hundred years. So has Gina's. Our families did everything together. Our joint properties date back to the days of Roosevelt."

"It didn't seem as if Harry and Gina even knew each other, or Sunflower, for that matter. They seemed distant, as a matter of fact."

"They loved each other but living side-by-side sometimes can cause difficulties, such as cattle branding and helping with the chores. Kind of like brothers and sisters."

"Oh. Never thought of that." I hesitated and sipped my drink. "I thought I saw a light on over at the house the other night, so I called the police."

"Oh my." She eyed me over her glass as she sipped. "Did you ever find a set of school books? Or ledger?"

"I did find a couple, but left them there." That's where the deed's hidden, the books. "Wait a minute. Actually, I do have them. I'd forgotten all about them."

"They belong to me." She glared at me. "When can I get them?"

"I'll bring them to the store," I said. "I see Aaron wants me to make a stop on the way home. Mind if I use your restroom?"

"Nope. Not at all. It's right to the left of the kitchen."

"Be right back." I hiked inside, and headed straight to the room. Once inside, I opened the cabinet and took several pictures of prescription bottles. I did my job and hurried back out. "Now I must get home. I have plenty to do."

"Okay. We'll have to do this again when we both have more time."

"Thank you."

We parted and I didn't feel at ease until the engine started humming and I had drove away from the curb. I didn't know why she'd put me so on edge, then realized that it was most likely caused from leaving my bottle unattended.

Chapter Twenty

I stopped into the store instead of going right home. Besides a few wood splinters on the counter, probably from Max's work, everything was fine.

Next on my list was to drop by my grandparents to see how Grandpa was after his fall. I hated knowing they were getting older. They lived up past the Calhoun Beach House and toward Lake-of-the-Isles. The greenery was beautiful around there, and if I'd had more time, I would've driven to the Rose Garden and sat for a minute enjoying the beautiful flowers. Grandma's Garden Club helped maintain gardens

I soon parked outside of their house and strode to the back patio where I found them sipping glasses of wine. "Hi," I greeted them. I dropped my bag and went into the kitchen for a glass for myself. I held it out. "I'm thirsty."

I sat beside Grandpa as he filled my glass. "Grandpa, how are you feeling?"

"Great. What brings you here?" Grandpa asked with a twinkle in his eye. "Out cruising? Shouldn't you be at the store?"

"She came to check up on you, Angus. Right?" I kissed Grandma's cheek in confirmation. "See?"

I peered closely at Grandpa's bump and declared, "You look fine." I smiled. "I came from Ida Gray's. She'd asked for me to previously look for some books. I did but never got around to telling her. Now that I told her, I have to give them to her. I'm going to bring them to the store for her to pick up."

"Why'd you hold back?" Grandpa asked.

"The police wanted me to look through them. The other day, I saw her leave the house, the police found my card on the floor. I hadn't been sure if it was her or not, now I know it was. What do you make of that?"

"Not sure, it could mean almost anything, honey." Grandpa rubbed his chin.

"Their ranches are joined. There's something about that and the oil company, that I've got to figure out." I waited a beat and continued, "She also said that their land dates back to Roosevelt."

"Well, if there's oil money involved, there's your motive," Grandpa said.

"I agree. It's exactly what I thought—greed."

"Have you tried to research her children? Weren't they at the expo?" Grandma asked. "That's where I'd begin."

"Harry is a Ranger at the park, and Sunflower danced in some of the performances."

"Anymore news about the drug?" Grandpa asked. "Refill?" He held up the bottle, but I held my hand over the top of my glass. He laughed. "Don't worry, this isn't drugged." He emptied it between himself and Grandma.

"I'm driving and haven't had much to eat so far today. Aaron's due home soon, too." I thought for a minute. "Maybe I should see what's in the park that had originally belonged to President Roosevelt."

"Yes, and what about the impersonators? Something's not right there, either," Grandma said.

"That's true, too." I emptied my glass. "I must get going. Oh! Don't forget brunch on Sunday. I'll keep you two up to date." I gave them each a cheek kiss. "Thanks." I left through their house, to take a look at Grandma's Dolley Madison sampler, hoping for inspiration. The sampler was a key in locating the Star Spangled Banner manuscript after it'd been hid for two hundred years. I wondered if the TR pieces in my possession held the secret to something valuable.

I took an alternative route home, winding around many parks and water bodies, enjoying watching children playing outside and families swimming. Eventually I parked in our garage and went into my house. I set the covered water bottle on the back counter away from everything else. I didn't trust that it was safe to drink.

I got another water bottle from the refrigerator, grabbed my laptop, and went out back to sit. It felt good to relax as I checked messages. Max had written to say that no one stopped in all afternoon, which is what I had expected.

While I waited for Aaron to come home from work, I did a search on Harry and found him listed in Medora at the same address as Ida's ranch.

I looked up when the backdoor opened and Aaron stepped outside with a can of beer, chips and dip. "Need anything?"

"Thank you. I'm kind of hungry. Got a notepad and pencil?"

Aaron held them up after he set the bowls on the table.

"How did it go with Ida?" He sat opposite and placed the pad and pen on his lap. "What's your impression?"

"It's like this—Max mentioned poison as I left—so I stopped for a bottle of water and drank from that instead of what she had ready. I believe it was ice tea. Now that I think about it, she didn't offer cookies or pie—nothing. Isn't that surprising? Grandma would've."

"Did you go inside at all?"

"Yes, I went to the bathroom and took pictures of the inside of her medicine cabinet," I said. "I left my water bottle with her when I did."

"We need to have the water in it tested."

"That's what I was thinking. I didn't drink from it after I left it with her," I said. "It's in the kitchen on the back counter."

"Okay. Now, what did she ask about?"

"The books. I said I'd bring them to the store."

"I bet there's something hidden in them." Aaron wrote on the pad. "Did she ask about the figurine?" I shook my head and took a sip. "That's interesting. She either knows it's unattainable or she's forgotten about it."

"We can't zero in on her, though. There's other suspects like that horrible woman, Pam. It makes no sense at all for her to walk through the store in a costume, and later threaten me, does it?" I frowned. "We're not any further ahead."

"We do know a few things, but nothing definite." He set the pad aside. "What were you researching?"

"Sunflower lives in Medora and Harry lives on the ranch. Ida said Harry, Sunflower and Gina quarreled a lot, similar to siblings."

"It stands to reason since they grew up living close."

I opened my laptop and continued with my search. I found that Sunflower participated in the jingle dancing a great deal of the time because her name showed up on a website featuring jingle dancers from that area, Harry was listed as a ranger on the park website, but with no other information about him. I began poking around the park's website, and found photographs of TR's cabin. Edith stayed there only once in the years following TR's death, and it had since burned down. A photo of the interior of the rustic cabin showed only a small trunk, a few items needed for personal use, and various odd pieces used in the course of living. I said, "Nothing much to investigate."

"Maybe we should go for a short trip out there? It isn't that far. We could go for only a few days, and maybe then we'd be able to figure it all out."

"Not yet, we need more to focus on. More specific clues." I turned my attention back to the impersonators and opened the bookmark for Buffalo Bill. I slowly read through his website and carefully read all the event dates and where he'd performed. "Write this down, will you?" I gave Aaron the dates. "I'm going to see if the dates coincide with Annie Oakley's." I found her schedule and read them out to him.

"They fit. Let's strike those two from the list because they couldn't have done it. They were working." He emptied his beer can and crushed it before dropping it into the recycling bin. "I'm going after another. Want something else?"

"A soda. Order a pizza, too, please."

"You got it."

I watched him walk away before switching back to the searches. The next one was for Ed Parsons, aka John Muir. He traveled the country with his act, but didn't have anything scheduled for the next two months. It made me wonder how he managed financially. I did a search for his girlfriend, Pam Simons, or were they married? Nothing popped up about her except that she was on Facebook. Aaron returned with our drinks and handed me my soda.

"I ordered a large- pepperoni and extra cheese."

"Great." I took another handful of chips. "Let's have Maggie and Tim come out."

"Already did. They're on their way."

I closed out from my account and shut down the laptop. "Let's pick a movie to watch with them."

"Sure." Aaron grinned. "Better go inside. The skeeters might carry us off."

It wasn't much longer before the pizza man arrived, followed by Maggie and Tim. After we'd finished gobbling down the pizza and drank a few sodas, we hustled inside to watch "Argo. Maggie and I snuggled into the sofa while the guys leaned back in the two recliners. About midway, I popped us a couple bags of popcorn. The movie was great, and hard to believe that the event really happened, and the Americans escaped without harm. Afterward, Maggie and Tim left.

"Nice evening, baby girl." Aaron kissed me, steering me toward the bedroom.

"Hmm." I let him lead.

Between his snores, neighborhood car doors opening and closing, and voices echoing through the open windows, I had trouble sleeping. I got up and meandered into the living room where I turned on the television. I covered myself with one of the sofa coverings, and closed my eyes while I listened to a PBS special that showed old commercials from the beginning of television. Some were funny, some boring. I fell asleep during a Hamm's Beer commercial. Later, I woke to a Colgate advertisement. I got up, went to bed, and slept through until morning.

When I woke, something nagged on my mind, but I wasn't sure what. I showered and dressed before catching up to Aaron in the kitchen. "Aren't Grandma and Grandpa coming out for brunch? I know that I that I mentioned it when I left." I poured us each a cup of coffee.

"I wondered about that. Better call."

We carried our cups outside to sit, and dialed their number. "Grandma? Are you two coming out for brunch? I promise that I've made the meal twice before and I've got it down pat. You won't get sick."

"Forgot. Grandpa got a call last night letting us know that his cousin, Sally—you do remember her, don't you? Well, she's flying in from Miami and needs to be picked up in two hours. We're just leaving. Grandpa is worried about the traffic and parking."

"Grandma, it only takes thirty minutes to get there and park." I took a sip of the hot coffee. "Would you like for us to get her?"

"Thank you dear, if it's not too much of a problem." I could feel relief in her voice.

"Tell me the airline and flight number." She did, and I saved it on the phone.

"Don't worry," I assured her. "We'll let you know when she arrives." I disconnected, and told Aaron. "We need to go to the airport and pick up Grandpa's cousin Sally."

"I'll finish getting dressed. We'll get going right away. If we're early we can watch the planes landing and taking off. That's always fun to do."

"Okay." While he was gone, my minded drifted to last night's vintage commercial program. Many were educational. Many taught girls how to dress and walk and take care of themselves. A few were about aspirins and other over the counter drugs. The logo for Northwest Airline had changed since the commercial, and now the company wasn't based in Minnesota anymore.

I brought our coffee mugs back inside and shut the coffee maker off, and filled the dishwasher. I figured I'd let it run while we were absent. As I finished pouring in the detergent, Aaron entered.

I put down the container and pressed the start button. The machine began humming nicely. "Let's go."

I took my bag and followed him out, and climbed into the passenger seat. I applied a bit of lipstick as he drove down the street. "I haven't seen Grandpa's cousin Sally since I was a teenager. I'm not sure if I know what she looks like." I gave Aaron the name of the airline and the flight number. "She was really, really nice. I know that. She bought me a doll when she stayed before."

"Anyone who bought you a doll, you'd like." Aaron smiled at me, and turned onto the main drag, which brought us over to 35W and to the Mall of America exits, and soon after that, the airport entrance. We found a parking spot in the close-by lot nearest the terminal, so we wouldn't have to worry about Sally walking very far. Since she was Grandpa's cousin, I figured she had to be in her seventies.

"What does she look like?" Aaron asked. I tugged on his arm to hurry as we crossed the parking lot and entered on the lower level. We hustled to the elevators and found our way to the upper level and found a waiting area.

"Let's sit here," I suggested. "Did you bring my water bottle in for testing?"

"Yes. Now, sit back and relax. Let's watch the planes."

We both sank into the chairs nearest the windows and watched as flights landed and took off. Our expected flight wasn't due for quite a while but it was nice to sit and watch the planes outside, and the people near us.

A number of attendants walked past, pulling their luggage. Then two pilots walked by, doing the same "Looks like a flight is due to come in. Maybe it's Sally's," I said. Sure enough, soon after that, a loudspeaker announced that her flight had landed.

We watched the stream of passengers eagerly, and then I recognized the same wiry hair and broad smile that was just like grandpa's. "Sally!" I cried, giving her a big kiss.

"Olivia, you look just like I remember, shorter with red hair and a beaming smile. You must be Aaron?" She gave him a smooch, leaving red lipstick on his cheek.

"Ready? Let's get your luggage and get out of here." We waded through the passengers and down to the luggage claim and after a short while, retrieved her suitcase. Aaron, ever the gentleman, picked it up and carried it for Sally.

"We're parked not far away. I don't think Grandpa likes driving out here, so we though we'd pick you up."

We wound our way to the car. "Here we are." Aaron opened the trunk and set the luggage inside of it, and closed the lid.

"You can sit in the front." I opened the door and helped her climb in. She buckled up while I got in the backseat.

Aaron followed the traffic signs leading us back out onto the freeway.

"The Mall of America," I pointed it out to her. "On your left—off over there! See it?"

"Oh my. I'd like to go there if I can. The attendants talked about it all the time."

We fell quiet as the traffic was tight and horns honked. Overhead another plane soared. Several minutes passed before we spoke again. Sally mentioned how much I had enjoyed playing with dolls when I was a little girl, and then asked when Aaron and I were going to have some children of our own.

"We will someday," I responded with a smile. We were already trying but nothing had happened. Changing the subject, I wondered, "Why did the airline attendants talk about the Mall of

America? Aren't they from all over? I bet that none of them are from here."

The car came to a sudden stop, and Aaron blasted the horn. "Stupid driver!" Traffic was a tangled mess for a minute. "That guy pulled right out in front of the car ahead of us," Aaron complained. "We're lucky that we weren't rear-ended." Traffic began flowing again.

"What were you saying, Sally? Something about the attendants."

"When I worked as one, I traveled all over and knew something about every city where we stopped. The passengers always like hearing such things, you know. However, one of the flight attendants was from this area. She sort of reminded me of you. You are about the same height and build. I wonder if you know her."

"A flight attendant with my height and build. I like to think that my memory's good but it's not that good," I said. "You don't know where she lives or anything like that, do you?"

"No, but she works part-time as a flight attendant," Sally said. "She said she only flies once a week. The rest of the time she works at a bar. Isn't that something."

Alarm bells went off in my head and I saw Aaron's eyes lock briefly on mine through the rear-view mirror.

We arrived at Grandma and Grandpa's house and soon had Sally safely unloaded and inside. Our duty done, we made our escape.

"There's something I want to check," I said to Aaron, as he started the car.

"I know what you're thinking." he replied.

Chapter Twenty-One

"We need to find out if Pam Simons is an airline attendant or not."

"Just because she looks similar to you, doesn't mean that it's the same person Sally spoke of, honey."

I stared out the window all the way home.

"Let's stop and see if she's working." I hoped we'd be able to drive through the parking lot. "What do you think?"

"Okay, we can do that."

Aaron made a detour that took us home by way of the Establishment. We circled around the cars in the lot and finally parked. The bright sun felt good when I got out of the car. The short walk brought us past an outdoor patio, filled with customers, and soon we were inside. Pam wasn't behind the counter, which only added to my suspicions. We ordered for outside, and went out to sit.

The soda was refreshing and the burgers hit their mark. I kept my eyes peeled, but didn't see anyone that I knew. After eating, we went directly home.

"I'll go ahead and send a message to the detectives, but I'm sure they've done a full background check on her."

"It's still pretty darn suspicious, if you ask me."

"Let's change the subject. How about if I go and fetch the books?" Aaron said.

"They're in the trunk. I put them there with the new Edith Roosevelt doll I bought. I've decided to build my own collection of First Lady dolls and display them in the store beside my Penny Doll collection."

I suddenly remembered the photos I'd taken of the prescription bottles inside Ida's bathroom cabinet the day before. I pulled out my phone. "Look, Aaron," and showed them to him. He leaned over me and we closely studied them. "This one has weird printing, and doesn't look as if it's American." I enlarged the picture. "See?"

"Let me look at that." He took my phone and studied it before sending himself the images. "I wonder."

"I'm thinking she picked up that bottle overseas while working as a flight attendant. If she did, maybe she picked up some of that other drug, what's it called? Sux?" I thought for a minute. "Yeah. That's it."

"You're jumping to conclusions here, Liv. You need to sit back and think about this. The detectives would've been all over her if they had any suspicions about her."

"That's the point! No one has any suspicions about anything!" Exasperated, I leaned back and looked out the living room window. I sent the images to the detectives. "There. Now they can look at them, too." It'd been a long day, and I was getting tired. "Let's look at the books once more."

"Yep! Be right back." I went to the front window while he was gone. It was a typical late Sunday afternoon. The neighbors across from us got in their car and drove away, and the kids who lived in the house next to ours played hopscotch on the sidewalk out front.

Aaron returned with the books. "Here." He handed me the Bible.

I handed it back. "I'm going to look closer at the plat book. It will tell us who the original owners were of the land back when this area was first settled."

"Suit yourself." He gave that book to me, setting the Bible on the table, and keeping the grammar book.

While Aaron perused his book, I carefully went through the pages of the county plat book, searching for anything unusual. "This all seems up and up except for the one notation that we'd found earlier where Teddy Roosevelt's land butted against the Gray ranch. I wonder if it isn't the deed itself that they're looking for?"

"It could very well be, but it's been so many years and there's ways to get around that. A good lawyer could do it."

"Unless there's a will someplace that usurps it." I shrugged. "That's very possible, too. We'll have to keep digging until the dots match." I continued sifting through the pages and was ready to set the book aside when something caught my eye. "Take a look at this." I showed him a jumble of numbers. "What on earth is it?"

"Not a clue."

"I'm taking a picture." I took two. "I'll send you and the detectives the images."

"Got 'em." His phone dinged.

"I'll also text them about the attendant idea."

I set the book aside when finished and stared out the window. The numbers and names seemed all different, like two separate people recorded them. What did all that mean? I didn't think Ida would treat herself with foreign medication. I turned back to Aaron. "Any thoughts about any of this?"

"Let's let it percolate until tomorrow."

"How about we take it easy and go for a drive. We'll let nature take it's course with ideas."

"You're right."

We jumped in the car and went for a pop at the local diner and stared out the window for an hour. It was great to relax and not think about anything in particular, time alone with my sweetie.

"How do you feel?" Aaron said.

"Much better. I don't feel bogged down with unanswered questions."

"That means, that new thoughts will come through," Aaron said.

"I know." I yawned. "Maybe I'll dream the answers."

"Keep the thought, baby." He reached across the booth for my hand. "Why do you think Ida is guilty of something? Surely you don't believe she's capable of murder?"

"I hope not," I said, "but my water could've possibly been poisoned." I shivered.

"Don't worry." Aaron released my hand. "Time to go home."

"I agree."

We drove home, and went to bed after a short while. I didn't sleep well. The full moon shone bright and silvery through the window, and I got up to stare out at it during the night. I looked out on the stars, and made a wish for the whole mess to soon solve itself. I was happy when morning came, and rose early.

Aaron drove me to work, and I went to greet the First Lady dolls.

"Ladies, the police will return but don't be alarmed. They wouldn't dare to bother any of you." I glanced at Dolley. "Mrs. Madison, you don't need to take out your spyglass. The British aren't returning. Good grief." I turned my thoughts to the job at hand.

Aaron helped me rearrange the houses. While we did this, I got a text message that the detectives would soon stop by. The front door opened and I glanced over to it as a tall young woman with a baby carrier walked in.

"Take your time, and if you have a question, just ask." She just smiled, and meandered around the displays.

"How old is the baby?" It appeared to be only a few weeks old.

"Four weeks," she replied. "She's a good baby. Her name is Magdalene. Maggie."

"Beautiful name." I went to take a look at the baby. "Beautiful baby." I stepped aside for the woman to continue looking. After a short while, she left the store.

The next time the door opened, it was for the detectives. I went over to the sales counter and sat behind it while Aaron stood beside it.

"Did you look at the pictures I sent? What do you think?" I asked.

"I'm curious as to how you obtained those pictures." Detective Erlandsen asked. "I don't supposed you had Ida Gray's permission."

"I went to the bathroom and snooped," I admitted.

"You shouldn't be snooping like that. Leave it us," Detective Mergens admonished me.

"However," added Detective Erlandsen. "We can confirm that it's a foreign prescription."

"You must be careful, Liv," Mergens said. "This isn't a game."

"I know it's not." I said.

"Where are the books?" Mergens asked.

"The trunk," I answered. "Don't forget the doll," I called to Aaron who was already heading for the back door.

"Now what's your take on this?" Mergens asked, leaning onto the counter. "I want to know if it's changed much from a few days ago."

I waited as both readied themselves to write, then began. "I believe there's a deed someplace. We have my figurine and the grass bowl of Inga's, which are in a bank security box. They both have symbols on them."

"Let's take a look at them. Can Aaron get them easily?"

"You have to speak to Inga about the bowl, but Aaron can fetch the figurine."

Aaron strode into the room and set the books down with the doll. "What can I get?" He glanced from me to the detectives.

"The figurine," I said. Detective Erlandsen had moved away from the counter and held his phone to his ear. "I'm sure he's calling Inga about the bowl."

"I can chauffeur her to the bank and run in for the jingle dancer."

Detective Mergens snapped his phone shut. "She'll lock up and come right down. Aaron, you don't mind, do you?"

"Nah. I want an end to this."

"Bring them around to the station," Mergens stated. "We've got another crime scene to investigate so we'll be taking off."

"Will do."

"I'm taking all the books. We'll get back to you." Mergens lifted them up and began walking to the door. "Be in touch."

"Liv, leave the investigation to us," Erlandsen said, and walked out the door.

"Ida is supposed to stop and get the books. Where is this all leading?" I turned to Aaron. "Are we missing anything? I'd still like to know more about Pam Simons, wouldn't you?"

"I'd like to know how Ida is connected to this. Does she poison people? It doesn't add up. That's what bothers me."

"She wouldn't murder her own niece or an attorney would she?"

"But who would?"

"I'd like another look at those two items before you take them to the precinct."

"Okay, but only for a few minutes."

Just then Inga breezed into the room. "I'm here Aaron, let's go." She stood jingling her keys before slipping them into a pants pocket. "Don't have much time."

"Alright." He held out his arm. "After you, ladies first."

I smiled as they walked toward the backdoor. I wondered where Max was for the day since he hadn't been down to the store.

I switched gears and logged into my accounts on the computer, checking the webmail first. Bambi , Gina's friend, sent a message that read: *Check this out, it's printed in our local paper.* I clicked on the link, and read the article. It said that a new drug had arrived in the US, deadly poisonous in too much is ingested. Its name was—I finished reading the article and realized that it was the same poison I'd suspected right from the start. Now all of my suspicions were confirmed. I responded: *Bambi, thanks. Now I know we were both right. Let's keep in touch. Liv.*

The confirmation put a whole new perspective on my thoughts. I knew that I had to find out for certain if Pam had brought the drug back with her on one of her flights. I wanted to close up shop and head to the airport and see what I could find out, but tabled the idea. Instead, I began a new search on airline attendants for the airline that Sally had flown. I wasn't able to find out any information, presumably because of security reasons. I closed from the site and decided to log out, and turn my attention back to my shop.

I was making room for my doll up high on a shelf when my phone rang. "Hi Grandma."

"Honey, I forgot to ask you two out for supper tonight."

"Does this mean we're invited? Should we bring anything?"

"Of course you're invited. That's why I called. Just bring yourselves."

"All right." I disconnected, and giggled. I was fortunate to have such a wonderful set of grandparents. Aaron, I was sure, felt the same. I had barely gotten started again on rearranging the shelf when the back door opened. "Max?" I moved around the corner to look. "It is you. I wondered what you were doing."

"I saw the cops were here, so I thought I'd stay away until they were gone." Max doesn't trust police, due some trouble he had when he was young. He took a long swallow from his water bottle. "Gonna tell me what's up?"

"While I was at Ida's-,"

"I knew it. She's up to something." He rubbed his chin. "I'm right, aren't I?"

"Settle down," I said. "I took pictures of the prescription bottles in her bathroom cabinet, and one looked foreign. Also, some writing in those books appear foreign. The pictures we forwarded to the detectives, and they now have the books."

"You still don't know how it all figures in, though?" Max said. He capped the bottle and set it aside.

"Nope. But I do believe it's about a land title that Teddy Roosevelt purchased, and Edith must've hidden for some reason. Both forgot all about it over the years. The estate must've continued paying the taxes, and Gina's family used the land."

"Very possible."

I finished setting the doll on the shelf, then stepped back. "Ida wanted the books, of course. I didn't stay long, only a few minutes before I left." I faced him. "The detectives want the jingle dancer figurine and Inga's grass bowl. Aaron is fetching them from the bank now. I asked to take another look at them before they go to the station."

"Thanks. Now that I know the scoop, I'm going back to boxing and labeling cartons so that we can get a little bit ahead."

I planned to follow him to the workroom, but the front door opened and a perspective customer entered. "Hello. I'm Liv. If you have any questions, just ask." I went to sit by the computer as the older woman began to circle the display tables.

"I'm interested in First Lady Bess Truman." She stopped near the FDR house. "Would it be this one here?"

I went over to join her. "She's one of our lesser known First Ladies. It was hard walking into Eleanor Roosevelt's shoes, and the house was in such a turmoil plus it was ready to fall apart. When the President was re-elected, the house went through extensive remodeling. It was almost entirely gutted."

"Thank you. I'll continue looking, if you don't mind?"

"Go ahead." I stayed with her, pointing out different features of each house.

"I did so like Jackie Kennedy."

I told her about the Rose Garden and the many changes in the White House, and the inaugural she wore. A short while later, it was decided that she'd purchase the Kennedy White House. I went to the computer, after requesting Max to help with carrying the boxes to her car.

"Thank you," I said, handing over the receipt.

When the customer left, Aaron returned.

"Funny thing happened," Aaron said upon entering. "We were followed when we left the bank. I took one side street after another until I finally lost the guy. I'm sure it was a male, but I couldn't tell who it was, or if the person reminded me of anyone. He was smart enough to know to stay a few car lengths behind."

"I wonder who it was?" I frowned, and pulled on a lock of my hair. "Do you have the items?"

"Sorry, but since we were followed, I thought it best to take them straight to the station. We didn't want to take any chances."

"Did Inga see the driver of the other car?"

"No. I told her not to turn around. I didn't want her to alert him at all. It wasn't until making the last turn when he drove around us and she caught a glimpse of him. By the way, she thought it was all very exciting."

"Then, whoever this person is, they must know that we have the items."

"Not really. For all they know, I could have gone in for regular store business."

"That's possible." I strolled toward the back room, and said, "I'm going to cut out dress pieces. Would you mind sitting up front for a while?"

"Sure. Why not?" Just then his phone chirped, and I waited to see what it was about since it was the work ring tone. When he clicked off, he said, "I have to work at five."

"We're invited to Grandma's. I'll have to go it alone."

"Sorry, honey."

And that is how the day ended, with me going over to my grandparents and Aaron going to work. The drive took a little longer than normal because of rush hour. Once there, I uncorked a bottle of wine, and sat on the patio deck with them and Sally, and enjoyed the evening.

Grandma served the most delicious grilled salmon, veggies and salad plus ice cream for desert. Sally let me know that her flight left the following evening, and I volunteered to take her to the airport. I decided that it'd give me a chance to snoop around to try and discover more about Pam's work as a flight attendant.

It being late, the drive home didn't take long, and soon I parked inside the garage. I was sad because Aaron wasn't home and I'd be alone. When I stepped into the kitchen, I hadn't expected to see the mess that greeted me.

I backed out the door, and fled across the street.

Chapter Twenty-Two

I'm sure it only took a few minutes for Aaron and police officers to arrive, but it seemed to me to take forever. Aaron found me sitting across the street on the curb, staring at the house – numbed by what had happened.

"Honey, I'm here." He plunked down on the curb beside me and pulled me into his embrace. "It's going to be all right."

"I...hope...so..." I said. He handed me a tissue, and I blew my nose. "It's a mess. The kitchen's a disaster."

"Don't worry, baby." He held me close.

We looked toward the house. The police were in and out of the house and canvassing the neighbors. We walked across the street back to the house.

We'd barely reached our front door when the two detectives arrived. "They're going to say something like, 'again?'" I said, and wasn't far off the mark.

"We meet again?"

"Twice in a day?"

The two went inside, leaving us behind.

"What'd I tell you?" I looked up to Aaron. "I haven't been inside. Called from back over there." I nodded toward the curb. "Don't know if I want to go inside."

"I'm calling Marie." Before I could protest, he had his phone out and was placing the call. "Marie?"

Of course what I heard was one-side of the conversation, but the upshot was that I would spend the night at Grandma's, on the couch since Sally was in the spare room. I gave in. "It's probably a good idea anyway."

Aaron put his arm around my shoulders. "I'll go in and get what you need."

"Don't forget my toothbrush and lipstick. My bag. Clean underwear."

"Yeah—got it." He walked away, and I watched him go inside.

I collapsed on the front steps and tried to stay out of everyone's way. I suspected that they were going over the house with a fine-tooth comb. It didn't take long for Aaron to reappear with a small suitcase filled with fresh clothing, personal items and pajamas plus my bag. "Thanks," I said after looking through everything. "Wow. You remembered everything. So, what are they doing in there? Tell me what it's like."

"Let's just say, you don't want to know." He drew in a deep breath. "Not sure what they were after, but whoever it was, they were angry at not finding it. Everything's overturned or messed up. Remember how bad your grandparents' bedroom was when the killer searched for the cuff links? It's that bad."

"It'll take days to get it sorted out and straightened." I frowned. "I'm calling Max to see if he'll take over the store tomorrow."

"Good idea." He kissed the top of my head. "It's time for you to go. The detectives know that you're not leaving town and know how to reach you. They'll be in contact. I'll let them know where you are, and make certain they have your cell phone number.

"All right," I said as Aaron walked me to my car, and opened the door. I placed the small suitcase in the backseat. "I'll call when I get there."

"Be careful."

I watched him through the rearview mirror as I drove away. I hated leaving him behind. I hated whoever was doing this. Fortunately, there wasn't much traffic at this time of the night because I wasn't in the mood for slow moving cars and stopping for pedestrians. I was happy to see the house as I turned the corner, parking out front. By the time I'd removed the suitcase and walked up to the front door, Grandma had the door open, and I entered.

"Liv, I'm so sorry," Grandma said.

"I know," I said. Tears flooded her eyes, which caused the same reaction in mine. After receiving her hug, I received one from Grandpa and Sally. "Thanks." I blew my nose again.

"Have a seat, dear girl, and tell us all about it," Sally said.

"I don't know what to say, really."

"I'll pour you a glass of wine," Grandpa said. He got up and went to do the chore, returning with a full bottle and filling everyone's glass.

"Thank you." I went ahead and relayed how I'd walked in the kitchen door, and the big mess in front of me. "That's all I know. Aaron said it'll take quite a bit to get it all picked up and sorted through."

"Now what, Liv? What do the detectives have to say?" Grandpa said.

"I think they're as lost as I am. We believe that they were after the books or else the jingle dancer figurine and Inga's grass bowl." I shrugged. "It's hard to know."

"You're safe here. Drink up and we'll make you a bed right here on the couch. It's time for us old people to hit the sack, anyway." Grandpa's mouth twitched. "Grandma will go to work tomorrow for you."

"Max will take over. I've already spoken to him." I said, and sipped my drink. "I'll need help cleaning up. I probably won't be able to get started until sometime tomorrow so I can still take you to the airport."

"Thank you," replied Cousin Sally.

It wasn't long before I was left to my own devices. I slipped into my pajamas, and threw a blanket on the couch and found a spare pillow. I scrunched up the pillow and slipped under another light-weight blanket and shut my eyes. When I closed my eyes I saw the messy kitchen again, and imagined what the rest of the house looked like. Each room and the mess was a vivid image. Car headlights shone brightly through the window at least twice as a car slowly drove past, shining right in my eyes. I pulled the drapes, and tried falling asleep. When car doors slammed, I sat up and peeked out from the curtains to the street and saw someone walking. When morning finally came, I wondered if I'd slept at all.

Grandma carried a tray of apple juice, and buttered toast out to me. I sat up, rubbed my eyes and yawned. "Is it always this noisy out here during the night?"

"What are you talking about?" Grandpa asked, coming from behind.

"First there was a car that drove by, twice, then another one dropping someone off and she went into the house across the street."

"The girl works late, nothing to it. Don't worry."

I went ahead and ate my toast, deep in thought. I wanted to trust them at their word, but too much had happened. The person who followed Aaron could very well have followed me here and waited to see if I'd later emerge or if I was alone. They may have broken into my car.

"Grandpa? Would you go out and see if my car is okay?"

"If it'll make you feel better."

"Thanks." I reached for my keys and handed them over. Grandma and Sally were out in the kitchen so I carried the tray out there. I set it on the counter and then sat down by the table. "I sent Grandpa out to check my car."

"I'm sure it's fine," Sally stated, sipping her coffee.

Grandma poured me a cup, and I hoped it would wake me up. It was going to be a very long day. I didn't want to go home and face the mess, but knew there wasn't any getting around it. Grandpa entered, and set my keys down in front of me.

"No problem. Tires are good. Started right up. Can't see anything wrong."

"Thank you. I feel better." With the coffee cup in hand, I excused myself and headed for the bathroom to shower. Pretty soon, I finished and joined the other three outside on the patio.

"Have you heard from Aaron?"

"No. I was just going to call him." I dialed him up and he answered in two rings. "How are you?"

"Great, but you want to hear about the house."

"Yes."

"Lipstick message on the bedroom room mirror that's threatening. It said, 'give it back'."

"The books? What?"

"Don't know. Otherwise it's just a big mess. Too much to fingerprint, but they took samples from the most likely places."

"I'll be home soon. You working?"

"Not right away. Let me do some cleaning. It's too much. Take Sally to the airport, and then come home. It'll give the detectives time to sort through stuff, also."

"You're right. I'll see you later. Love you."

"Love you, too."

We disconnected, and I relayed the message, but left out the part about the lipstick message. "I guess I'll be here for awhile. Max is busy in the store."

"I'm calling Inga," Grandma said, reaching for her phone. "See what she has to say."

"Maybe she was also broken into last night?" I wondered, because when something happens to me—it's like a domino effect. I sipped my coffee and listened in on the one-sided conversation.

"Who'd a thought all of this murder and mayhem would happen right here in Minneapolis? Unbelievable." Sally shook her head. "I'm ready to go home. It makes me fearful."

I felt sorry for her, and placed my hand over hers. "It'll be all right. Just wait and see."

"Someone did break-in last night at Inga's. They didn't take anything other than her TR photos." Grandma set the phone down. "Too many strange happenings." She rubbed her chin. "Now, where were we?" You were going to ask me something."

"I've got some free time. Do you need some errands run, or maybe do some weeding?

"Weeding, definite."

I groaned, and wished I hadn't asked. "Okay. I'm right on it."

After finishing my coffee, and I went for the sunscreen lotion and slathered myself up before going out in the hot morning sun. I stayed in the shade as long as possible, stopping for a glass of ice water when necessary. Grandma made egg salad sandwiches for lunch and I took a breather. After lunch, it was time to shower and get ready to take Sally to the airport, Soon we were heading down the road toward the interstate.

"I hope you had a nice time," I asked as I entered the I-94 entrance ramp.

"Oh, yes. The time just flew by." Sally glanced at me. "Tell me about your store. I never did get to see it and I feel bad about that."

"It's a delight. You'll have to come and spend time looking around." I told her about the houses and all the different eras that were represented. She seemed enthralled, until I realized she'd fallen asleep. We drove in silence until I'd parked in the area near where we had two days ago.

Her head bobbed up and she said, "Here? Already?"

"Yep. I'll get your suitcase." I walked around to the trunk and lifted it out, setting the wheels on the ground. "By the way, you don't happen to remember if the attendant who reminded you of me came off your plane, do you?"

"No, she didn't. I'm sorry I can't be more help to you with your mystery." Sally took my arm, and we walked close to the airport. "I wish that I could've stayed longer. August looks well."

"They're both doing well."

We entered the airport. After checking in the baggage, we followed signs to the correct terminal. Only a few people were waiting. Sally and I sat in much the same area as before to wait for the attendant to call passengers for boarding. More people began arriving, and tt didn't take long for the room to fill. I tried to keep my eyes peeled for the look-alike attendant, but found it difficult. If it was Pam, her short height would make it even more difficult.

Once Sally was walking out to board and we had waved goodbye for the last time, I took time to explore the airport. As I walked, I read all the posted departure and arrival destination times. My main concern was for flights with Middle East destinations. I meandered slowly up and down each terminal until at last coming across a listing for Saudi Arabia. I decided to sit for a while.

I texted Aaron to let him know what I was doing. He replied, *ok*. As I watched the distant planes come and go, I began to wonder if this was worth my while when I noticed an attendant about my height, with red springy hair walk by. Few people had red springy hair, so I realized that she was probably the woman that Sally had seen. I stood up so that I could keep an eye on her, but just as I was about to follow her, a voice from behind whispered, "Take this as your second warning. Three is fatal."

My eyes opened wide with fear, and I turned to stare into the flow of passengers but missed seeing anyone familiar. It sounded like a male's voice, deep and low. Anger swept through me, and I wanted to scream and shout. Instead, I turned and walked away.

I purchased a beverage on my way out the door, and quickly walked to my car. I paid the parking fee and headed right onto the freeway. I also wanted to get home and discuss this latest development with Aaron.

The threat was solid, and scary. I found that I was driving over the speed limit and made myself slow down, even though I was becoming more and more frightened. Fortunately, traffic moved right. The garage door was open, and I parked right beside Aaron's car.

I rushed inside, found him in the living room asleep, and gave him a big kiss.

"Hey hon." He opened his eyes. "Missed you."

"Ditto." We kissed again.

"You look scared. What happened?"

"Someone threatened me again." Aaron sat up, and pulled me beside him. I told him what the person had said. "I looked around, but didn't see anyone that I recognized."

"What on earth does this person think we have? All you did was watch the planes." He frowned, and reached for his phone. "I'm telling the detectives."

When Aaron's call was answered, he told the operator what had happened, then disconnected. "You're to have someone with you at all times."

"Figures. It's the answer to everything. In the meantime, I'm scared to death." I got up. "My suitcase is in the car, I forgot to bring in. I'll be right back."

"No. I'll go. You stay right here." Aaron stood, and walked past me. "I'll bring it in and then we'll walk through the house."

In the bathroom, I stared at the mirror's reflection of myself and saw a frightened woman with dark rings under her eyes. Aaron returned and led me from the room.

"I've pretty much straightened our room, so we can sleep here tonight. All the drawers were upside down." He guided me into the spare room, where my period dresses lay in shambles across the spare bed and the sewing material thrown into a large pile.

The kitchen still had a few drawers tipped over, but most of the pots and pans had been put away. "Thank you for doing all that work. It's not so bad anymore." I shook my head and squeezed his hand while he led me down the kitchen stairs into the basement. I stood in awe, looking across the vast, un-partitioned room, straight to the laundry area, where our clothes were scattered on the cement floor. "I didn't bother down here yet, as you can tell. It's last on my list since no one usually sees it, except us."

"You're right." I sighed, balling my fist. "These threats are going to end."

"And, not soon enough."

"I'm going to come up with some sort of trap, if it's the last thing I do."

Chapter Twenty-Three

The rest of the day and into the evening was spent putting stuff away and straightening. Aaron worked in the kitchen and I finished what was left to do in our bedroom before moving onto the spare room. I hung each of my period dresses carefully. They were authentic and I prized them. I picked up the dress that had been owned by Edith Roosevelt, and ran my hand down its rich velvet fabric and something crinkled under my fingers. I turned the material over and found a small pocket stitched inside, and inside the pocket was a slip of paper. I gasped. *A hidden message?* Plunking down on the bed, I carefully opened the yellowed paper., The ink of the handwritten note was barely visible but I was reluctant to hold it under the light for fear of further harming it. It read:

Dearest Alice,
Don't forget the jingle dancer.
Lovingly,
Edith

"Huh?" I dashed out to the kitchen. "Look. You'll never guess in a million years what I found." I held up the note. "It's incredible."

"Let me see," Aaron said. I set the letter carefully down on the counter top, and watched as his eyes opened wider. "This is a find. It'll have to go to the heirs of TR."

"People hid treasures inside of all sorts of things. Why not a figurine of a jingle dancer?" I said.

"True," Aaron said.

Gently, I refolded it and placed it on top of my laptop. "What on earth did she hide in it? A million dollars?" I shook my head. "I think this is what we've been waiting to discover, and it's been right in front of us all along."

"I wonder..." Aaron said. He rubbed his chin.

"It could be something hidden in the jingle dancer, that the police have." I took the paper and placed it in a baggie and dropped it into the refrigerator freezer between the TV dinners. "Should be safe."

"And, frozen."

Soon after, we headed for bed and fell asleep immediately. I woke to the noise of the garbage truck at five a.m. Groaning, I rolled over and tried to go back to sleep, but was unable to so I got up and went to the kitchen. With a cup of fresh coffee in hand, I sat down in front of the laptop and logged in. It didn't take long to send a message to Bambi asking if she knew of anyone in her area who had recently traveled overseas. I checked through my most recent messages and responded, then logged out. I logged into my business account and website and opened the webmail. I let out a sigh of relief to find that no one had written a nasty letter. After logging out, I went to the bedroom and put on a pair of jogging shorts and t-shirt.

I went for a run and collapsed on a chair upon my return.

"It's good to see that you're returning to your old self," Aaron said.

"Thanks. Do you work? Who's my bodyguard?" I got up and went for a drink of water.

"It'll have to be Max. Your grandparents will be coming out for a time, also," Aaron said.

"Okay. I'm going to shower and get ready," I said.

I hurried down the hallway and jumped into the shower. I'd hoped Aaron would be with me all day, but understood that he had a job, too. Max wasn't much as a bodyguard, as he always had his head in his work, or was smoking outside. ON the other hand, he didn't hover over me like Grandma.

After sharing a quick breakfast of toast and orange juice, Aaron and I said our 'goodbyes', and parted for the day. I drove rather than walked, because I felt it safer, and parked right beside Max's truck. As soon as I entered the back door of the store, I felt like someone had invaded my space.

"Hello." I whispered, making sure the door locked behind me. Straight ahead, the countertop looked fine, nothing seemed out of place. The floor needed more sweeping, but that was a normal occurrence when Max carved in here. I decided that I was creeping myself out and walked in. The rest of the room looked as it should, and I felt relieved. I placed my bag in its usual place and continued a slow scan of the room. All the boxes were in line and nothing appeared to have shifted.

I walked into the showroom and stood near the entrance and studied the room. Nothing was out of position, nor looked different or out of the ordinary. I took a deep breath and made my usual rounds of the display tables. I straightened and rearranged a few items, but I always did that. By the time I got to the door, it seemed as if all was well. It was too soon to open the shop, and I decided to use the time to check my email. I went to the sales counter and sat down behind the computer. I heard a noise once again from the basement, but remembered the women making quilts down there, making made me feel better.

I opened the cash drawer and began counting. I made out the deposit, and smiled. Each month, the sales outdid the previous month. Looking at the clock, I realized that I had time to make the deposit and return before the store was due to open. I sent a message to Max, telling him what I was doing, then left.

Since the bank was just down the block, my errand only took a few minutes, but upon my return, I felt the same eerie feeling when I entered the store earlier. I shrugged it off and checked my messages on the computer. Max hadn't answered, which was odd.

I sat by the computer and gave him a call. When he didn't answer within a few rings, I raced out the back door and up the outside steps to his apartment and pounded on the door. I had a key since I owned the building, and let myself in, calling, "Max! Max!"

I found him on the floor and when I placed my nose next to his mouth, it smelled metallic or different, definitely not food. He was unresponsive when I checked for a pulse. Immediately I called the emergency line, and then began resuscitation. I hoped it was doing some good. Within a matter of minutes, an ambulance crew invaded the small apartment with their gurney and other equipment. As they carried him out the door, I followed. Aaron and the detectives had just parked out front.

"What happened?" Aaron asked, rushing toward me.

"I think he's been poisoned. Not sure." I bit back tears. "When will this end?"

He pulled me close. "We'll wait right here, and when they want us, we'll go together."

I nodded, curling my fists from anger. I'd like to slug the person who did this to Max. After a few minutes, Detective Mergens walked toward us. I stood up, holding Aaron's hand. "How's he doing?"

"Too soon," he said. "Come on inside and tell me what you touched."

"I'm coming with her," Aaron steered me in front and we followed the detective.

Once inside the apartment, I said, "Really, besides opening the door and administering CPR, I didn't touch anything. I knew as soon as I saw him that he looked like Gina had."

"Did you see anything unusual?"

Noticing a bottled water, I said, "Max usually doesn't walk around drinking coffee, and I didn't leave any here. This is too weird."

Mergens picked up the bottle with care, and placed it in an evidence bag. "We'll have it analyzed."

I slumped onto the bed. "I wonder how he's doing?"

"He'll be fine." Aaron hugged me. His cell phone chirped and he broke away to answer it. "I'll let her know." He sat beside me and clasped my hand. "Max is starting to come around."

"Finally some good news." Mergens took a deep breath. He looked at Erlandsen. "Have Ida Gray brought in for questioning." When Erlandsen left the room, Mergens asked me, "What about about the threat you received at the airport. Anything more to add?"

"Someone came from behind, and said that it was my second warning. The third one is fatal. Something like that." I shivered. I told him my reasons for being at the airport and noticing someone my height with red springy hair and wearing a uniform, but was unable to learn any more. "Thank heavens it's working out for Max. I shouldn't have left Gina, then maybe she'd be alive, too."

"It's all coming to a head. Whoever it is, is getting bolder. But so far, they haven't made a major slip-up. Maybe the next time."

"I'd like to set a trap. Last night I found a note once belonging to Edith Roosevelt. I'd like to put news of it on the website." I thought. "I won't state verbatim what's on it. I'll make something up, of course."

"Too risky."

"Well, okay." In my mind, my fingers crossed. I smiled. "Can I leave? I'd like to get back to my store. I'm sure Grandma and Grandpa will be with me until closing."

"Go ahead."

Aaron walked me out and back to the store where I sat in the workroom, where my grandparents found me five minutes later.

"What a nightmare. He's going make it, isn't he?" Grandma said. I knew that Grandma meant Max.

"Yes, he'll be fine."

"Wow!" She held her hand to her chest. "What a relief!"

"I'm going to leave now." Aaron looked me square in the eyes. "You are only to eat or drink something store-bought.

Don't eat or drink anything anyone brings. I don't like where this is all going." He squeezed my hands. "Do you understand?"

"Yes." I nodded. "I'll follow orders."

"Good." He kissed my forehead and stood up. "I'll call or text you as often as possible."

Grandma took to straightening the workroom and we chased Grandpa out to bring back sandwiches and beverages to tide us over until closing time. I went out front and sat at the computer. Aaron contacted me every half-hour to make sure I was okay. Police patrol officers stopped by several times through the day. I didn't expect to hear much more that day, so I was surprised when Erlandsen stepped inside the store.

"What's going on?" I asked. "Any news about Max?"

"We don't have much to hold Ida Gray on, and she, of course, denies it all."

"Maybe someone brought it up to his apartment?"

"Anything's possible." He shrugged. "Do you know if he's spoke with anyone lately that ticked him off? Trouble with customers?"

"I've no idea. Beats me why anyone would try and harm Max. He's a great employee and trusted friend." I blew my nose. "I don't understand any of this." As we talked, I realized that it was up to me to bring this to an end. They'd find the drugs, but the problem wouldn't be solved. The killer would still be after the source. I believed it was a land title and still in TR's possession but this person was still unable to discover its whereabouts. The person could easily get out on bail and come searching for it or else have other family members do it for him.

The detectives left, leaving me alone with Grandma. Grandpa returned with food and left with a promise of returning at the end of the day to pick her up. A customer came in and Grandma helped by answering questions. I went ahead and posted a message on my website stating that I'd found a new letter from Edith Roosevelt. I made certain to not mention its contents except that it was addressed to Alice.

Once the customer left, I looked up at the clock and knew Grandpa would soon arrive. "I'm going to pop popcorn and watch a movie. Aaron will be home about seven or eight at the latest. He's pulling an extra shift because they're short men."

"I suppose everyone wants a vacation this time of year, and this is what happens. It's unfortunate that it's now, right when you need him the most." Grandma stood by me at the sales counter. "We'll be in tomorrow and every day until this mess is resolved."

"It's as complicated as the other two mysteries." I reached for the phone. "I'll call the hospital."

"No, dear. The hospital is busy enough without having to answer telephone calls about patients. Aaron will keep you updated."

I replaced the receiver. "I suppose that you're right." At that moment, Grandpa parked out front and honked. I gave Grandma a kiss and she waved as she left. I felt like crying like a baby now that I was alone, but knew that wouldn't solve my problems. I locked the front door and headed to the back workroom where I retrieved my bag.

As I walked out to the car, I felt glad that I'd driven and not walked. I certainly never expected a day like today. I started the car and drove toward home, debating whether to drive through the Establishment's parking lot. My curiosity got the better of me, and I decided to do it. I looked carefully for out of state license plates and found one from Florida. There was nothing about the other cars to catch my attention, so I continued my drive home.

Once inside of our house, I made sure all the doors and windows were locked before shedding my clothes and getting comfortable in a pair of shorts and t-shirt. I microwaved a bag of popcorn, grabbed a bottle of soda and sat down in front of the TV. I remembered what Aaron had said about being careful about I ate. Both the popcorn and soda hadn't been opened before, and came directly from the supermarket.

I found an old movie, *Arsenic and Old Lace*,". I usually enjoy watching this movie, but, funny as it was, it reminded me too much of my current situation. I gave up on television and went to my laptop, and checked my e-mail. One message caught my attention immediately. It was from Bambi. It said: *Liv, haven't seen anyone. Harry was reportedly home one day with the flu. Don't know anything else. Keep me informed. Bambi.*

I responded with another question, *What about Sunflower?*

I closed out and ate the rest of my popcorn, peeking out from behind the closed drapes at Gina' house. I figured that it was locked up tighter than a steel drum, now that the police were involved. On one hand, that was a relief, but on the other, I would've liked another walk through of the house. My thoughts circled back to the impersonators and their websites. The only for sure known facts was that Ida was Harry and Sunflower's mother, they lived in Medora near the National Park, and that Harry was a Ranger and lived on a ranch.

I tried to remember the harsh words that was spoke between those two at the beginning of the exposition, but couldn't. I recalled that they stood quite a distance from where I stood. It had surprised me that they hadn't treated Gina warmer or acted as if they were related. If not knowing any better, I would've thought they were squabbling.

Gina and Bambi were good friends. Bambi had been helpful in my search. Ida wanted something right from the start. She hadn't wanted to raise suspicions so she'd asked me to walk through the house and search for the books. As a neighbor and the person who found Gina's body, she figured that I'd be above suspicion.

Gina was diabetic. Her medication must've speeded the reaction to the drug otherwise it would've caused Max's immediate death. I believed it was his strong constitution that had kept him alive. Was the lawyer who died a diabetic or in poor health? I tried a quick search of him, but got what I expected—no information. I sent another message to Bambi and asked if she knew if he'd been sick or on medication.

I started to clean up my mess when Aaron walked in the door.

"Thank heavens you're home."

"Good news. The detectives are narrowing it down."

"So am I."

I peeked out the window just as the same car that had circled outside of Grandma's, drove past on our street and stopped, at the far end of the block.

"Aaron? I think, you need to come here and look—someone has us under surveillance."

Chapter Twenty-Four

"You're kidding!" Aaron hurried over to my side.

"See?" I said. "It's the same car I saw by Grandma's."

"I'm calling for a squad car to check it out," Aaron said.

I watched as he called the precinct.

"A squad car will come by every hour on the hour," he said after disconnecting.

"Good. I feel safer," I said. "Now, It's time for us to get going."

During the drive to work, Aaron told me that Ida was questioned and released. The photos I'd taken from her bathroom cabinet couldn't be used against her since they weren't lawfully obtained. The contents of the water bottle will be released sometime today. I crossed my arms and clamped my jaw tight, and stared out the side window.

I didn't say anything until we'd parked and climbed from the car. "I have to be dead before they find evidence, is that it?"

"Don't worry." Aaron tried to grab my arm, but I broke away. "We're watching her. She won't do this again. She's on our radar."

"Not good enough." I chased ahead, letting myself inside the door. Aaron stayed close behind, but I ignored him. I set my bag down, and walked around him and headed toward the showroom. "I've got work to do."

"So do I." Aaron stayed right with me. "How about if I go down to the corner and buy us a bagel and coffee, then we can sit and talk this out?"

"Okay." I plopped down on the chair by the computer and stared over at the houses. "Ladies, if anyone sneaks in here, let me know!"

I looked back at the blank screen. Frowning, I listened as the back door opened and closed as Aaron left. He had certainly taken his time. I needed to know about Max. I dialed the hospital number. "Please pass me through…" I heard the floor squeak, and I turned—gasped—dropping the phone. "Oh my God!"

"How dare you get Gina to legally grant you the right to value her antiques? How dare you? You conniving little thief! It should all have gone to me!" Ida wagged a small pistol right at me, inching closer. "Sic'ing the cops on me like that." The closer she came, the fire in her eyes burned brighter. "You were supposed to drink that—you thief."

"She asked me to look after her historical items and so forth! I have a legal document!"

"Another reason to kill you!"

"You're crazy!" I stared at the end of the pistol. At that angle, and that close, it looked like a cannon. I glanced around the room, hoping to see something to throw. I remembered Aaron saying something about keeping the crazies engaged. "Tell me."

"The deed. It was supposed to be right here in the purse— Edith gave it to Alice," Ida said.

"Who gave what to whom?" I noticed that a heavy set of pliers on the floor. Max must have left them there when he was assembling a house for me. I plunked down on the chair. "Explain." Keeping my eyes locked on hers, I tried to maneuver the pliers with my feet for easy access.

"No more talk," Ida said.

I ducked as she aimed. Grabbing the pliers, I sat up quickly and threw them as hard as possible. They hit her right on the shoulder, and the gun went off. The shot went wild. I ran toward her, knocking her down just as Aaron raced into the room.

"What in the-- ?" Aaron dropped the coffees, bagel bag, and joined in. We soon had her in handcuffs.

"Now do you have enough?" I asked, with my hands on my hips. I marched over to Ida, and raised my hand to slap her. She cowered. I lowered my hand. "That's what you ought to get." I turned on my heel and walked away.

I went into the workroom and sat down. My heart raced while my head felt as if it was spinning. I wanted to lie down and sleep for an eternity as my thoughts spun in circles. I couldn't get it out of my mind that she hadn't worked alone. Was Harry her partner? Was Sunflower involved? I closed my eyes for a few minutes before going after the mop and cleaning up the floor. I ignored Ida, who was slumped on the floor, her handcuffs fastened to a heavy shelf.

Aaron sat near the computer talking on his phone, probably either to his sergeant or Tim, his patrol partner. I finished mopping and placed the dirty mop in the back room.

"Tim and Maggie are coming over for a barbecue. We're locking this place up after Ida's out of here." His concerned eyes warmed me. "You're not staying here today. There's too much going on." He raised my chin and ducked his head to kiss me.

"Okay." We embraced and I stayed in the workroom. I picked up a nearby magazine and thumbed through it. I heard the front door open and familiar voices, the detectives. Soon another set of voices, unfamiliar, wafted to me, and I figured they were from the patrol officers. Ida hollered, "Thief!" as they took her away, and that's the last I heard from her, much to my relief. Still, I couldn't resist asking, "she gone?" when Aaron came in.

"Yes, the officers took her away," Detective Erlandsen said, coming in behind Aaron. "How about a statement, and then we'll go?"

"Sure." I told him what had happened and he wrote it down.

"Is that all?" I asked when I'd finished.

"Yes. A team will soon come to remove the bullet." I nodded. "Good. You two can leave soon."

"That was Alice Roosevelt's gun so she must have had the purse since they were together. She probably stole the TR figurine from Inga, too. I'm glad that our jingle dancer is safe with you guys and the grass bowl. Will they be returned soon?"

"We're waiting for the case to close." He nodded, and left me alone with Aaron.

"I feel sick and want to go home, right now," I stated. "I'm glad that's over and done."

"These people are crazy." Aaron sat opposite me. "Tim and Maggie will meet us back at our house."

It didn't take too long before the detectives found the bullet and picked up a few other odd pieces of evidence. We locked up the store when they left and went home. Aaron suggested a short stop at the hospital where we found Max asleep, but doing well. We wrote him a short note, and left.

I smiled once our house came into view. Maggie and Tim wouldn't come for another hour so I curled up in bed. All sorts of thoughts went around in my head as I tried to make sense of the turmoil that had just happened. The ringing phone brought me out of myself, and I answered.

"Hi Grandma."

"I need to know if you're okay?" I nodded, and I'd swear she saw me. "You're not hurt?" I shook my head. "Since you're doing fine, I'll hang up."

"Tim and Maggie are coming out."

"Don't let them stay long. You need your sleep."

"Yes, Grandma." We disconnected. I placed the phone down and rolled over. *The woman knows everything. How does she do that?* I slept another few minutes, and felt better. I met Aaron in the kitchen.

"You're not going to believe this, but Marie ordered chicken wings, deep fried mushrooms, and some other things from the nearby restaurant for Tim to pick up on the way over here. The woman's unbelievable." He shrugged. "She's a wonderful Grandma. I wish that I'd had a grandma just like her when I was growing up."

"We already share her."

"She reads minds."

I poured myself a glass of cold water and stood by the sink, looking out. "I'm going to sit outside and read a book until they get here."

"Best news I've heard yet."

We kissed and I went to change clothes. I put on a pair of shorts and another T-shirt. I found the book I had begun before the expo, and took it with me outside. The fresh air and sunshine instantly put me to sleep. I woke to the sound of Maggie's voice.

"Should have known she'd be sleeping." Maggie held out a glass, I sat up and took it. "Drink up! I picked up two bottles on the way, and by the time we stopped for the food--, well it took forever!"

"To us!" I cheered, clinking our two glasses together. The men arrived, each carrying styrofoam containers that they set the on the table.

"We're going to enjoy this day!"

"I hope. It sure didn't start out so hot." I sipped from my glass and reached for a toothpick to stab a mushroom. "We need plates."

"Forgot." Aaron rushed away and we dove into the food.

The afternoon passed by and soon we were sitting in front of the TV watching a movie. When it finished, we sat around and talked about all the events that happened lately. A few more beers hit the spot. It was close to midnight before they left and we headed off to bed.

"Got any plans for tomorrow?" Aaron asked. "I'm going to mow the lawn."

"I'm going to finish putting thing back in order, but I also want to keep an eye on Gina's house. I want to see who comes and goes, if anyone."

"Try not to think about it."

"Just wondering when it'll be put on the market." I gave him a kiss and rolled over. I tried to tell myself that I wasn't being a snoop, that there really was an unknown clue in the house. There had to be motive for Ida to want me dead. Did she act alone?

I woke in the morning to the phone ringing, and answered, "Hello." When no one responded, I hung up. After slipping on my slippers, I shuffled into the bathroom to shower. Aaron was already outside mowing. I dressed and went to the kitchen. When I saw him wheeling the lawn mower into the shed, I began scrambling eggs, and dished them up as he entered.

Aaron had a few errands to run and I wasn't to let anyone in the house and to stay indoors with the doors closed and locked. Personally, I itched for one last walk through Gina's. I hadn't been inside since before they packed some things up, and then it was a peek.

"You're not to go to Gina's. Understood?"

"You read minds too?" I fumed. "What is with you people? I'm not a child!"

"I know you too well."

I stomped off toward the back room where I had a few more things to finish folding and returning to their correct drawers. It saddened me that my Mary Lincoln dress had been bunched up, and I didn't want to think about the mess made of the pantaloons and hoops plus the corsets. They were a tangled mess.

I set about straightening and fixing messes and arranging it all, carrying all of the period dresses down to the basement and placing them in a storage wardrobe. I liked to have First Ladies days when I would dress in the featured First Lady period style clothes. The customer enjoyed it. However, I tried to not do the earlier First Ladies frequently because of the difficult styles of clothes. The corsets squeezed my breath out from me, and who can move wearing a hoop?

I needed a breather and sat and read my book for a little while, enjoying the story. It was from the *White House Chef* mystery series by Julie Hyzy. I enjoyed her novels since they were about the White House, and complemented my First Ladies White House dollhouses. After I finished reading it, and then looked online for messages, but Bambi hadn't replied yet. On the business webmail, there were two short comments. They read: *Are you sure it's from Edith Roosevelt? She's been dead a long time.* The next message read: *Where was it hidden? You need to give it back to the family. It's too valuable to keep for yourself. It belongs to history. Thief!* I wondered if Ida hadn't sent the message? I cringed.

Even though Aaron was home, I felt frightened. The phone rang once more without a response when I answered. Grandma called a number of times. Aaron came and went on his errands during the afternoon. Every time he left the house, I shivered. I kept all curtains closed and the television blaring so that anyone who came to the door would know that someone was home and wouldn't try to break-in.

Late that afternoon, Aaron asked if I wanted to go with him down to the station where he had to go over a report. I declined. I feared going in there. Feared seeing that woman even though I knew she was locked up in another facility.

"I'm not ready to face people at the moment."

I went back to straightening up, and decided it was time to face the world by opening the drapes and curtains. I turned the television sound lower, and didn't think anymore about being alone. I was relieved, however, when Maggie called.

"I'm doing fine," I told her. "Aaron had to go and make out a report. He'll be back a little later."

"Do you need company?"

"The doors are locked. I'm not letting anyone in." I hesitated, and said, "What's odd is that it doesn't seem like Ida worked alone. I wish it was wrapped up."

"I know, but it's best to be careful until they're sure they have the right person and that she acted alone."

"I know." We disconnected, and I got busy once again. Finally, the kitchen was as I liked it. Aaron had switched a few drawers around, now they were back in their rightful places. A dog barked out back, and the neighbor guided it by leash across and over to his yard. It was a peaceful day until the front door bell rang. I jumped and looked out the room window peering at the figure in front of the door. I took in the tall, brown uniform of a man. It reminded me of a Ranger's uniform. I gulped. The doorbell buzzed once again. I decided another look was necessary. I went to another window and chanced a closer look, and saw a delivery truck parked two houses down. I opened the door.

"Yes? We didn't order anything."

"You know the Olson's?" He nodded toward the house two doors down. "Would you sign for this, and then I'll leave a note for where their package is."

"Sure." I signed, and accepted the small package and he left. I closed and locked the door, and then watched from the window as his delivery truck drove away. I set the package on a nearby table, and stared across the street. *Now's the time.*

I grabbed my phone and keys, locking the door behind me. I ran across the street and around to the backyard. I felt confident that I wouldn't be seen since few children were out front playing. At the back door of Gina's house, I glanced around me before trying to turn the doorknob with my hand covered by my shirttail. When it didn't open, I felt above the doorframe for a key and also under the flowerpots with wilting flowers. Then I picked up a stone, found a key, and tried it in the lock.

The door lock popped open, and I quickly entered. I slipped the key into my pocket for easy access in case I needed to come back. I took the time to open and close the cupboard doors, finding them empty. I opened all closet doors and found them all empty of items. I didn't know what to look for, but continued onward. In the bathroom, I took the time to open the cabinet and found that room devoid of items, also. I was ready to give up my notion of finding a clue when I ran across a small doll box, and opened the lid. It held trinkets. I let myself out and went back to my house to look through the box.

Chapter Twenty-Five

As I sat going through the small items, I wondered how to explain them to Aaron, and then he walked in, and I found I couldn't say anything.

Aaron put his hands on his hips as he surveyed the scene. Me at the table with the open box in front of me. "You went over there, didn't you?" He sat beside me on the sofa. "Tell me that you didn't break a window. Tell me that you found a key and entered."

"A key under a rock." I shrugged. "This box sat on a bed-room floor. It's like it slipped from someone's pile and they forgot to go back for it."

"What all do we have here?"

"Actually, I just opened it up." I lifted a tiny candlestick holder and stared at it. "Was this for a kid or what?"

"Probably for the top of a baby's dresser or rocker-, or back of the commode." He took it and held it to the late afternoon light. Setting it down, he asked, "What else?"

"Old granny buttons, thimbles." I set them aside, deciding to sort through the pieces as we looked. "An old pair of spectacles similar to Teddy Roosevelt's." I started another pile with them. "A cigarette holder. A rather long one, like Franklin Roosevelt's." I placed them next to the spectacles. "Nothing is of consequence from what I can tell. How about you?"

"Look at this old photograph. You can barely make out the people, it's so old and grainy."

"Oh my." We both studied it against the light. "You're not thinking the same as me, are you?"

"It's got to be," Aaron said. "Teddy Roosevelt standing in front of his cabin with Edith beside him."

"Yes, with little Alice between them and look at what she's holding." I pointed to the spot. "The jingle dancer." My eyes opened wider. "Look at this closer. Doesn't it look like Edith is holding a sheet of paper? The picture is so grainy that all I see clearly is a big stamp on it. I wonder if it is the deed she's holding?"

"Let's look at the deed in the freezer."

"This calls for a celebration! We've made a break-through."

"You have. A breakthrough to what, though?"

"You get the sodas. I'll get the letter. Let's hope that the picture letter is the same."

We did a hip dance in the kitchen while Aaron poured the beverages and I fetched the letter from the freezer. "Call the station. Tell them you're coming for the figurine and books."

"Yes, ma'am." He set his filled glass back into the refrigerator.

I hurried to the living room with the letter, sitting down and taking a sip of my drink. The sun hid behind the trees. I hesitated opening the letter since it was cold. I left it on the coffee table and decided to take in a shower to the pass the time until his return.

As I walked from the bedroom after putting on my jammies, I walked back to my place in the living room. I figured it wouldn't be much longer. No sooner had I flipped through the stations and found a suitable program, when the garage door opened and Aaron walked inside, calling out, "I'm back!"

"I'm in here!" I reached for the letter, removing it from the baggie. "Bring a clean towel, too!"

When Aaron strode into the room, he handed me the towel and set the figurine down in front of me. "I'll unwrap it. Give me a sec."

As he slowly removed it from the package and I spread the towel out, we looked at each other and smiled. "We're soon over this ordeal," I said.

"I hope you're right," Aaron said. "The books, too."

I removed the letter and reread it. "'*Don't forget the cookie jar.*'" I set it back on the towel. "That's all it says on the letter."

"How strange," Aaron said.

"Let's take a closer look at the figurine."

"To have the deed hidden inside of this china doll, is crazy." Aaron shook his head. "This all seems highly unlikely that a land title is inside of this thing." He held it up. "It's not chipped at all." Slowly he turned it, holding it up against the light. "There's nothing here except the blanket symbol."

I took it from him and did the same thing. "It's such a small symbol, too. Hand painted. Straight lines." I set it down. "Interesting." I picked up the photo. "Blanket—blanket—see it? See the connection?" I jumped up. "That's it! The blanket!"

"Honey, the blanket is wool, probably. Moth ridden. Probably destroyed or long gone. We're at the end of the line." He scratched his chin whiskers. "That's my opinion."

"I don't believe that. We don't know." I picked up the figurine again and gave it a last inspection. "Nothing drilled into the bottom, either." I placed the letter back inside the envelope and plastic bag before placing the figurine inside another baggie. "These are going into the freezer. I'm putting the bread, and frozen veggies in front of it."

"All right." Aaron picked up the remote control.

In the kitchen, I hid the items and picked up Aaron's bottle of soda from the fridge before returning to the living room. We each sipped from a full glass and I retrieved my laptop and checked the business webmail plus my personal e-mail account. Finally, Bambi responded. She said that Harry had been gone somewhere for a couple days, but she didn't know where. She didn't know about Sunflower. I replied, and asked if she had knowledge about a blanket in the TR cabin, which he may have kept. I sent the message and hoped for an instant response. I reasoned that if he'd kept the blanket, then it would mean something to him, and in that case, it may be part of the museum's inventory. I hoped that would be the answer.

"Bambi responded. Harry's been out of town, but she doesn't know about Sunflower."

"Did you ask about the attorney? If he was poisoned?"

"No."

"I wonder if Mergens knows that?" He reached for his phone and sent a message.

"Ida's still in jail, right?"

"Right."

I was certain that without me, the mystery wouldn't get solved. Positive. I sent another message to Bambi and asked if she knew anything about a figurine or grass bowl, then set the laptop aside to watch the movie. We curled up and watched John Wayne knock down cowboys and shove them into jail or shoot down a crook. Before going to bed, I checked my e-mail and reluctantly, logged out and shut it down for the night.

I was safe and warm. Ida was in jail, and I didn't have a worry, so I fell asleep. I woke during the night to a car door slamming and looked out. The neighbor girl dashed to her house and went inside. I crawled back to bed, sleeping until morning.

After rising early, I went for a morning run, upon returning home, I showered and made ready for the day. Aaron drove me to work, then left right away to pick Max up from the hospital.

While the computer hummed to life, I strolled around the display tables, straightening things and doing my usual tidy chores. Sitting by the computer, I checked the webmail, and someone responded to the letter notice, stating—*it belongs to the TR estate. Give it back.* By the time I'd checked my personal e-mail, I heard the back door open.

"Hey you," I called, stepping out from my place. "How are you?" I met Max in the workroom, sitting on his usual perch. "Finally, I feel like this place is back to normal."

"I'm happy to be here, that's for sure." Max grinned. "I must tell you, though. This has got to quit, or I will."

"You're blaming me for this happening?" Crushed, I collapsed on a stool.

"No. Well, maybe I am." He scratched his whiskers. "It was meant for you. Just like the other time. It was because of you."

"You can't blame me for this!"

"Listen. I'm going to bed. We'll talk more later." Puzzled, I watched him walk out, and stared at his back.

"I hadn't expected that." I looked at Aaron. "It's not my fault."

"It's no one's. He'll see that after he's had a decent rest."

"I hope so."

I turned toward my sewing and started stitching up more inaugural gowns for the various First Ladies. Once I got going, it didn't take long to stitch the seams, what took the time was the hand stitching of lace and buttons, which covered the snaps that I'd also sewn onto the fabric. Making the button holes I'd found were quite hard to do because the fabric pinched and since the costume was miniature, it added to the problem. Aaron read through a magazine as I sewed, and ever so often, he'd move to the showroom to keep watch. I sighed, knowing how much I appreciated his presence. I stayed focused, and forced myself to ignore Max and his threat to quit. I'm not sure how to cope without having him around. He did so much.

I should've heard back from prospective employees from the ad, which I'd placed last week. With the unemployment rate high, I thought someone would've applied by now. When Aaron called my name, I called, "Just a minute!"

I hiked out to the showroom, and saw him speaking to an older gentleman and young woman, and all three stood near the World War II White House. I walked over to them, and said, "Hi. I'm Liv. Like the house?"

"It brings back memories, ma'am. Your husband was just telling me about the house and how it's all set up for Franklin. Very accommodating. Eleanor sure looked after him, making sure that the hallways were made wider when he'd visit the storage area. Another tray was added also for him to use for writing. The staff worked around him, and made sure everything was convenient for him."

"What fascinating thing can you tell me about First Lady Roosevelt?" the young lady asked. "Something that Grandpa may not know?"

"That she once flew with Amelia Earhart." I smiled when her eyes opened wider. "Isn't that fun to know?"

"Yes. I can tell my teacher."

"I'll take it," the gentleman stated. "It's for my lovely bride of fifty-two years. This is our last grandchild after nine children."

"How sweet." I looked over to Aaron, who slightly blushed.

"I'll get the boxes."

"Let's get it all rung up." They followed me to the checkout counter where I rung up the sale and took care of the paper work. Since Max already had several boxed, it didn't take long for Aaron to return. He helped carry them out while I went for all the furnishings. Within an hour, we had it all loaded and the happy customers left.

"That felt good," I chimed. "I needed a sale. It's been slow and then after the few hours of hell from the other day with Ida."

"I know."

I took a moment to check through my e-mail and Bambi had responded. She said that there had been a beautiful blanket in the cabin, but was not sure where it's now located. She didn't know anything about a figurine or a grass bowl. I told her, 'thanks', and logged out of the account.

"Bambi remembers a blanket, but not a figurine or grass bowl."

"Okay," Aaron shrugged. "You don't mind walking home, do you? It should be safe. Nothing should happen. Ida's in custody."

"You're right. We don't really know if she acted alone, but the police don't have any other lead."

"Now, you're right in line with me." He removed his key from his pocket and started the car by remote.

"I'll see you at home."

After kissing, he left. I toured the houses once more before going to the back workroom and started to remove furnishings for another FDR house. When I'd checked the inventory list to make sure I had all items, I labeled and boxed them up and stacked it. The store phone rang, and I went to answer.

"Hello. First Lady Dollhouse store. How may I help you?" The heavy breathing made me weary, and I replaced the phone receiver in its cradle. Instantly, it rang again. "Hello." I tentatively said, "How may I help you?" I replaced the receiver. I stared at it for quite a while, holding my breath. I convinced myself to take several deep breaths. I thought of calling Aaron, but wasn't sure if it was anything worth being scared about.

I wanted to make sure that Max felt better, so I called him.

"Did you sleep? How do you feel?"

"Don't mind me at all, Liv. I'm doing fine. I'm just tired and worn-out."

"No quitting?"

"Nope. I'm happy. I could use a raise after this, and help. Anyone answer the ad?"

"Not yet. It just came out. Sold an Eleanor Roosevelt."

"Good. I'll get on it tomorrow."

"Night."

As I prepared to lock up, I kept thinking about the phone call and decided to text Aaron about it. Afterwards, I headed out the back door and began walking toward home. At the corner stop light, I glanced over toward the store and felt comforted at seeing it. I continued walking toward home.

A small mom-and-pop lay just up ahead, and I stepped inside and purchased a bottle of water. Standing by the counter, I glanced outside and noticed a familiar looking car, but thought nothing of it. After taking a swallow, I stepped out and began my journey home. At the next light, while I stood waiting for it to change, I noticed the same car only it was coming from the side street.

My palms began sweating, and my heart beat harder. I started walking faster. At the first opportunity, I slipped inside the door of a local second-hand shop. I pretended to search through clothes racks near a window, but off to the side. I noticed the same car, but still couldn't make out the driver because of the sun always in my eyes.

I stayed inside the store for quite awhile. I hadn't planned to buy anything but felt guilty after awhile because the clerk kept looking over at me. I found a pair of shorts my size and went up to the counter, purchasing them. I figured by now that this person had lost sight of me so I walked out into the sunshine.

The car wasn't in view, and I easily continued my walk. I held tight to my purchase and finished drinking my water. As I drew near to the Establishment, I walked down and around to see if the car had parked, but didn't find it. Relieved, I continued. At the following corner, Aaron texted back, stating that he was on his way home. As I walked, I sent him a message telling him I was almost home, too.

At the corner of our street, I hurried to our house and quickly entered. Once inside, I made sure that the door was locked behind me. I dropped my belongings on the counter, went out to the living room, and watched out the window as the same car drove past...

Chapter Twenty-Six

That does it. I stayed lower than the windows, went back to our bedroom and slipped into darker shaded clothing. Armed with my phone, which had a camera, plus a table knife and house keys, I headed out the backdoor. Once in the patio area, I sneaked to the side of the house and hurried to a vantage point behind a large shrub. I silently praised Grandma for planting it, and keeping it watered. The car had moved, and now was parked further down and near the main road. I wondered how to reach it without being discovered. The man's profile still was unrecognizable. I decided to inch my way closer with hopes of taking a picture of the license plate.

The best way to accomplish my goal was to cross through neighboring yards. I hurried to the other side of our house, and crossed through the yards easily until coming to the very last one, which was fenced. I took a chance and stayed down as I hiked the perimeter until coming closer. Once near, I leaned out from my hiding spot behind a large, old, oak tree and took the picture. I took several, then slipped the phone into my pocket.

I raced the same way back to my house, as I'd come. After fumbling with the keys, I entered and sat down to look at the images. "Yes, gotcha." I stared at them, but the man's face was unclear due to the sunshade and the windshield glare. Also, he was wearing sunglasses and was that the beginning of a beard on his chin?

Before getting up, I sent the images to Aaron along with a brief message explaining them. Afterwards, I took a drink and retrieved the letter and figurine from the freezer, setting the items on the living room coffee table. I headed to the back room to get the plat book, Bible, and grammar book.

That's when I heard the unmistakable sound of the back door opening and closing. *I thought it was shut.* "Hello?" A chill went up and down my spine. "Aaron?" I took the knife from my pocket, and with sweaty fingers, held it tight. On tiptoe, I inched to the kitchen only to find that the back door was wide open. *I must not have shut it tight.* I locked it, and took a moment to open and close the broom closet door. Securing both doors, I made my way back to the living room and sat down.

As I held the figurine up for further scrutiny, the phone rang. I dropped the figurine and it landed on the cushion beside me. "Hello," I said but no one responded. Frowning, I set the phone aside and held up the figurine. The weight of it struck me as odd, I thought it would be heavier. Very carefully I studied each and every jingle bell as well as the painted cloth around the waistline and headband. The painted feathers, which were made to look like an eagle, were well done. The lines were perfect. The flowing dress and the lines painted for the skirt were made by a steady hand. I was impressed. Just a slight crack caught my attention. The only noticeable symbol was the blanket on the base. I set it aside and reached for the letter.

The handwriting certainly appeared a match to the samples given over the internet of Edith Roosevelt's. The broad strokes and steady hand making her loops were from a strong woman. I picked up the figurine again and compared the strokes from the writing with the paint strokes of the feathers and wondered if they were made by the same hand. I set the pair aside to give it further thought.

It couldn't have been Edith Roosevelt's handwriting in the in the grammar book, or was it? That made me wonder who wrote in the book? I wasn't any closer at figuring things out, but my ideas began to make sense.

The search led me right back to where I'd started and without a conclusion. My phone rang again, only this time the voice was Aaron.

"Hey! I'm stopping at the station to see if Ida has said anymore."

"All right. I'm looking up things, but can't seem to pinpoint anything worthwhile. I feel live I'm blowing in the wind."

"I'll try to be home soon."

We disconnected and I flipped through television stations until settling on another old movie featuring the Marx Brothers. I opened the Bible, and noticed notations concerns about property rights in the back of it where family members jotted tidbits about deceased relatives.

I stared at the television set until Aaron walked in the door with the plat book.

"Great! I want to compare handwriting. Take a look at the Bible and the page here in the grammar book."

"Why would someone write about the land deed in these two places? Because of Teddy Roosevelt?" Aaron said. "I have to go back to the station to write up a few reports. I'll be home in an hour. I had planned to take care of them in the morning, but no such luck. My sergeant told me he needed them asap."

"That's fine. I'm just going to sit here and look through the books. Maybe I can make some sense out of it all."

"All right, sweetheart." Aaron kissed me before he left.

I picked up the plat book and looked at it once again. I knew that the properties were adjoined, but didn't see why Ida would poison people over the deed.

Had Ida acted alone? Could she have really killed the lawyer plus Gina, and now almost killed Max? I was growing desperate. I typed in a search for the courthouse to obtain the County Treasurer phone number. Were they behind on taxes? As the monitor began displaying the links, I heard the floor squeak from behind.

A shadow flashed across the television screen.

I threw the laptop up and over my head, ducking at the same time as someone reached for my head. I grabbed one of the books and flung it at him as I rolled further from his grasp.

I didn't have time to scream as he reached further and grabbed my arm from behind the sofa. Soon he cornered me from the open area around the furniture, where I'd planned to make my escape.

"What do you want from me?" I scanned the surface of everything, looking for an instrument to throw or harm him with.

"I want that deed." He wore the uniform of a desperate man, dressed in worn-out jeans and T-shirt with a beer logo on the front. Whiskers covered his chin but behind his sunglasses, I saw the eyes of Harry.

"Why? And what deed are you talking about?" I hoped to keep him talking as I tried to think of what to do. "You did the poisoning, didn't you?"

"We aren't selling to no oil companies."

"Ahh! So that's what this is about. I thought so." I crossed my arms. "Oil and greed." I almost smiled. "What about Gina?"

"She wanted to sell it. The land was rightfully mine."

"How does Teddy Roosevelt fit into this?"

"Bought it back in the late 1800's, and never handed over the title. Great-Granddad paid full price, but the deed never showed."

I kept my eyes on his, and tried climbing over the sofa's back, but Harry reached out and grabbed my arm. Pulling me close, he tightened his grip by yanking my right arm to my back and making me face him. Instantly, the point of a knife pricked me under my chin.

"Ouch!" I wiggled, but the point went in further so I stopped.

"You're gonna tell me," he growled.

My right arm twisted, sending a sharp pain throughout my body. I screamed, and reached for the figurine. Immediately, I managed to hit him on the side of his head. The figurine slashed right next to his eye cutting him. Next the figurine dropped onto the hard table, and broke apart. A slip of paper shown through the pieces. We saw it at the same time, and his eyes opened wide. I bit into his hand and he let go immediately. We scrambled for the paper. I grabbed it, clenching it in my fist.

"Give it to me!" He jerked my arm and started prying my fingers apart.

"Ouch!" I brought my knee high, kicking him in the groin. "You're not going to get away with this." I clenched my teeth.

"That's it for you!"

He lurched after me as I raced toward the door. He grabbed for my arm, but I pulled away. "Oh no you don't!" I said. My prayers were soon answered when the garage door hummed open. "Aaron's home. Give yourself up!"

He rushed out the front door, with me hot on his heels as he ran toward his parked car.

"Aaron!" I called. "Get him!"

Aaron chased him, but Harry jumped into his car too fast. Aaron called it in with the license plate numbers as I stood beside him out of breath.

"They'll get him." Aaron placed his arm over my shoulder, and pulled me into his chest. "I'm here. I'm not going anywhere." I looked up at him. "Good grief. You're bleeding."

"Come back to the house. I'll show you what happened." Together we walked back to the house, and into the kitchen.

"I'm getting a bandage and some ointment for that cut. You'll have to see a doctor," Aaron said.

"It stings." I touched it with a tissue and looked at the blood, and frowned. "I've got to catch my breath," I said, sitting. Soon, he returned and wiped my sore and applied ointment and the bandage. "I feel better now. How about a glass of water?" I drew in a few quick breaths and drank from the full water glass he handed me. "Thanks."

"It was Harry, wasn't it?"

"Yes. The dirty bugger followed me all the way home, too." I sipped the cool water, and stared at the glass. "Yikes. Hopefully, they'll catch him soon." My heart pounded, and head throbbed. "He's after a deed."

"It's just as we thought." I watched him rub his chin. "We're one step ahead of him." He smiled. "Where is it?"

"Oh dear God." I jumped up and headed outside with Aaron right behind me. "I think it's out here somewhere. I know he didn't get it."

"The wind is blowing from the west." We stood in the middle of the street, scanning the boulevards. "I'll look on this side, you over there."

"Okay." I strode to my area and slowly combed the bushes, trees and flowers while Aaron did the same. My chin throbbed and my head hurt. I reached into a pocket for another tissue, and pulled out the crumpled ball of paper. "Found it!"

Aaron rushed toward me. "Where was it?"

"In my pocket. Must've forgot." I shrugged.

At the same moment, the detectives turned the corner and drove toward our house. We met them at the door.

"I found it." I smiled. "Got what he was looking for." I held it in my hand. "I'll explain inside."

"Huh?" Detective Erlandsen said, looking at me. "It's a crime scene, again. Let's enter from a different door."

"You're right." We stopped outside of the front door. "I think he must've entered through the kitchen garage door, not the back door leading to the patio. I remember hearing a noise, and checking it out and then locking it."

"What else?" Detective Mergens asked.

"He followed me home from work. I tried losing him by going inside various stores, but he'd always reappear." I waited a minute, then continued, "I did sneak over and take photos and sent them to Aaron."

"I showed them to you."

"Affirmative." Mergens looked at me. "Continue."

"He must've sneaked in the garage and then waited for me to take out these things." When he got a puzzled look, I said, "The books, figurine and letter."

"That's what you were doing?"

"Yes. The TV was on and I was looking through it all. He also must know my hiding place in the freezer."

At that moment, a squad car parked and the officers walked up to us.

"Secure the living room. Prints from the kitchen and garage door as well as the living room. I'll call the team. You don't touch a thing."

"You two stay right here," Mergens stated.

"Is it all right if we go to the patio and sit?" I asked.

"Of course."

Aaron and I walked around the house to the patio and sat, staring off into the distance. I still had the crumpled paper in my pocket, and brought it out. "I don't suppose the air is good for this, but neither are all the wrinkles." I waited for Aaron to brush the table top clean of dust. "Your shirt is clean, isn't it?"

"Don't we have towels in the basement?" Aaron got up. "I'll go and get one."

A shiver raced up and down my spine the moment he left my sight. I glanced around the yard, and searched the nearby yards for a glimpse of Harry. I wondered if he'd been caught? Fortunately, Aaron returned quickly.

"Do you know if Harry's been picked up?"

"Hold on." Aaron put in a call to his station.

I took the towel and spread it out, smoothing out all wrinkles. I removed the deed and carefully began the arduous chore of unfolding it. When he disconnected, I asked, "Have they?"

"No. They've got his house staked out and a few other choice places. Don't worry. He'll show up."

"Let's hope." I groaned inside. I didn't care for the turn of events. Harry could pop up at anytime and anyplace. I wasn't safe.

I switched my focus to the deed. Gradually, it spread before my eyes. "You can see how it was rolled and folded into the doll."

"Yes, but is it the deed? The paper's too small for that."

"Good point." We both studied it. "It's getting dark and that makes it harder to read it, but it almost seems like a treasure map."

"It has bullet points."

"Yes, like it should be checked off." It began with the grass bowl. "We've got the first. The second is the blanket symbol on the figurine." I read further down the list. "The cabin is emphasized."

"Which must be where it's located?"

"I believe so."

"We're due for a vacation after this escapade."

"It's not over with yet," I reminded him. "Harry needs to be behind bars."

"Let's plan one week from today for a road trip out to the Theodore Roosevelt National Park." Aaron's eyes glistened. "Sound good?"

"You betcha." That man had better be behind bars, I thought, as I rolled the letter inside the towel beside the photo.

It took another forty minutes or more before we were allowed back into the house. The mosquitoes were making a nuisance of themselves, and I was happy when we walked back in. The detectives were just wrapping it up, and we sat down by the kitchen table. I reached for my half-empty glass of water, and topped it off.

"Walk us through what happened," Erlandsen said. "We've had fingerprints lifted from the doors, including the broom closet where he must have hidden. Anyplace else in this room?"

"I don't believe so." I finished my water. "We weren't in here together. I had removed the freezer items and brought them into the living room, as well as the books from the back room. The entire skirmish happened in that room. We heard the garage door open—he had his hand on my arm and yanked me closer before that happened—I took the moment to knee-kick him in the groin. That gave me the chance to break free."

"When did he try and get the paper?"

"Oh yeah. I also knocked him over the head with the figurine once I'd kneed him. It broke from landing on the table. He reached for it at the same time—then the garage door went up, and he chased out the door with me behind him."

"He got in the car before I could jump him," Aaron finished the story.

"Right," I agreed. "Any news about him?"

"No, not yet." Mergens shook his head. "The team will make another sweep in the morning. I suggest you two hit the sack, and we'll call."

"Good night." Erlandsen made for the door. "We'll be in touch."

Once all the policemen and the two detectives left us alone, we took the advice and got ready for bed. Neither of us had eaten, so we cooked up an omelet before going to bed. Aaron was sound asleep when my head hit the pillow. I'd first showered and checked all the windows and doors-twice-before jumping into the sack.

Sometime during the night, I heard a strange noise, like voices yelling. I reached for Aaron but found his spot empty. I slid my feet into slippers, and cautiously walked down the hallway, following the voices. I stopped at the top of stairs where Aaron's and Harry's voices became louder.

I grabbed the frying pan from the stove, and began climbing down the stairs when there was a sudden crash of broken bottles. Aaron groaned. My eyes focused in the dim light coming through the basement window. I inched further until at last reaching the bottom step.

"Give me the deed," Harry shouted. He had Aaron in a stronghold, and held a small weapon next to his throat.

"Oh no you don't!" I rushed straight at him and hit Harry on the head with the frying pan, causing him to collapse. Aaron regained his composure and took over subduing Harry.

"'Bout time you got here." He took the small gun which had dropped on the floor, and slipped it into his pocket. "Call it in, will you?"

"Can't you knock him on the head or something? He looks too alive." I left him to his devices and went upstairs and got his phone, and called it in.

I'd barely had time to put my robe on before the police returned. It seemed forever until they finally left.

"Case closed," Erlandsen stated on his way out the door.

"That's what you think."

At least to them, it was closed, but not to me.

Chapter twenty-seven

One week later

It didn't take long before we'd crossed the Minnesota border and entered North Dakota, on our way to the Theodore Roosevelt National Park. We'd thought about beginning our road trip with a drive through Yellowstone because it's our first National Park, but decided to head straight for TR Park after we discovered the land title map. Was it the land title deed or clues to finding the land title?

The very first place we stopped was at the Court House, only to discover that there wasn't a record of a deed sale on that parcel of land between Roosevelt and the County. Yes, he'd purchased the ranch land, which was recorded properly.

"I wonder what the cabin will tell us?" I asked as we hopped back into the car and buckled up.

"Get the picture out." Aaron glanced over to me, and I reached for my bag.

"I'm texting Grandma." I did that, to keep her up to date. I brought out the picture and studied it as Aaron began driving toward the entrance of the park where the former President's cabin stood. "It's just Alice, Edith and Teddy standing in front of the cabin and baby Alice holding the figurine."

"Even if there's no land title, the matter will be set to rest." Aaron drove further until at last turning into the site. "No buffalo nearby!"

"We'll drive through the park afterwards." I smiled because I wanted to see at least one buffalo, too.

Inside the Visitor's Center, we signed the guest book and inquired about the cabin tour since no one was allowed to enter it without a Ranger present. We had ten minutes to wait, so we glanced through the many photos and other wall hangings featuring the President.

"The tour will begin right here. All those interested please line up over here." The Ranger stood tall and proud. His silver mustache and sparkling eyes reflected mischief, giving me a feeling that he would've had a great time with the President hunting or wrestling cattle. "We'll now begin."

The small group followed him out to the cabin in single-file fashion. The three room Maltese Cross Ranch cabin had a steeply-pitched roof. One room had a small, fold out table where the President wrote his memoirs under a kerosene lamp, or else read. His favorite piece of furniture was his rocking chair. He had a small bedroom where his trunk is still located. Upstairs, there was a loft where his ranch hands slept. The cabin had withstood many moves, until its permanent move by a stroke of Harry S. Truman's Presidential pen. In 1959, it became a permanent site at the park.

We were barely allowed to look around or touch anything. As the Ranger spoke, I took the moment to study the wall hangings for a sign of the figurine, grass bowl, or another photo, but didn't find anything worthwhile. I raised my hand, and asked, "Did he own any other parcel of land besides what's part of the park?"

"No. There's been a huge discussion lately about that in the papers, but no, to answer your question. The historical society has researched that extensively and found no copy of any land entitlement or deed in the President's name or any of his family."

"Thank you."

After walking around for a little while, we stopped once again to look at the front of the cabin. It did appear to have Alice Roosevelt's initials engraved in it, and also we heard that when he passed away, she came and stayed for a short while. It wasn't recorded though—the information was word of mouth.

"Dead end?" I said to Aaron as we walked to the car.

"It seems like." He opened the car doors.

"Two people killed for no reason." My eyes welled with tears. "It's a dirty shame. The courts will have to sort out everything now."

"Off to Yellowstone?"

"First, the buffalo--, then Yellowstone!"

"And, maybe we can witness a pow-wow or a jingle dance while on vacation."

THE END

Afterward

I've never found evidence that Theodore Roosevelt purchased land to set aside for Alice. Most of what's in the novel is a work of fiction, which means that I made most of it up in my head to fit the story.

I honor him as a wonderful President, who propelled us on the journey of our National Parks system and holding the land dear to our hearts. It's the one true thing, that we as Americans, did right.

About Barbara Schlichting

Barbara Schlichting was born and raised in Minneapolis and graduated from Theodore Roosevelt high school in 1970. She and her husband moved their family to Bemidji, Minnesota, in 1979. She attended Bemidji State University where she earned her undergraduate and graduate degrees in elementary education and special education. Ms Schlichting has been married for forty-four years and has two grown sons who have blessed her with five grandchildren and one great grandson.

BONUS SAMPLE CHAPTER

The Blood Spangled Banner
A First Ladies Mystery

Chapter One

The front window rattled against the wind as I unlocked the door of the First Lady White House Dollhouse store and walked inside toward the dollhouse tables. Dolley Madison and I were distantly related, so greeting her first seemed natural.

I wore a new pink dress to match Dolley's inaugural gown. After two months of interest in several White House dollhouses for her national chain store's toy department, Jackie Newell, was coming to get a firsthand look. She was scheduled to arrive within the hour, which left me with just enough time to spruce up the showroom and ensure that my 1814 White House dollhouse arrangement was in perfect shape. This was my chance to make the big time.

"There, there, now Dolley." I straightened her because she'd tipped slightly. "Mr. Prez? You need to be on your best behavior today. No chasing Dolley around the house with my perspective buyer coming soon! No pinching her bum." I wagged my finger at him.

"Mrs. Lincoln? You're looking marvelous today. How's the headache after that awful carriage ride? It was an attempt on your life, wasn't it?" I'd had an awful one after the car accident that killed my parents when I was eleven. Now, it's an ache in my heart, still—twenty years later.

I glanced over to the First Lady pictures hanging on the wall. "Why are you crooked, Barbara?" I stopped to straighten the first Mrs. Bush's portrait.

"I'll return shortly to fix your hair."

"Mrs. Carter, I hope last night was worth it. All that Billy Beer." Something isn't right. Mrs. Carter has never been this tipsy.

"Don't worry, ladies, you're back to looking good." I winked while passing.

Near the backroom, I gasped at a crunch underfoot. Another step. Another crunch. I gazed across the hallway floor, and the bottom sank from my stomach. My eyes opened wide, I'd walked across broken furniture.

"Hello?" I flicked on the light in the workroom. Boxes and boxes lay strewn across the floor. Miniature chairs, tables, dolls, vases, desks, and beds were scattered. The workbench was littered with broken dollhouse pieces. My sewing items were tossed about.

I screamed.

I was sure that it reached the psychic shop next door. Mikal, the proprietor, kept his window open for fresh air.

I heard a noise, as I began backing out toward the bathroom. Meaty, strong arms came from behind and covered my mouth, pulling me against a firm chest. I smelled a slight vanilla scent as I bit into the assailant's fleshy fingers. I struggled, biting harder, trying to stomp his feet, but he held tight.

Grandpa's open toolbox full of hammers, nails, and box cutters lay almost within reach. I tried inching closer, but my captor jerked my head back, clutching my hair. I twisted to see him. A black ski mask covered his face.

"NO screaming." His icy tone sent fear up my spine. "You hear?" He slowly brought down his hand after I tried to nod.

"Where are they?" He wrenched my left arm up behind my back. Pain seared up my arm, as I leaned closer to the toolbox. "I want them now."

"Ouch! You're hurting me!"

"Where are they?"

"You're breaking my arm." He loosened his grip. "I'm not psychic here. Just tell me what you want." Slowly I moved my right hand while inching closer to the toolbox. "I don't understand." I grabbed a box cutter from the workbench and quietly snapped it open. "My fiancé is a cop, so——."

"Shut up!"

The toolbox tumbled over, sending its contents skittering across the floor. My assailant's hand loosened from my back, giving me enough time to turn and thrust the blade into his forearm. He yelped and grabbed at his bleeding arm.

I dashed out the back door. "Help!" Scrambling down the alley and rounding the building to the front of the store, I screamed again then ducked inside the doorway of Mikal's shop.

"Liv, calm down. What's wrong?" Mikal walked toward me with a client following. "Another mouse?" He grinned and glanced at his client. "Stephanie, my neighbor, Liv."

"I don't have time for this stupidity," I said.

"Excuse me!" Stephanie said. The short, stocky client peeked out from behind Mikal, narrowed her eyes and crossed her arms over her flat chest. "Listen, missy. I was in the middle of a reading. It was just getting good! I found out about my husband's little girlie friend with the big boobs. Now this!" She threw her arms in the air. "My reading is botched. I want a refund."

"You haven't paid." Mikal glared at her.

"I won't either." She marched away, but not before giving me the finger.

"Hey! I'm in trouble, loser! I was assaulted just now." Just because I'd evicted a live-in mouse family from my shop a few weeks ago didn't mean it was back. "Someone trashed my shop and grabbed me." I pulled my cell phone from my pocket and called Aaron, my fiancé.

"Sit down, right here," Mikal ordered. "I'm calling the cops."

My boyfriend picked up the call. "Aaron, someone just attacked me at the shop." I sank into the chair.

"Are you hurt? What happened?"

"I'm fine, I'm at Mikal's."

"I'll be right there," Aaron said. "Have you called 911?"

"No, I called you."

"I'll take care of it, then I'll be right there." Aaron disconnected.

"I'm going back. The Gorilla must be gone by now." I took a deep breath and headed for the door.

"Stay and wait for Aaron," Mikal urged.

"Nope. I've got to check on the store." I had to protect the ladies. The First Ladies had already been through so much in their life, now it's up to me to make sure nothing else happens to them. Mommy always said they were special, like being the Nation's Mother. As First Lady, she'd make sure that the President looked out for our interests and needs like food for the hungry.

"I'll stay outside, I promise."

I texted my best friend, Maggie, as I walked out the door. My knees felt weak, like I might sink to the ground. *Where were the police?* My feet crunched in the snow, and I started to shiver. I could've been badly hurt. *Where was Aaron?* My arm ached as I massaged it, trying to ignore the pain. *Was the man gone or still in the store? What did he mean? Where are they? Where's what?*

I stood to the side to wait.

Where was Max?

Max worked part-time for me and rented the apartment above the shop. He should be around here someplace, but who knows? Max often gambled away his money. I was always getting cryptic messages from parts unknown, asking how to reach him, presumably to remove body parts.

A reassuring chuckle from behind made me grin. Max's voice boomed from above. "Livvie! Now what? Another mouse in the house?"

My headache suddenly grew to the size of Texas. I glanced up and massaged my temples.

"Someone broke in, and assaulted me. The workroom's a mess." Tears streamed down my cheeks. I wiped my nose with the sleeve of my heavy sweater just as Aaron's squad car drove up.

Aaron's smile made my toes curl. I knew that I could make through this day.

Tim, Aaron's partner, went around to the back while Aaron stayed out front.

Finally, sirens blared in the distance and soon stopped. Two police officers climbed from the car, as Aaron and Tim secured the premises. People gathered to stare at the building while other shopkeepers popped out to gawk.

"Everyone move on and go about their business. Now!" Aaron said.

Max walked down the outside steps. He gave me a puzzled look, lit a smoke, and stood near me as an officer approached us.

"You the owner?" the officer stated.

"Yes."

"You?" he turned to Max.

"He's my upstairs renter and employee." I noticed two plain-clothes officers approaching, one older with gray hair, the other younger and blond.

"We'll take over. There's been a rash of burglaries in the area," the detective stated, showing his badge. "Detective Mergens. Ms. Anderson? Olivia Anderson? You called it in?"

"My fiancé called it in, but I'm Olivia, Liv, Anderson."

"Ms. Anderson," he said. "My partner, Detective Erlandsen, and I, are curious about this theft because of its nature."

"Yes, let's go inside for some privacy," Detective Erlandsen said.

"I'll follow." My phone buzzed, and I read Maggie's message, "Stay safe. Keep me updated." The showroom appeared unscathed. I took a deep breath and looked toward the historical White House and saw Dolley. I breathed relief, knowing it was unharmed. The other houses appeared unscathed, but I'd check on the Ladies as soon as possible. *Hold on girls, I'm coming.*

"How does the showroom look?" Mergens asked.

"Great, actually. This morning is very important to me." I stuck my hands in my pockets and went back to the front window.

"Jackie Newell of *Jackie of New York!* Department Store is due here in less than an hour." I shook from deep inside.

"Who?" Mergens asked.

"She is the owner of the national department store chain, *Jackie of New York!* You know, from the Home Shopping Network."

"Oh! My wife would probably know," Mergens said, rolling his eyes.

"I hope her interest in the houses will spike sales."

"The back lock was picked," Erlandsen stated. "Know anyone who'd want to break in? Have anything valuable in here besides dollhouses?"

"Plenty. Look around the room. I have my Penny Dolls and First Lady photos, and they sell for several hundred dollars, at least." I nodded at them, placing my hands on my hips. We stood by the glass counter in front of the register and computer. I swung my attention back to the officer's question, and crossed my arms. "Max carves doll heads in here or his apartment at night. He sets his own hours. I tell him what style of house I need and which First Lady. The pieces need to be glued and, in some instances, stapled together. They're fragile, but sturdy. He fills in when needed."

"You trust him?" Mergens asked.

"Absolutely. He has a key. He lives here. I've known him for years." I crossed my arms. "His workbench is in the workroom— underneath all that wreckage."

"I see." Mergens wrote in his notepad. "Was he home?"

"I don't know."

"Where do you live?"

"With my grandparents, Marie and August Ott." I scratched my head. "I've never given Dorrie a key. She's my other employee."

"Any cause for alarm?" He studied me. "You know. Anything unusual. Pattern change such as misplacing a key?"

"We want this Dorrie's info," Erlandsen said.

"I can't think of anything unusual at the moment." I shook my head. "I keep my purse in the workroom, and it's usually hung on the clothes tree." I quickly looked up Dorrie's contact information from the list beside the computer. "Here's her info. I'm sure it was a man because of his strength and low voice. Now can I see the damage?" I became more worried with each passing minute.

"Anything you can tell me about the guy who attacked you?" Detective Mergens cocked his head. "It's pretty nasty in there. We thought we'd get all the information before you see it." He frowned. "It'll be a shock."

"I saw some of it before he grabbed me." I sank into the nearest chair and reached for the tissue box. I thought of Jackie Kennedy and all the pain she'd endured as I wiped my nose. "He was big. A gorilla. HUGE. His fingers and hands were beefy. His biceps pumped up when he tightened his grip on me. He wore a ski mask. His voice sounded like it had potholes and icebergs." I glanced at the clock and suddenly my brain kicked into gear. "Can we hustle here? I'm expecting a very important client pretty soon." I blew my nose.

"One more question." Erlandsen held up a finger. "Anyone you might have a beef with?"

"I can't think of anyone." I frowned, massaging my chin. "Unless this has something to do with Max. He gambles and often loses." I thought a moment. "The beefy guy asked, where are they? I don't know what he was talking about. Where is what?"

"He was after something in particular. Now, we're getting somewhere. That's more than what the other victims could tell us." Erlandsen glanced up at me.

"What other victims?" I stared at him. "I'm not the first?"

"There's been a rash with break-ins," Erlandsen said. "Ongoing investigation."

"Dollhouses?" I asked. I glanced at each detective. "Good grief. This doesn't make sense. I'll keep a closer watch."

They closed their notepads.

"Now are we done?" I asked. "I've plenty to do."

"Almost." Erlandsen stepped aside. "We're in the process of checking for prints."

I waited a beat, my stomach tied in knots, as the door opened and closed. They left. I got up and forced myself to go to the workroom, stopping just outside the doorway. My gaze swept across the floor of the workroom. *The poor first ladies. Broken china dishes. Pieces scattered from one end of the room to the other. Poor Mrs. Monroe with the French furniture.* Tears streamed down my cheeks. It'd take hours to sort through everything and decide what was salvageable.

"What a mess. It's a disaster," I whispered. "What were they after? Will they be back?"

I went into the restroom, glanced in the tiny mirror, fluffed up my hair, dabbed on some red lipstick, and noticed a chipped nail. A file was handy and soon the chipped nail was smooth. *Hopefully, I look presentable for Jackie Newell's arrival.* The back door opened just as I stepped from the bathroom.

"Hey, babe." Aaron walked toward me. "Don't worry about a thing. I've requested a few days off but don't know for sure if it'll be approved. I also wouldn't be surprised is if the sarge calls me in for a half shift. We're short officers right now due to the flu season."

"Thank you." The front bell jingled.

"I'll call you later." Aaron tweaked my chin. "By the way, I put a box of chocolate under the register."

"Another, among many reasons why I love you," I said.

He left.

I tried to calm my nerves by taking deep breaths.

Aaron stepped back in. "Don't forget to call the insurance agent."

"Already on my to-do list."

He walked to his patrol car and drove away. I noticed a familiar car parked out back, and realized that it belonged to an old schoolmate, Ronnie. He earned his living by taking pictures and writing news articles for the local paper. I cringed.

I went to the register, slipped off the box cover and removed two chocolate pieces, stuffing both in my mouth. A third piece sounded good, so I shoved it into my mouth before setting the box under the register. A car door slammed and I went to the front window.

A long, black limousine was parked in front of the store. Jackie Newell and a thirtyish woman climbed out, followed by a big, burly man wearing aviator sunglasses and a black suit. I figured him as a bodyguard or escort.

"You can do this," I told myself, gulping. Opening the front door, I willed my racing heart to slow down. "Good morning."

Both women stood about the same height. Ms. Newell wore a ritzy black dress coat and the younger woman was dressed in a simple navy suit. Ms. Newell's practiced smile shone as she walked toward the store, the other woman following two paces behind. The bodyguard had his eyes glued on the passersby. *Why does she need a bodyguard?* I swept the hair back from my face, smiling.

"Ms. Newell, I hope that you'll like the store." I pretended as if all was well as my fast beating heart slowed to a normal pace. I jutted my hand out. "Olivia Anderson, but you can call me Liv."

"Call me Jackie. So nice to meet you." She shook my hand before glancing around the room. "Very nice. Yes, indeed. Love your pictures of the First Ladies. Who is your favorite?"

"Dolley, of course."

The woman beside Jackie cleared her throat.

"My secretary, Wanda Brown. She's invaluable. Don't know what I'd do without her." Jackie gave a winning smile.

Calm my pumping heart. Yes! Maybe a dozen or more houses purchased by her highness.

Wanda held out her hand. "Nice to meet you." Her eyes shifted around the room. "Nice store you have."

"Thank you."

Jackie's eyes lingered on the heritage-style White House.

"I see you have Dolley Madison as the First Lady in this house." Jackie tucked her small pouch under her arm before reaching into the house. "May I?" She picked up the doll and began examining it. "Tell me about the gown. It's gorgeous. I see it's layered with crinolines and even has pantaloons."

"I sew the clothing with as much authenticity as possible." I smiled. "The dress Mrs. Madison is wearing is representative of what she wore for the Inaugural Ball. It's made of buff-colored velvet with ropes of pearls and a fashionable turban with Bird of Paradise flowers. She was the first to have an Inaugural Ball. Leave it to Dolley."

I spoke with confidence. I had studied the First Ladies in college, read the history books as well as the gossipy ones. I could have entertained Jackie all day with my grasp on White House minutiae, but I wasn't sure if she was an enthusiast like me.

"Very informative." Jackie's eyes lit up as she gave the doll a closer inspection. "I hear you're a descendant of Dolley Madison."

"Yes, I am, as a matter of fact." I glanced outside. Max was passing by with a cup in one hand and a bag in the other. "Are you?"

"I am as well. She's amazing."

"Who's your favorite?"

Wanda was also watching Max pass by, and a smile crossed her lips. Go figure.

"Dolley too." Jackie grinned. "It's beautiful." She carefully placed the piece back in its original position. "Ever hear of the family secret?" She removed a magnifying glass from her purse and knelt down to peer closely at the interior walls.

"A family secret? No. Never heard of it." I furrowed my brows.

"Are you certain?" Jackie eyed me suspiciously.

"Yes." I nodded. *What is she talking about?*

"Most interesting." She looked me square in the eye.

Is she trying to figure out if I'm telling the truth?

"How long have you known you're a descendant?" I returned her stare.

"Last year. I've done plenty of research into it. There's definitely a family secret," she said. "Back to business." Ms. Newell straightened up. "Are the wall decorations identical to how Dolley decorated?"

"What do you mean?" I asked, raising a brow. "Of course they are! The wall hanging is quite similar to my grandma's."

"Gorgeous." Wanda leaned closer to Jackie. She held up china from the Madison house.

The bell jingled. The bodyguard entered and stood in front of the door. He crossed his arms. "Problem solved."

Wanda nodded.

What is he talking about? Problem solved?

These people from New York seemed to talk in riddles, or else I was losing it. This conversation is giving me the jitters. I glanced across the street to the park. When Wanda cleared her throat, it jerked me back to attention.

"She's concerned about historical accuracy." Wanda looked me in the eye. "She's interested in all things Dolley, including Mr. Madison."

"No family rumor or 'secret' heard of, eh?" Jackie stood and dropped the magnifier into her little purse. She glanced at me once again. "Sure?"

"Positive."

"Is every adornment on the clothing accurately portrayed on both Mr. and Mrs. Madison?" Jackie asked.

"She wants to know if this is exactly what was worn during the inaugural ball," Wanda clarified.

"Yes. Dolley's dress. Everything on it is accurate as well as his, but his is purchased. Men's clothing is very tough to sew." *What is with the tag team between the two?*

"I'm interested in a 'secret', but if you don't know of one—," Jackie said.

"I don't." I shook my head. *What is with her? What secret?* I had to change the subject to get back in control. "All the dollhouses are made by hand. I have two employees, one who carves the dolls' heads and my showroom assistant who helps arrange the interior settings." *Isn't she going to purchase a few houses?*

Jackie held up President Madison and scrutinized his cufflinks. I blinked.

"Mr. Madison's cufflinks have been missing from the duPont museum for years. You know? Montpelier? The Madison home? It's part of the 'secret,' my dear." She cocked her brow and stared right through me. "They need finding."

"I don't know what you're talking about," I said, running my fingers through my hair. "I know the duPont's purchased the estate some years after it was sold by Dolley."

"Excuse me," Wanda interrupted. "You have thirty minutes until you're scheduled to meet with Mr. Carlson." Wanda looked at me. There was something in her eyes, but I wasn't sure what. Curiosity? "We're booked at the Twin City Hotel. It makes getting around easy. Only a couple blocks from here."

"May I take Mr. and Mrs. Madison with me today for further scrutiny? I'll place my order on Wednesday and then return them. Day after tomorrow." Jackie opened her little pouch and dropped the dolls inside before I could say, "Boo."

"Wait a second, here. I need a credit card number." I was beginning to think she was a magician, the way she made those dolls disappear.

"Here." Wanda handed me the card.

"I'll make out the sale, but hold the charge until they're returned." I took care of the paper work before they left, leaving me confused. "How many houses do you think you'll purchase? I'd like to know so that they'll be ready."

"Maybe two heritage houses, but I'm not sure."

At the window, I watched them leave, Jackie with her purse tucked tight under her arm like a million dollar bank vault. First Jackie, then Wanda climbed into the car. The bodyguard held the door open, shutting it behind.

What family secret?

Order your copy of The Blood Spangled Banner today!
Available in paperback from Amazon and your favorite local bookstore.
Available in ebook format for Kindle, Nook, and Kobo.

About This Book

The typeface in this book is 11.5 Garamond and Helvetica (for the headings). It was laid out using Adobe InDesign software and converted to PDF for uploading to the printing facility.

About Darkhouse Books

Darkhouse Books is dedicated to publishing entertaining fiction, primarily in the mystery and science fiction field. Darkhouse Books is located in Niles, California, an inadvertently-preserved, 120 year old one-sided railtown, forty miles from San Francisco. Further information may be obtained by visiting our website at www.darkhousebooks.com.

Also by Barbara Schlichting

The First Lady
White House
Dollhouse Shop

The Blood Spangled Banner

by Barbara Schlichting

A First Lady Mystery – Dolley Madison

LAWN ORDER

A Margaret & Bitsy Mystery

MOLLY MACRAE

Author of *Wilder Rumors*

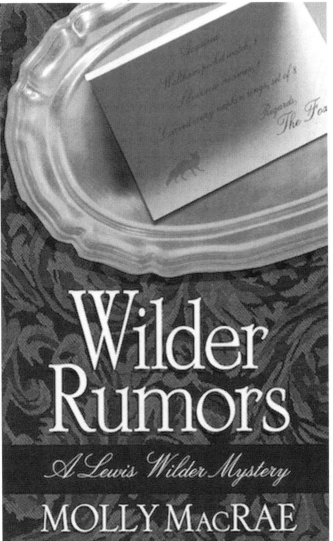

Wilder
Rumors

A Lewis Wilder Mystery

MOLLY MacRAE

Molly MacRae

My Troubles

Ten Cozy Tales
Of Mystery & Murder

The Anthology of Cozy-Noir

CRIME SCENE DO NOT CROSS

CRIME SCENE DO NOT CROSS

CRIME SCENE DO NOT CROSS

Edited
by
Andrew MacRae

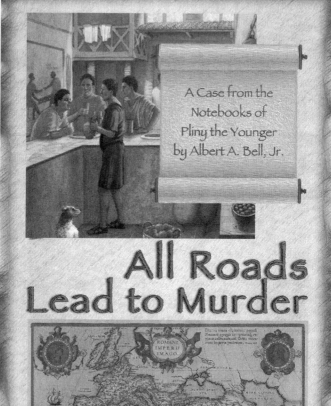

A Case from the
Notebooks of
Pliny the Younger
by Albert A. Bell, Jr.

All Roads
Lead to Murder

Made in the USA
Lexington, KY
15 January 2018